Martian Flight

Martian Flight

Broken Cosmos Volume Two

Ian Kennedy

Copyright Notice

Special Thanks

Beta Readers:
Geoff Kwitko
Jenna Harper
Hannah Climas
Janina Kennedy

Cover Art:
Courtney Egan (Eucafox)

Chapter 1

"The rumour is that High Command is livid about the *Green Dragon's* escape. There's talk that there will be executions, treason charges!" Trooper Grox was busy stowing his personal effects in the overhead locker in his section of the barracks number 037 aboard the *Iron Bastion*, one of the two main Collective Zone flagships. He was a standard soldier, medium height and muscular, there was nothing remarkable about him physically.

Trooper Althar, another standard soldier, responded curtly, "Look, Grox, we all know that there were major stuff ups recently, but there's no need to spread rumours and talk about things that you cannot possibly know anything about. Besides," he hefted a heavy pack and stuffed it into the overhead locker, "the lieutenant will have your guts if he catches you talking about such things. He's a hard-arse, and he doesn't like loose talk."

They had their backs to each other as they each stowed their personal belongings and prepared for the long cryo-sleep.

"Is it true we're going to Mars?" Grox said again after a short pause.

Althar grimaced. "There you go again! We won't get the briefing until we get where we're going so I tell you to shut it and you keep talking about gossip and rumour!"

"But why do they only tell us when we get there? Surely they could let us know before we get into cryo-sleep?" said Grox, a childish whine appearing in his voice.

Althar shook his head. "They do because they do. That's all there is to it...but yes, the rumour is Mars." He smiled to himself.

Grox let out a small chuckle in triumph, "See, you like the gossip just as much as me...damn pack won't fit! Why do they always make these cabinets too small for our shit?" Grox gave a large heave and forced his belongings into the overhead locker.

"Because you always pack so much shit that's non regulation." Althar indicated his neat locker. "See? Mine fits perfectly."

"Yeah but you're a swine who doesn't like books!" said Grox with a laugh. "Give me a hand would you?"

"Books!? What use do we have of books? We're soldiers, trained to fight and kill, not read books about...what's this?" Althar picked up a book that fell down from Grox's locker. "*The Collected Works of...William Shakespeare*? Who the hell is Shakespeare?"

"It's poetry, and plays, good stuff!" Grox snatched the book back. "You wouldn't understand, you barbarian..." Grox said with a grin.

"Yeah, whatever, I see no need in books. You can't kill with a book." Althar gave Grox's stuff a shove and a particularly heavy and large book fell out of the locker and hit Althar on the head before falling to the floor with a loud thud.

"OW!" Althar swore for a while.

Grox's grin widened. "You sure about that?"

"Fuck's sake," said Althar quietly and picked up the heavy book. Without looking at it, he shoved it back into the locker and helped Grox stow the rest of his luggage.

When they had finished storing their possessions, they picked up their rifles that were leaning next to their everyday beds and began to clean and strip them.

Grox paused mid clean and looked around the barracks. He watched their section getting ready for the long trip to wherever they were going. The men and women of 3rd Platoon were all busy storing their luggage in overhead lockers above their normal beds, the cryo-pods were elsewhere in the ship, but when they were not travelling between worlds they slept in normal beds. The room was spartan, gunmetal walls and lockers with simple and uncomfortable beds beneath them lined the walls. Everyone was busy and prepping for the exciting journey. 3rd Platoon were all pretty new and had not really seen much combat other than the pacification of the Moon. And there they had only fought against rioting prisoners and some tech-slaves.

"Hurry up, the lieutenant will be here in a minute, it's nearly time!" ordered Althar.

Grox checked his chronometer. He saw the time and swore, and he began cleaning and reassembling his rifle in double time. He just finished as the lieutenant entered the barracks and everyone stood and snapped to attention next to their beds.

Lieutenant Vauz marched into the barracks and surveyed his soldiers. He was a short man with lots of battle experience and the scars to prove it. He was missing his left eye, which was replaced by a mechanical prosthetic that had a piercing red glow. People were afraid of Vauz, even his soldiers were afraid of him, but they would follow him through Hell, as they knew he was the consummate commander and tactician, and he cared for every one of them. He wore the standard grey-green of a ship's soldier. All the soldiers in the fleet wore similar.

He moved to each in turn and inspected their lockers and weapons. He said little except for a few dressing downs of tardy gun maintenance and poor locker storage.

He came to Althar's locker. "Trooper Althar." He nodded to the trooper.

"Sir!" Althar saluted and opened his locker for inspection. Then he presented his rifle for inspection.

"Good, good," said Vauz. "The professional soldier. You could all learn something from this man!" Vauz's voice boomed around the barracks as he raised his voice for the instruction.

Althar's chest swelled with pride.

Vauz moved on to Grox who was the last soldier in the line. "Trooper Grox," Vauz said a little warily.

Grox opened his locker for inspection and a book fell out onto the floor. Grox froze. Althar froze. They knew that the lieutenant had certain views about books.

Vauz paused, staring at the book on the cold metal floor. He bent down slowly and picked it up, looking at it in his hands. He opened the old and worn cover and read the title, "*The Collected Works of William Shakespeare*." He paused again. "When people had two names, how inefficient." He looked down his nose at Grox. "Well?"

"Sir, I can explain..." said Grox, his voice a squeak.

"Good...then do..." replied Vauz.

"Sir, I uh, like poetry and the battle plays. He was an ancient Earth playwright, see? *Henry V* is particularly good!"

Vauz snapped the book closed in one hand and stared at Grox for what seemed like an age. After a time, Vauz spoke, quietly at first just to Grox. "From this day to the ending of the world, / but we in it shall be remembered / we few," he turned and addressed the barracks, his voice booming again, "we happy few, we band of brothers; / for he today who sheds his blood with me / shall be my brother." Vauz raised his arms, the book still closed in one hand.

Grox could not believe it. He stood slack jawed as his lieutenant quoted part of *Henry V* to him, to all of them.

Vauz turned on his heel from addressing the barracks and threw the book back at Grox who caught it roughly. "Stow it away carefully," Vauz said. "We can't damage the greats now can we?" He grinned and then silently and quickly exited the barracks. "Cryo-pods in thirty minutes!" he shouted over his shoulder as he left the room.

Grox let out a breath, he felt as if he had held it for minutes. He looked at Althar. "Well, how's that then?" He grinned.

Althar shook his head, and let out a disbelieving chuckle.

Grox placed the book carefully back into his locker.

3rd Platoon and the rest of the military in the ship were filing towards the large banks of cryo-pods in the specially designed cargo bay. A squad at a time, the troops were placed into cryo-sleep and their vital signs monitored by the onboard computers and tech-slaves. Soon the whole of the *Iron Bastion* would be in cryo-sleep, and they would be heading for Mars, so the rumour went.

***

"CEO? Sir?" The thin voice came from the small frame of the messenger who had been tasked with bringing the latest news of the Fleet's departure from the Moon. She was terrified of the ancient man standing with his back to her as he stared out of one of the large windows from the boardroom at the top of Atraxa Prime. He seemed not to hear her.

She tried again. "Uh, CEO Sir?" She noticed him almost imperceptibly tilt his head and turn towards her. She continued, "The Fleet has loaded up its troops and has started the long journey to Mars. Fleet Commander Boltha is confident of her success at apprehending the criminals and bringing them to swift justice by your mighty hand..." She froze. He had raised his left hand. "CEO Sir, they took the red hard drive and..."

"Come here," Uxus rasped. He indicated a position beside himself at the window with his gnarled left hand. "I need you to...understand something."

The messenger moved like an automaton. She was terrified of what was about to happen, not that she knew what that was, but also terrified if she did not obey. She stopped exactly where he had indicated and looked up at him with wide eyes.

At this close distance she could see all the lines and creases in his face and his thinning grey hair. She wanted to look at the marvellous view out the window in front of her, but she could not bring herself to take her eyes from her leader.

Uxus raised a hand and indicated the smouldering ruins of where the cloaked weapon had been and the large portion of Atraxa Prime destroyed in the blast from its energy stores when they overloaded.

"See that?" Uxus rasped. It sounded, to the messenger, like he would need longevity surgery soon. The messenger nodded meekly, just managing to look away from her commander and down to where he was pointing.

"We will--" she said.

"WE WILL CRUSH THEM!" Uxus bellowed with a strength and rage of a body much younger than his. He bunched his fists and slammed them into the glass window wall.

The messenger flinched and shied away. She had never seen him so angry. She felt as if it were her fault, that something she had said was causing him such anguish.

"I will bring death to their pathetic sector of the system, and I will destroy the Solar Solutions Corporation!" Uxus yelled, "I will see them destroyed...I will get the drive back...I will have my war...I have my catalyst...the Collective Zone will be victorious..." Uxus trailed off, suddenly quiet.

"Perhaps," he said quietly to himself, somewhat calmer. "Perhaps this will give me the reason I need to take the war to Solar Solutions. Perhaps...the stealing of the hard drive..." He paused in thought.

The messenger still stood beside him, not knowing what to do or say. Her commander had calmed down, which was good, but she did not really understand what he was talking about.

"Prepare a shuttle craft for me; get me my personal pilot; I will be heading to the *Old Monarch* command ship. Inform the commander of the *Old Monarch*, I will see him. I will be making a long trip soon. Now go!" He waved his left hand in her direction while running his right hand through his grey hair.

The messenger bowed and scurried away, pleased to be out of the gaze of the man she revered. As she descended in the lift from the boardroom, she pondered to herself. What did the CEO mean when was going on a long journey? Was he going to pursue the Great Fleet in the *Old Monarch* ship? However, the *Iron Bastion* was already leading the Great Fleet. Never did both capital ships leave the Earth. And it had been ages since the two corporations had been in all-out war.

As she descended in the lift and headed to the command communications room to relay the message to the *Old Monarch* and prepare a shuttle, she shivered. Things would not end well.

Chapter 2

Draz dreamed. Draz saw her parents. She saw her mother scavenging in the rad-wastes. She was a beautiful woman with long brown hair and brown eyes. She was athletic and muscular from a lifetime of scavenging in the harsh environment of the rad-dunes. Draz would grow to look like her, in time.

Draz was little again. She ran around making whooshing noises in the main room in their family home.

There was her father. He was not muscular; he worked in the administration of the Corporate Wing. He was tall, thin, and had a head of red hair. Draz ran around and he scooped her up as he came home from work. He moved her through the air, and she put her arms out like a jet plane and he joined in with the whooshing noises. She was happy. Draz was happy. As were her two parents. They were very much in love, and they loved the fact that they had a young daughter to share the world with.

Draz saw the tanks and troops. There was killing and death. There were explosions. Draz was older, eighteen. The troops broke into their apartment. It was another Shipping Wing invasion of Corporate Wing territory. Part of the civil war that had raged since before her birth. Her father died trying to protect her from the soldiers. He was no soldier. They easily shot him. Her mother was out scavenging and had made it back in time for the main assault. She had fought against the invasion. But in the mess, she had been killed in an artillery strike. Draz had got the news from the news boards that were put up around the Corporate Wing main compound and she had seen the name of her mother listed as missing.

Draz saw herself older. She was snorting drugs. She saw herself turn into a walking corpse. She saw herself scavenging in the wastes and the Shipping Wing attack that had torn her recent life apart.

She was on an empty, enclosed hover train. She looked around. She could not see anything out the blanked windows. She got up slowly and moved to the door between carriages. In the next carriage there was no one either. Nor was there anyone in any carriage. She was stuck, alone in an infinite train. Inevitably heading to somewhere she could not see.

Suddenly the covers dropped from the windows, and she saw that she was flying through space on this train. Ahead was the Moon.

Draz screamed the silent scream of a dream. She saw herself on the Moon prison. She saw her life flash around her. She dreamed terrible nightmares.

***

The *Green Dragon* cut through the void on autopilot with the computer in control. It forged a path through the nothingness. Its windows glittering white against the backdrop of black. They mirrored the stars. The graphic symbol of a green dragon emblazoned on the prow of the craft sliced into the void and carved its way silently through space.

They were heading to Mars: a planet of pirates and disorder: the buffer zone between the Collective Zone and the Solar Solutions corporations.

The Great Fleet proceeded millions of kilometres behind. It chased the *Green Dragon* through the void. The *Iron Bastion* was at the front of the formation of the thirty ships of the Fleet. They spread out in a wedge like the tip of a spear and forged a vengeful yet silent path through the ether, windows glittering to mirror the stars that shone so far away.

***

Alfred dreamed. He saw Blinky again. He saw her clothes, her face, her eyes. He heard her laugh. He saw her smile, or at least he thought he did. He was starting to forget. He clung desperately in his dreams to her form and face, but things were starting to become blurry. He could not quite remember her laugh, her voice, her smile. Her eyes were slightly less clear in his mind. He grasped desperately for the images. It was like grasping at water. In the dream it was impossible to control things.

He saw her on top of the cooling towers. He saw her turn and jump off. He heard his scream of anguish. He was moving as if in slow motion.

He was forgetting. He was forgetting her smile, her hair, her laugh, her eyes: her. He was forgetting her. He did not want to forget, but where there should have been clarity, as in the past, there was fuzziness. In his mind things were becoming a memory of a memory. It was all starting to fade. He was forgetting, in his madness, he was forgetting.

Chapter 3

Shuttle 734 approached the *Old Monarch* as it hung in orbit off one station of the Earth Ring.

"This is shuttle 734, we request permission to land," said the pilot mechanically as she had done many times before. She sat in her black pilot's uniform at the cramped controls at the front of the shuttle.

Uxus sat in the passenger seat behind the pilot, and Uxus' personal Black Guard sat behind him. Uxus wore his standard grey uniform that he was accustomed to wearing almost everywhere. It was simple yet effective and it designated him as different from the others around him but it did not stand out too much in case there was an emergency and he had to be extracted. His six guards wore black, like the pilot, but they also wore black helmets and visors that covered their faces so they could not be recognised.

The pilot dared not look back at her passengers. The gaze of Uxus was scary enough and the fact that she was carrying the CEO of the Collective Zone on this shuttle was always nerve-wracking, but she could never get over the guards. The faceless guards that the rumours said were genetically modified not to feel pain and who were cybernetically altered to be fearless and ruthless in all forms of combat. They would readily die for their CEO, and they would protect him to their last drop of blood. The pilot shivered. She wanted to get back to regular shuttle work as soon as she could.

The pilot looked out the window of her shuttle and saw on either side that angular fighter craft had formed up on the wings of the shuttle and were guiding it towards the gaping maw that was the docking bay at the front of the *Old Monarch*.

"Permission granted shuttle 734. We acknowledge your cargo, and everything is ready," came the crackly voice over the radio. The pilot sighed with relief; soon she could get back to normal work.

Shuttle 734 was guided at slow speed into the docking bay mouth at the front of the *Old Monarch*. It landed in the designated area in the middle of a full military detail of hundreds of soldiers all standing to attention. They were waiting for their leader.

The fighter craft that had formed up on the wings of the shuttle peeled off and flew back to their patrol routes around the *Old Monarch*.

***

Uxus thanked the pilot and unbuckled his safety harness. He got up stiffly and left the craft down the access ramp in the side. The guards followed their leader closely and silently out of the shuttle and formed up around him. The surrounding area was full of soldiers at full attention, all in their green-grey fatigues.

Uxus noted the small man who stood ahead of him in the centre of the mass of soldiers. Uxus towered over him by at least six or seven inches, and as Uxus approached, he could see the man was visibly shaking and looking very nervous while trying to hide his terror.

Uxus approached the man and bowed. The small man also bowed, rather awkwardly. Uxus never liked the man. He was too jumpy and scared of Uxus to be an effective ship commander. However, he had an exemplary record and the company had voted that he be commander of the *Old Monarch*.

Uxus preferred the command of Boltha on the *Iron Bastion*. She was not scared of him and could easily hold her own, even if she did test his patience at times. However, he had to send the *Iron Bastion* with the Fleet on ahead to pursue the *Green Dragon* and because of that, he was left with the *Old Monarch* and its commander to deal with.

"C-commander Vorthox at your service, CEO," said the little man with a stutter of terror, and a second, even more awkward bow.

"I know who you are, Vorthox," said the CEO icily. He could see Vorthox visibly turn a paler shade of white.

"To what do we owe this pleasure, CEO?" whimpered Vorthox, with another bow.

"I have come here to requisition this ship to follow the Great Fleet out to Mars and beyond," ordered Uxus.

"B-but, CEO, the *Iron Bastion* has already left. Surely you don't mean to deprive Earth of the other..." Vorthox's voice failed him under the steely gaze of Uxus. "I-I mean, CEO..." he failed again.

"I intend to follow the Great Fleet in this craft. I had to send the Great Fleet immediately on its pursuit, as I had to get a few things in order back on Earth. But I want to follow in this craft. I intend to be there when the final blows are struck against the Solar Solutions Corporation. I have left instructions for the other board members to carry on our great work without me but I must endeavour to bring home the *Green Dragon* and crush the Solar Solutions Corporate Empire. Is that clear?" ordered Uxus.

"Perfectly clear, CEO," said Vorthox, swallowing.

"Now, I would like a tour of the ship," said Uxus in a more civil tone, as if all problems had been forgotten.

Uxus bowed again to the man he detested in front of him, simply out of protocol. Vorthox bowed again too. Then Uxus made a sign to his personal guard and the six black clad and visored soldiers fanned out around the pair and they made their way out of the docking bay and through the ship.

After the grand tour, they headed to the bridge, during which Vorthox snivelled and prostrated himself to his CEO with such abandon that Uxus had to stop him at times, as he was being made uncomfortable.

Uxus liked the fawning and adoration of his corporation's lower members, it boosted his ego and enforced obedience, but there was a point where the whole grovelling act became ridiculous.

On the bridge, Uxus' personal Black Guard fanned out to stand around the edges of the room. Then Commander Vorthox took the command out of habit and Uxus watched on with some concealed amusement as the man realised that it should be Uxus taking command.

Vorthox, realising his faux pas, visibly shook as he bowed the lowest he ever had and vacated the command position with multiple bows as he backed away from the CEO. Vorthox backed into one of the Black Guards mid bow and the guard shoved him away. Vorthox fell over in a heap. Uxus just managed to stifle a laugh.

"Thank you Vorthox," said the CEO, not wanting to embarrass the man any further. "I can take it from here. Please, advise me on the correct procedure for leaving the Earth Ring's docking arms. I believe this is most important for you to show me." Uxus despised the man, but he knew that if Vorthox felt humiliated then that was bad for morale. Uxus needed Vorthox on his side and if he placated the commander of the *Old Monarch's* idiosyncrasies then the whole journey to Mars and beyond would be much more pleasant.

"Yes, CEO!" Vorthox had picked himself up and, all embarrassment forgotten, began to instruct the CEO on how to disengage from the Earth Ring and move out into open space. Uxus could see the man was grateful for the saving of face, and smiled as the small man instructed him on the commands, that Uxus already knew. Uxus however wanted the *Old Monarch's* commander to feel like he was instructing him.

"Now, I will require a medical unit to attend me," continued Uxus, when the ship had cleared the Earth Ring. "I will undergo longevity surgery on the way to Mars. The time should give my system long enough to heal. I will also await a message from a trusted confidant. Tell me if there is a message from somewhere around Jupiter. Be sure to wake me no matter what if such a message comes in."

***

Under instruction, the *Old Monarch* left its port on the Earth Ring and moved out into open space. The patrolling fighter craft docked, and procedures were begun to put the majority of the military and crew on the craft into cryo-sleep for the long journey to link up with the Great Fleet in its endeavours.

From deep within the ship in the medical wing, Uxus underwent longevity surgery. It was a brutal affair of poking and prodding with needles and chemicals while skin was stretched and teased and organs were revitalised with state of the art techniques. The subject was oblivious to what would normally be an excruciating operation as he was under sedation. The procedure had to be repeated numerous times over some days and weeks, but eventually the procedure would increase the life span of the recipient by a number of decades. Both corporations limited the procedure to only the most valuable company members. The long trip and cryo-sleep after the surgery would allow Uxus' flesh to heal and when he emerged, when they had reached Mars, he would be a new man.

Chapter 4

"Trader Virtus, Commander Anya will see you now." The crisp voice of the intercom sounded in Virtus' newly assigned quarters in the special guest wing of the command structure of the Europa Colony.

Virtus, who had been recovering from his long sleep in cryo-storage since the destruction of *Florida Station*, was lying on his bed in his newly assigned clothes that were black and green like colony command staff as he insisted that he only wore his white robes when he was saving people on the trading floor in a Church.

The Europa command structure had been very sympathetic to him about the destruction of *Florida Station*, and they had believed everything he had said about what had happened. What else could they do? He smiled to himself. They had been treating him very well, with the assignment of the special guest quarters and now he was going to discuss being installed in the Church here on Europa. His job was not yet finished. His smile widened.

Virtus swung his legs over the edge of the bed. He was still stiff from the prolonged cryo-sleep, but he was also an older man and the stiffness in his joints could not really be avoided. Perhaps he should go for longevity surgery, he mused to himself. However, that would take time out of his work, and he had so much work left to do.

He paused for a minute while he sat on the edge of the bed, his bare feet feeling the warm carpet between his toes.

There were computer cores on all the colonies, stations and ships in the system. He knew that his Sect spread beyond *Florida Station*. He had made sure to send emissaries out to the nearby stations and moons to spread the word. He did not know, however, how effective his missionaries had been in spreading the word. It was difficult to communicate between stations and moons about something like that without totally secure communication links. He would have to see for himself here on Europa what had happened to his message.

"And now, we continue," he whispered to himself as he slipped on his shoes and achingly stood up. His white robes hung on a hook on a large floor to ceiling cupboard near his bed.

Virtus stretched for a second and then moved towards the door. It slid open at his touch, and he moved down the empty metal corridor that led from the special guest apartments to the main transit system that moved people around the Europa Colony. A Guide was waiting for him a respectful distance down the corridor and Virtus greeted him kindly. The Guide was dressed in a dark red jump suit.

"This way, sir," said the Guide with a nod.

As he moved through the structures a little distance behind the Guide, Virtus noted how clean and new many of the features of the Europa Colony were. It was almost as old as *Florida Station* was but it had obviously seen more funding and favour with the Solar Solutions high command and many of the systems were new and revamped from their old state.

Virtus paused on the platform of the transit system that worked basically like a hover train system around the colony. The Guide waited for him; there was no rush. The platform he was on was clean and well maintained. The metal walls and floor were well cared for despite the flow of traffic across and through them.

A train arrived and the Guide mentioned to him that it was not going in the right direction, so they continued to wait.

17

"How do the systems run here?" asked Virtus suddenly. The question was aimed at his Guide.

"Sir?" said the Guide, a little taken aback. He did not really understand.

"I mean, do the computer controlled functions of the station, like these trains I assume, do they run well?" Virtus' piercing eyes bored into the Guide.

"Well enough, sir. I mean, we have been having some troubles with some lower tech-slaves and some of the automated systems do malfunction occasionally, but the station is rather old and it always needs maintenance," replied the Guide. He smiled meekly.

"Excellent..." said Virtus, not paying any more attention to the Guide. His mind was elsewhere.

The Guide looked puzzled, but did not question his superior.

Another train arrived and the Guide motioned that they should board this one and so Virtus moved onto the train. It was also clean and well maintained, given its use. Virtus sat on the nearest empty seat and the Guide sat behind him. The chairs were metal and cloth. They were rather uncomfortable but functional. The train accelerated away from the station and reached top speed quickly.

Virtus marvelled at the speed that they were going as he saw stations zip by outside his window. Then the train moved into a glass lined tunnel so that the occupants could see outside of the colony. Virtus, who had seen a lot in his life, still felt awed by the sight he saw. Stretching away in all directions from the train tunnel was the manmade colony, and then beyond that stretching to the horizon was the ice sheet of Europa: the frozen surface to a moon wide ocean. Beyond that, Virtus looked up and there was the great gas giant of Jupiter hanging in space; the silent guardian of all it surveyed.

Virtus marvelled at the sight. He felt energised to continue his work having seen such a spectacle. The system must be free.

After about ten minutes of fast travel, the train passed back into an enclosed tunnel and began to slow. It stopped at a couple of stations and the Guide did not indicate that they should get off, so Virtus became lost in his own thoughts.

A few more minutes passed and then the Guide got to his feet. He touched Virtus on the shoulder to indicate their stop was approaching. Virtus looked up and got to his feet. The train stopped and the Guide and Virtus disembarked. Virtus noted that the platform was empty other than a large, guarded door.

The Guide moved to the secured door on the platform and, after showing the guards a security pass, was allowed to pass through. Virtus followed the Guide through the door.

The duo proceeded up a flight of steps and then came to another guarded door, the same procedure was observed again and then the pair moved into a larger open space with various guarded doors dotted around the edges. Virtus looked up at the large glass dome above him and saw Jupiter again looking down over all it ruled.

"This is the main command structure. It connects to all different areas of the colony through the doors around us," whispered the Guide reverently.

Virtus was unsure whether the whisper was because of him or because of the structure. "Where do I go now?" he asked.

The Guide pointed to a large door over to the right. "Through there is the command room itself," said the Guide, again in a whisper.

Virtus nodded and moved towards the door. He noted that the Guide did not follow, and Virtus wondered how he would get past the armed guards at this secured door.

As Virtus approached, one guard moved to intercept him. "Identify yourself," he said.

"I am Trader Virtus, summoned by Commander Anya, to talk in the command room." He had not lost his authoritative voice, as he saw the guard recoil slightly and then bow.

"This way," said the guard and let Virtus through the final guarded door with a few key presses on a computer terminal.

Virtus wondered how the guard could be sure of his identity but then he saw a number of cameras dotted around the door and made the assumption that he had been identified through those.

As the door slid open he was ushered through, and he walked into a large room lined with computer terminals and colonists working on them. There were multiple levels to the room and walkways leading around the edges of the chamber with stairwells on each side so that people could move between levels.

Virtus stood stunned for a moment. He observed the commotion of the command structure. Suddenly at his left shoulder appeared Commander Anya. Virtus took a step back from the edge of the walkway and turned to talk to the person who had summoned him. He recognised her from the time he awoke from the long cryo-sleep on Europa.

"Ah, Commander Anya," Virtus said appreciatively while clapping his hands in delight.

"Trader Virtus," replied Anya with an outstretched hand. Virtus took it and shook it warmly. "Thank you for coming so promptly, I realise it must be hard to function after the long cryo-sleep and the destruction of your home." She released his hand and indicated for him to walk with her around the walkway around the edge of the command structure. He graciously accepted the invitation and they walked together, side by side.

Virtus listened respectfully as Commander Anya outlined the workings of the colony on Europa and as they circled the command structure. He did not say a word other than the occasional agreement with what Anya said.

"...but we have noticed something of late," said Anya as she passed one of the zetting terminals lodged in the side of the command structure, the chair occupied by one of the zetters who was sitting bolt upright with the zetter's grin.

"Oh yes?" said Virtus, almost nonchalantly.

"Yes, something had been going strange with our computer networks lately." She paused and checked one of the terminals near her. "You see? There!" She pointed at a blip on the screen.

Virtus leaned over and observed a slight discolouration on the zetting map that the current zetter was navigating. It was displayed on a computer screen above the zetting terminal. He smiled almost imperceptibly.

"Oh?" He made a movement with his hands as if to indicate he did not understand such matters.

"Yes, it's weird. The networks are starting to malfunction more than before. Every time there's a zet the integrity of the system falls a little rather than rising."

"How are the tech-slaves behaving?" asked Virtus calmly, but he was excited. His job may be a little easier than he thought.

"They're all right, but there have been some malfunctions and disobeying of orders," Anya said, still looking apprehensively at the projected zetting plan on the monitor in front of her. "Nothing we cannot handle with normal persuasion methods..."

"You mean electro-shock them?" said Virtus a little accusatively.

"Yes, well, they are mindless creatures, or at least, mostly mindless now," said Anya turning back to face Virtus. Virtus' brow furrowed slightly, but Anya seemed not to notice.

"Why are you telling me all this?" said Virtus, regaining his calm demeanour.

"Ah...well the thing is, I wanted to know what happened onboard *Florida Station* to cause such a major malfunction and core detonation. As you're the only survivor; or at least the only one we recovered, I hoped that you could tell me something and I was a little troubled about what was going on here." Anya looked up at the man who was looking rather thoughtfully out over the edge of the walkway around the command section.

"So, you have no idea why *Florida Station* exploded?" Virtus asked, testing the waters.

"None, there was not much left when our salvage crews arrived after the distress call from the *Green Dragon* ship..." Anya trailed off when she saw Virtus' face at the mention of the *Green Dragon*. "What?" she asked.

"Oh, just that the main culprit for the destruction of the station was sent to the Earth Moon Prison on board the *Green Dragon* and I have heard nothing more about him." Virtus stared into space, trying to add emphasis to his words. "He sabotaged the reactor with a zet and the whole thing exploded. I was lucky enough to be near a cryo-pod when the alarms sounded, and I managed to survive the jettison into space." He looked at Anya with a calm expression. "He'll be on the Earth Moon now, or maybe he's dead--"

"That's it? It was some sort of terrorist?" interrupted Anya.

Virtus nodded. "Indeed, he was a terrorist that worked with a few accomplices, and they are all in prison now."

"What was his name?" asked Anya.

"Theta 7B, or Alfred," said Virtus with a sigh and a shrug, as if he had no idea why the man had blown up the station.

"I remember him; he sent some communications to this base. Huh, strange, he never seemed the terrorist type in his communications. He always seemed rather...meek." Now it was Anya's turn to stare into space.

"No, no, he was a traitor. I was at his interrogation," said Virtus.

"Huh...well, good riddance to him," said Anya.

They had walked a few circles of the command centre on the outside gantries when after a while of silence Virtus tried his luck with a question.

"I realise that this is imposing on your well run machine, and I realise that you probably have a head priest here, but I was wondering if I could be installed in the Church as some kind of Trader?" He stopped mid walk to add emphasis to his situation.

"I'm glad you asked that. In fact, our Head Trader has had to leave the colony on a business pilgrimage to Neptune. I did not broach the subject because I thought you might be too weak after your ordeal." She looked into his face. "But I see that you are resolved to continue your calling and I admire that. We can have you installed as a temporary Head Trader for the time being. Our old Head Trader won't be back for another few years or so yet. I would be pleased to make the arrangements for your work."

"Thank you," said Virtus, a fire behind his eyes, and he shook her hand again.

"Would you like me to get a Guide to take you to your place of worship?" Anya snapped her fingers before he could respond and, he did not know how, but the same Guide he had had before appeared by Commander Anya's left shoulder.

"Well, thank you that would be marvellous. I have one final question, though; does the Church have a zetting terminal? I need it for my work..." He paused, hoping to be cut off.

Commander Anya looked at him carefully, "Yes, of course, I realise that some Head Traders are zetters and go about their worship with the markets in the network." Virtus looked relieved. "Our usual Head Trader was not a zetter, but I can have the terminal that is there made operational soon," she continued and smiled. "Now if you'll excuse me I have work to get on with, please wait outside the security doors and I will have this Guide join you shortly." The Guide next to Anya bowed.

"Thank you, Commander," said Virtus emboldened by the ease of his encounter. He moved around the outside of the command centre and out through the guarded doors that he came in and he waited in what he realised was the foyer of the command centre. He looked at the many guarded doors that were spaced around the outside and wondered to which areas of the colony that they led.

**

Back in the command centre, Anya whispered in the Guide's ear, "Keep watching him carefully as you have been doing, there's something I do not trust about our so called Trader. Report any misgivings to me." The Guide nodded and Anya gave him the indication to leave.

**

Virtus saw the Guide approaching and he fell in step beside the Guide as he was led back to the train station. Firstly, they journeyed back to Virtus' rooms so that he could change into his newly cleaned white robes of a Head Trader. They then journeyed on a different train to the heart of the commercial district of the colony.

24

The Guide led the Trader through the winding streets to the front of the Church. It was a large metal building with the symbol of Solar Solutions emblazoned on the front and it had a large board of numbers and symbols where the religious devotions of so many could be tracked with ease. There was a large group of people clustered out the front of the building watching their contributions with interest.

Virtus noted that there was a lot of green on the board. The Bull must be ascendant, he thought. He smiled.

The Guide opened the front door for him and Virtus entered the Church. His heart sang as he saw the familiar sight of the trading floor and the computers around the edges, with the dais at the far end where he would make his speeches. He saw the brown robed priests moving through the crowd collecting donations and making sure people were saved by investing. He smiled wider.

Virtus noted that the Guide had disappeared, but that was all right. Virtus knew his way around a Church. It was similar to the one he worked in on *Florida Station*. He moved through the crowd, which seemed to part for him like water. They had not seen a white robed priest in a while. He approached the dais and the crowd fell silent and looked with upturned and expectant faces in his direction as he stood on the platform above them.

"My friends," he said, "the Bull is ascendant, and we have a lot of work to do!" The crowd erupted into applause.

Chapter 5

Lights blinked and flickered on throughout the *Green Dragon*. Computers booted up after a nine-month sleep cycle that saw the *Green Dragon* draw near to its intended target of Mars.

On the rows of cryo-pods, signs of life were beginning to return. Tech-slaves moved from one pod to the other triggering the wake cycle and the occupants were waking from their nine-month slumber and staggering out of their pods to a new year.

Draz felt the warmth on her face. She tried to open her eyes. They were stuck together after nine months closed. She tried to move her arms and she managed to rub her face with her right hand. She opened her eyes.

"Cycle. Complete," said the tech-slave to her in a staccato voice. "Welcome. To. Mars." It moved off to the next pod.

Draz shivered, not because of the cold, the air scrubbers had been warming the craft up after powering down for the long journey, but because she never liked those tech-slaves. They made her feel uneasy. She watched it trigger the wake cycle on the pod next to hers. She knew it was Alfred's and she looked forward to seeing him, even though to her and to him it was only a moment since they saw each other, it had really been nine months.

Draz staggered out of her pod. The floor was still cold under her bare feet even though the ship had been on warm up cycle. She heard a hiss then a cough and a splutter in the pod next to hers and Alfred staggered out.

"See? Totally safe," he said with a wheeze.

"What's up with you?" asked Draz as she dressed into the clothes she retrieved from the nearby locker.

"No-no idea," said Alfred, coughing. He straightened up, unpacked his clothes, and dressed.

Draz noticed as he was dressing that the flap of skin on the side of his head that held the implant had come loose and she could see the needle insertion point and the wires and circuitry implanted into his skull.

Alfred caught her looking and put the skin back. Draz looked away quickly and felt a little embarrassed that she had been seen gawping.

"It's not so bad," Alfred said quietly. Draz knew what he was talking about, but she did not reply. She kept her eyes on the ground.

After they had dressed, they stood around for a minute wondering what to do.

The other crew and military contingent of the *Green Dragon* were dismounting from their pods, dressing, and moving back to work immediately.

"Now what?" asked Alfred. He looked around rather puzzled. "Where's Artisius?"

"The captain will be on the bridge already; he would have been woken up a while ago with the first of the crew," said a passing crewmember, who overheard and then disappeared into the crowd before either of them could ask any questions.

"I guess we go to the bridge," said Draz.

Alfred nodded.

They moved out of the cryo-pod bay and made their way, rather unsure of their whereabouts in the ship, towards the bridge.

After a few minutes of walking, and when there were fewer members of the crew around, Alfred asked, "Did you dream?"

Draz stopped walking and paused for a second. Alfred stopped too, waiting for her. "Yes," she said. "I think, I'm not sure..." Draz screwed up her face trying to remember the fleeting memories in her head that seemed to be from dreams. "Yes, yes I did," she said after a while. She looked at the ground.

"Were they all right?" asked Alfred again. He was simply making light conversation as she had mentioned dreams before they got into the pods.

"No," Draz said after a while. "They were horrible." She looked back up at Alfred and there was sadness in her eyes. "They weren't nice at all. It was about my childhood and my parents and their deaths." The dreams came flooding back into Draz's memory. "I'd rather not talk about it. How about you? Any dreams?"

"Yeah..." Alfred said staring off into the distance down the corridor. "Blinky."

"Who is this Blinky? You've mention this person before..." Draz said rather troubled.

"My sister. She was my sister. She killed herself years ago," he was still staring down the corridor past Draz. He shifted his gaze to the floor, studying his feet. "I couldn't stop her..."

They both paused a while in silence and then Draz began to move down the corridor again. Alfred did not follow; he was still looking at the ground. Draz paused again to wait for him.

"You know, I used to know her exact face. Every detail of it. In my dreams and in my memories. Now it's fading. She's slipping away and I can't do anything about it." Alfred pointed to the implant on the side of his skull. "It's this, I know it is. One day I won't even know she existed," he said and grimaced. Then he smiled a sad smile at Draz. "But you don't need to know all that."

28

Draz looked concerned but said nothing. They moved off silently down the corridor and through the lift system up to the bridge of the ship. They reached the bridge and as the door slid aside, they saw Artisius pacing the command dais and issuing orders to his crew.

Artisius turned as he heard someone approach and he smiled. "Aha! Good you're awake." He was dressed in his blue dress uniform with gold trim and braid, and red epaulettes.

Draz and Alfred both nodded and stood at the edge of the dais respectfully out of the way as it was obvious that Artisius was busy.

Artisius moved over to them and addressed them both. "I trust you had a good rest?" He smiled.

"In a manner of speaking," Alfred said with a chuckle. He smiled at Artisius' blustering yet positive attitude.

"Good!" Artisius slapped Alfred on the shoulder. Then he spun on his heel and addressed one of the crew on the bridge. "Final count?"

"99.8 per cent success rate, sir," said the orderly.

"Success rate of what?" asked Draz.

"Survival rate of the cryo-sleep. We only lost a few this time..." Artisius trailed off when he saw Draz's expression.

"WHAT? You said it was safe. By lost do you mean dead?" She glared at Artisius and then at Alfred.

"Well...as safe as a nine month sleep can be." Artisius tried to defuse the situation, and failed.

Draz smouldered. She was angry that to assuage her fear they had lied to her. She fell silent.

Alfred looked apologetic.

Artisius pursed his lips and raised a hand to his brow, but also said nothing. He spun around again and faced the red planet that was taking up a large portion of the vision in the observation dome. He took a few steps towards it.

"Look at that! Have you ever seen anything more magnificent? The Red Planet! Mars!" Artisius opened his arms wide and let out a guffaw. He was obviously in a very good mood. "It was the second planet to be colonised by the human race; and the second planet to be destroyed by it! This was the planet many fled to when The War engulfed the Earth and nuclear fire scoured the Earth's surface. This was the planet many still flee to, to hide and disappear from their lives and from themselves. Mars is in the buffer zone between Collective Zone and Solar Solutions territories. It was originally inhabited by enthusiastic colonists from the Earth and then operations moved in to mining and terraforming. Then The War happened, and humans by the millions fled to Mars for peace and security. But with no government prepared to deal with so many refugees and then the corporations taking over after The War who really did not want to deal with the people who fled to Mars, the planet devolved into a massive pit of criminal activity and black markets. Mars was once the nearest neighbour to Earth and the God of War. Now, due to Earth and war, it is a crime infested cesspool where people go to be forgotten and almost anything could be bought, for a price. We should fit right in!"

Draz had remained silent as long as she could, letting Artisius carry on. "Why are you so pleased to see that dump? We all know about Mars being a centre of crime and black markets. And you've obviously seen other, better planets in your life. Why the good mood at all. We're supposed to almost be out of fuel too, remember?" Draz snapped, still hurt by their deception.

"Because, Draz, we've evaded the Collective's Great Fleet so far! That's worth celebrating! It shouldn't be too hard here to find fuel and provisions for our next venture into the Solar Solutions spaceways around Jupiter." Artisius smiled a charming smile and faced Draz. "And," he took a few steps towards her, "we should be able to disappear in the criminals and thugs of this planet. It will be easy to blend in; we are officially criminals to the Collective Zone after all. And I'm sure news of our little exploit on Earth will have reached here by now. Whether that helps with securing supplies or hinders as people will want to report us for a bounty we'll have to see..." He pursed his lips again. "Whatever the case, it's going to be fun!"

Alfred, who had been standing to the side and silently for now, gave Artisius a sideways glance but still said nothing.

"Sir, the planetary defences are hailing us," said the Communications Officer.

Draz, Alfred and Artisius all sighed in relief at the break in their conversation.

"Good," replied Artisius, moving to the computer terminal to talk privately to the docking commander on the nearest Martian space station. "I'll take this communication in private," he said putting on the headphones.

Draz moved over to Alfred. They were both staring out of the observation dome at the red planet in front of them. It was a giant orb of red sand and steel-like human construction. There seemed to be a large amount of debris floating around in orbit as if something had exploded and spread itself around the planet. There were numerous space stations in low orbit that looked like very large chunks of debris, as they were irregularly shaped and angular. Around these stations were large bulk cruisers and capital ships of all descriptions. Some were bristling with weapons, that Draz and Alfred could see, others were more civilian craft that simply moved slowly and low around the planet.

As the *Green Dragon* edged closer, they saw smaller ships darting in and out from the main space stations and capital ships on whatever missions that they had been assigned. The whole spectacle looked like a total mess.

"How are we going to get through all that?" whispered Draz. "I mean, we need fuel, but this place looks nuts. Have you ever seen anything like it before?"

"No," Alfred said eventually, "never," he added, his voice betrayed that he was shocked by what he was seeing. Mars was a chaotic mess and even Earth's spaceways looked ordered and regimented in comparison.

Artisius came back to them and stood on the command dais. "Ship wide broadcast please," he said. The Communications Officer nodded and gave him the signal. "Men and women of the *Green Dragon*, we have reached Mars. They have agreed to let us dock, for a price. We should be able to seek repairs and stock up on fuel here. All hands will be required with the repairs and refuelling. This is not a holiday stop. There will be no ship leave. I want all hands to work on this ship's repairs and refuelling."

Draz and Alfred detected a rather sullen nature come over the bridge crew at this announcement.

Artisius ignored it and continued. "Those are my orders. The Collective Zone fleet is pursuing us. We can lose no time. Oh, and the docking authorities have no idea the Great Fleet is pursuing us, so I would be grateful if you did not tell them. They are welcome to that surprise when they arrive." Artisius smiled at this. "They deserve it with the cost of this landing. Artisius out." He gave the signal to the Communications Officer and the link to the ship's speakers was cut.

"So, as you're not crew, you can investigate this planet, if you want to..." said Artisius turning to Draz and Alfred. They looked at each other.

"Isn't it a bit...dangerous?" said Alfred.

Draz smirked.

"Well...yes, but you might like the adventure!" said Artisius, a smile growing over his face. "I mean, the next trip is through the asteroids and to Jupiter, which will take another good deal of months...in cryo-storage. I just thought you'd like to stretch your legs a little."

"I'd rath--" said Alfred.

"We'll go to the surface," said Draz. "I can't stand cryo-sleep."

Alfred looked at her rather annoyed, but submissively.

"Oh, and that's good, because I might, it's not certain, but I might, need you two to help with negotiations...I've made some enquiries to some contacts, but we'll see..." Artisius added as almost an afterthought.

"Uh? But you said--" said Draz

"Yes, yes I said the Docking Master and I had agreed on things, but that was just for landing. We still need fuel and repairs..."

Alfred chuckled.

Draz glared at Artisius. "How much do we need? How much money do we have to work with?"

"Oh, a good frigate's worth of fuel. We have average fuel tanks, but above average reactors. As for currency, well, as I didn't get paid for my last mission on Earth, due to some stowaways." He looked at them for a moment. "We don't have much in the way of money..."

"Oh great, so we're supposed to bluff our way in and out?" said Draz, throwing her hands up in the air.

"In a manner of speaking. Look, they probably know a frigate blasted its way away from Earth by now, but they might not know which one, and even if they do, they probably don't care. There's no love lost for the Collective here." Artisius paused and scratched his brow. "We do have a rather large stockpile of ferkis powder...and some potential tech-slave candidates..."

Alfred stepped into the conversation, "No, I will not be a drug dealer and a slave trader in one go. No!" He emphasised his position with his hands by chopping the air.

Draz looked at him. Her eyes agreed with his position, but she was more practical. "We have no choice..." She looked at the planet out the glass dome, and then back at Alfred and Artisius. "We have no choice!" she said more resolutely.

"We have no choice," agreed Artisius.

Alfred stood resolute for a while, then his resolve cracked as he thought about their position. "All right, but we sell the drugs first and try to keep the slaves. I'd rather get rid of the drugs than become a slave trader."

"Agreed!" said Artisius. "I'm not that bad a person..."

Draz considered the position. Her facial expression gave away she would rather sell the slaves, but that was her addiction talking. "Deal!" she said eventually. "None of us are bad people; we just have to do questionable things sometimes..." She smiled at Artisius and Alfred. "How long until we dock?"

"About an hour," said Artisius. "I've organised a dock on that," he pointed out of the dome, "space station. It's called *Challenger 2*. We should be safe there for a bit. The Collective Zone fleet shouldn't get here for another month, by that time we'll be gone. Easy!"

"I admire your optimism, but things often don't work out like that," Draz said with a chuckle.

"No, well, we'll see. We've been all right so far!" Artisius smiled charmingly. "Oh Alfred, would it be possible, in the period before we dock, for you to zet for a bit and clear the system of anomalies? It's been nine months since last time and something may have gone wrong."

Alfred nodded and moved to the zetting station. Draz looked on concerned and as Alfred was preparing, she took Artisius aside and said to him out of earshot, "I'm worried about him, his condition seems to be worsening and it's due to the zetting. He said to me that he's forgetting things in his memory now..." She looked over at Alfred who was busy preparing the terminal.

"He seems all right now..." whispered Artisius.

"That's because he wants to zet, but afterwards he's said to me that he's forgetting things," Draz whispered, her face showing more concern than she intended.

"Noted," Artisius said. "But he's the only zetter onboard and it needs to be done."

"I know," said Draz, "but we can't use him up and then throw him away..."

"Station ready, permission to begin?" said Alfred loudly. Draz thought it was certain that he had overheard them, but he seemed not to care. Alfred would have to live with the consequences later.

Artisius moved over to him and tapped him on the shoulder in agreement. Alfred inserted the needle into his temple and rode the waves of pleasure as he soared through the ship's system again.

Draz stood on the bridge. She looked at Alfred, bolt upright with the zetter's grin, she looked at the red orb filling the observation dome, and she noted her tingling craving for ferkis powder.

"If we get out of this place and into Solar Solutions territory at all it will be a miracle..." she said quietly.

Chapter 6

The *Green Dragon* skilfully avoided the myriad pieces of debris that littered the space around Mars. The debris consisted of old spaceship parts, satellites, and general space junk that had accumulated over time. The ship came into dock at one of the many platforms that was suspended in low orbit around the planet. From here, people got shuttles to the surface and carried out repairs on damaged vessels.

Artisius addressed Alfred, who had just finished his zet and was calming down from the rush, and Draz, who was trying not to look distressed at both Alfred's condition and the fact that she was starting to look sketchy. Artisius knew this was from the ferkis powder and he reasoned she was feeling withdrawal, especially as they were going to trade away much of their surplus supply.

"So, Mars! Now all we--" Artisius began, in an attempt to sound grand.

"Why's there so much junk? Isn't that dangerous?" interrupted Draz.

Artisius, somewhat annoyed by the interruption, explained, "Around Earth the space junk had been cleaned up in the 23rd century after a number of collisions had rendered space ships of the newly formed corporations severely damaged. After The War, the newly empowered corporations had agreed enough to clean up the space around Earth for security and commercial reasons. It was not so for Mars. Mars had always been Earth's poor cousin, and had never had one cohesive government system of any kind. Many factions fought constantly over the red surface and one faction could not gain enough traction or influence to clean up the surrounding space. Besides this, they thought it was fun sport to watch craft explode and add to the circles of garbage that orbited the planet." He paused in his speech to see if Alfred and Draz were paying attention, they were. "There was some agreement between the warring factions that there should be some sort of control of what enters and leaves the planet, therefore a rudimentary customs system was set up on each entry port space station and is funded by all the large factions that control the surface," Artisius said, amazed that he had not been interrupted again. He could see that what he had said had made the pair rather nervous.

"Uh," Alfred piped up eventually, "I take it that ferkis powder is illegal here, as with everywhere else in the System?"

Artisius nodded. "Indeed," he said after a pause.

Draz looked stubborn.

"Then how the hell are we going to pass through customs with kilos of that!?" Alfred sounded annoyed.

"Easy," said Artisius with a smile.

Alfred gave him a sidelong glance as if daring him to explain himself.

Draz looked blankly at Artisius, and then a thought occurred to her, and she broke into a smile. "Ah, of course!" she said with a laugh.

Artisius smiled at her and they enjoyed their private joke. Alfred stared blankly at them and added after a while, in a somewhat annoyed tone. "Can you explain your in joke, please?"

"Oh dear, so innocent," said Draz, laughing. "Should I tell him, or do you want to?" She turned to Artisius.

"Please." Artisius raised an upturned, open palm in Alfred's direction encouraging Draz to continue.

Draz turned back to Alfred, who, it was apparent, was in no mood for jokes, and who voiced that he just wanted to know how they were not going to be sent back to the Earth Moon for smuggling ferkis powder.

"We pay them," said Draz with a chuckle.

"Pay?" said Alfred.

"Bribe," said Artisius, blowing the whole joke wide open.

A look came across Alfred's face, a look of understanding, disapproval, and embarrassment all at the same time. He blushed. "Oh," he said, "but? Oh...How'd you get it so early, Draz?" he asked.

"I've dealt with drugs before, and corrupt police before. Long story..." she trailed off. "You've really never bribed anyone in your life?" she said amused.

"Nope," said Alfred, he seemed not sure whether to be proud or embarrassed. "And Artisius, I assume you've done this a lot?"

"Countless times," he said, smiling.

"So, we're safe?" Alfred asked, anxiously again.

"Well...maybe," Artisius said with a wink.

"Hah, well with assurances like that!" said Draz with a laugh. She rocked back on the heels of her boots.

"Hrm," said Alfred, and left it at that, his brow furrowing with annoyance. "Slave trading, drug trading..." he said.

"Criminals?" said Artisius, a little annoyed to be spoken about harshly; he had saved Alfred after all.

"Hah, yeah, we are all criminals I guess," sighed Alfred, his anger deflating. "Come on, let's get this done." He shrugged

They all headed out of the bridge and through the *Green Dragon*. On the way they stopped in with the *Green Dragon's* armoury. Artisius armed himself with a pair of ornate pistols that strapped around his waist and made him look like some kind of gunslinger of old. They went with his dress uniform smartly and it was plain that he liked the way he looked. Draz chose a large calibre pistol, similar to her family one that she had lost on Earth. Alfred, reluctantly and with some protest, picked a smallish pistol that, although low in calibre, he would be able to fire quickly and accurately due to his lack of skill with a firearm.

Artisius also picked up three communicators and threw one each to Draz and Alfred. "If we get separated these should allow us to talk to each other, they're also computers with maps, if we need them."

After this, they headed to the docking tube that had been extended and connected in airtight fashion to the large platform above the Martian surface.

***

"Okay," said Artisius when they reached the end of the docking tube, "beyond these doors normal space laws of the corporations do not apply. The law is might makes right, remember that. Act tough; be confident; don't be afraid to threaten with your pistol and don't give anything away." He looked at both of them squarely in their faces. "We need fuel, repairs and supplies. We have drugs and slaves to trade, but don't give them away too easily. The Collective fleet will be here in a month, and then we have to leave, fast."

Alfred and Draz nodded.

"Do you understand?" Artisius said.

Draz fingered her pistol. "This will be just like scavenging in the Omega Quadrant and the towns out there." She smiled. "I know how to behave in this kind of environment."

Artisius nodded. He was confident that Draz knew how to behave in this situation. He was more concerned about Alfred, although he was an expert with computers and zetting, he was not inspiring confidence in the other two with his attitude and his anxiety. The last thing they needed was for someone to blow the whole operation wide open due to ineptitude.

39

"You good, Alfred?" Artisius looked anxiously at Alfred, who looked nervous.

"Not really, I'd prefer to zet rather than be a smuggler, but let's go." He smiled meekly.

Artisius looked at him a little longer and then turned to the airlock hatch. He pressed a few keys and the whole door slid to one side and out of the way. Ahead of them was the Martian Customs Union.

The trio stepped out of the docking tube and onto the surface of the platform. A tech-slave was waiting for them, and it asked them sharply what they were visiting Mars for.

"Business, and repairs," said Artisius to the half machine. The tech-slave looked blank as it processed the information and then rasped a series of instructions. Artisius turned to Draz and Alfred as the tech-slave stumbled off. "We need to head to customs and line up. They will ask you questions under lie detector conditions, so don't lie, or if you do, be good at it," he said as he led them through the throng of people milling around.

"What if we are caught," asked Alfred, trying to keep up with Artisius.

"You die," said Artisius over his shoulder. He realised he probably worried Alfred a lot with that comment and stopped in his stride and turned to face Alfred. "Look, they won't ask you anything hard; this is a criminal planet, after all. Just be calm and look confident." Artisius added a smile to soften the situation.

Alfred scowled.

Draz looked neutral; she was looking around in awe and the scale of the platform they were on and the clear, transparent roof of the space station that afforded a great view of the Martian surface a few hundred kilometres away. "This is amazing, not a dump at all!" she said, turning around to see as much as she could.

She stared at the people she saw walking past. Some were outlaws and miscreants from the corners of the Solar System. Others were military personnel. Artisius explained they were gang officers. Still others were traders and smugglers and all sorts of passengers from all over, and they were all in one giant melting pot.

Artisius smiled at his passengers' naiveté. He remembered when he was just as awestruck. He waited for them to stop gawping.

The trio moved off again. They walked past stores and food houses where exotic smells wafted out from different types of cooking that only Artisius of the three had experienced before.

As they walked a little too close to one of the stalls, Alfred was accosted by an elderly woman, speaking a language he did not understand. He tried to extricate himself from the situation by signing that he did not want the food she was trying to sell him, even though it did smell delicious. Draz and Artisius walked on and only recognised the lack of their companion after a little time had passed. They returned to see Alfred raising both arms to block the woman from force-feeding him something. Draz sighed. Artisius laughed.

"Help!" cried Alfred, blocking another attempt to force feed him. He backed away again, but the woman had him in her grasp with one hand, and a menacing spoon in the other.

Artisius approached the old woman and said something to her in her language and she instantly let go of Alfred and started yelling at him. Alfred staggered back, free from her clutches.

"Come on," said Artisius to Alfred as he grabbed him by the arm, and they made their way through the crowd again.

"What did you say to her?" Alfred asked after a short time.

"I said you were a drug mule and could not eat anything at the moment," Artisius said.

Draz let out a guffaw.

Alfred glared at Artisius, and then chuckled to himself.

They reached the customs check and ahead of them stretched a number of long queues that ended in counters where they could see people working to process the new arrivals.

"Okay now here are the customs queues. We join one and then get questioned independently when we reach the end." They joined a queue that stretched for a few dozen people and waited.

"What about our guns?" whispered Alfred.

"Oh, they're fine. Guns are fine. Everyone has a gun here. It's drugs and other illegal trades they're after," said Artisius.

"Oh, great," Alfred replied.

"That doesn't mean there are no drugs on Mars, by the way," Artisius added. "There are plenty, but they like to use their own planet produced ones rather than imported ones."

Alfred nodded vaguely. He looked at Draz who was looking around wide eyed and not really paying attention to anything Alfred or Artisius had said.

The queue moved slowly, and as it did, Draz and Alfred looked at all the types of people entering Mars. Artisius, who had seen it all a number of times before, looked blankly as the queue moved.

"First time off world?" asked Alfred as he saw Draz looking around, "apart from the Earth Moon?"

Draz nodded, awestruck at the difference between Earth and Mars. "I expected to be used to something like this due to my smuggling, but this is off the scale. And it's only one of the space stations above the planet. This is amazing. So many different kinds of people and things. I was wrong when I called it a dump earlier!"

42

"But surely you experienced something like it on Earth with the zone-cities and the Earth Ring?" asked Alfred.

"Well, yes, but I was only on an Earth Ring space station as a prisoner and the Atraxa Prime Zone-City was second nature to me. It was a lot different from this." Draz said, still looking around and craning her neck up to see the Martian surface through the transparent roof of the station. "I'd always expected to stay on Earth my whole life. I never expected to see other planets."

Alfred nodded.

"The air, it smells, different," said Draz. "I noticed it when we stepped out of the docking tube but now..."

"That's all the spices and chemicals used in the cooking and manufacturing on this space station," said Artisius. He was not marvelling at the environment, which they were in. He had seen and experienced all this before. He looked anxiously at Alfred and Draz. He was anxious about them getting through customs unscathed. He could see Alfred was anxious too.

The queue moved slowly onwards. Draz and Alfred marvelled at the diversity and variety of people and languages that were in the lines. There were parents and children talking away in their own languages; people bringing strange animals through that Alfred and Draz had never seen before; there were people from all over the Solar System. The majority seemed to speak a form of understandable System Normal speak but there were others speaking languages that were unintelligible to Alfred and Draz. There were also all different colours of skin tone on show. There were all manner of people trying to gain access to the Martian buffer zone between the two great corporations.

Draz tapped Artisius on the shoulder. "Why are there so many people trying to get access to Mars?" she asked.

He turned and replied simply, "To escape; to be forgotten; to start a new life; to make their fortune. Mars is the last truly free place in the Solar System, except for Pluto, and it's placed perfectly between the Collective Zone and Solar Solutions."

"But if it's run by gangs, how is it free?" asked Draz, her brow furrowing with confusion.

"You're still stuck in that 'the corporations are the best option for humanity' mindset from your days on Earth. Even after all they did to you, you still hold onto the idea that the corporate governance of every aspect of someone's life is the best option?" replied Artisius. He raised his eyebrows at her. "That everything can be solved with advertisements and iron control of the population."

"Well..." she began.

"No, they are free because on Mars you can do what you want, so long as you don't cross all the factions and Families. You are a lot freer here than anywhere else. It is lawless and dangerous, true, but that breeds its own kind of freedom. It's not for everyone, but I've seen a lot of this system in my life and there's nothing quite like Mars. On the other hand, almost every Solar Solutions station is the same, as is anything Collective Zone. They are all homogenous. Whereas Mars...Ah, it's my turn through customs. The light has gone green meaning I have to approach. Good luck! See you on the other side!" And with that Artisius reached the head of the queue and moved to the counter for his interrogation.

***

Draz waited next, not quite sure of Artisius' answer to her question. Then it was her turn, the light went green above the counter where people went in to be checked. Artisius had passed through the gate with little trouble.

Alfred waited third in line. He was nervous. The light above the counter went green and he took a deep breath before moving forward to face the customs guard.

"Name?" said the guard mechanically as Alfred approached. He was staring at a computer screen and did not look up as Alfred moved up to the counter. The guard was a large, brutish man with a big scar across the left side of his face stretching from his eye to his chin. He wore what Alfred assumed was a standard customs uniform of blue and black with a strange symbol of Mars on his left shoulder sewn into the fabric.

"Alfred," said Alfred, with a little bit too much of a tremor in his voice.

The guard looked up for a second, scrutinising Alfred as if to question the authenticity of his answer. Alfred swallowed hard. Then the guard went back to filling out the form on the computer.

"Reason for travel to Mars?"

"Business, and repairs," stammered Alfred, trying to remember how Artisius had put it to the tech-slave.

"Repairs?" asked the guard.

"Uh, yes, um, we ran into...hostile forces!" Alfred was pleased he had thought he had saved the situation without lying.

"Pirates eh?" said the guard, pressing some keys. "Name of your ship?" snapped the guard.

"The *Green Dragon*." Alfred suddenly felt very nervous as the guard stopped what he was doing and looked directly into Alfred's face. Alfred could not take his eyes off the vicious scar on the man's cheek.

"I see," said the guard carefully. "We've had reports that a ship matching that name blasted away from Earth, and that the Collective Zone military is searching for it!" He raised the one eyebrow above his good eye.

"Um..." is all Alfred could manage.

"Relax, mate," said the guard, smiling and leaning back in his chair. "We're no friends of the Collective. We aren't going to turn you over to them. It takes balls to blast away from Earth."

"But aren't you scared of them?" said Alfred, not quite knowing what to say.

"Nah, we have some space defences if they do come after you."

Alfred did not confirm or deny this.

"Don't you think they would have attacked us already if they could?" the guard said, smiling wider.

Alfred was mesmerised as the scar moved.

"Look, what are you trading for repairs? Perhaps we can come to an arrangement?" the guard said and cocked his head to one side.

"We could." Alfred nodded, unsure. "Um, various supplies; human resources, chemicals..." he stopped when the guard nodded.

"Well how about we say...you give us twenty per cent of your resources and...chemicals...and we call it even and I don't report you to the Collective? Fair trade eh?" The guard smiled, but Alfred could tell he was deadly serious.

"Okay..." whimpered Alfred.

"Good, you're clear. Remember our deal! Send your products to the Customs Union. Next!" The guard pressed a few keys on the computer and a gate opened next to the counter.

Alfred moved past the counter, and through the gate. He was shaking. He had sold away twenty per cent of their trade. He felt a fool and a failure. He saw Artisius and Draz waiting for him a short distance away.

"Aha! You made it," said Artisius. "How much were you stung?"

"Eh?" asked Alfred.

"How much of our 'produce' did you bargain away for your freedom from Collective Zone slavery?" Artisius said, laughing. Draz smiled at him.

"You mean, you too?" stammered Alfred.

"You thought we'd get through without having to bribe?" said Draz, her smile widening.

"Oh." Alfred felt a fool, and embarrassed. He looked at the ground, "Twenty per cent."

"WHAT?" bellowed Artisius.

Draz moved the palm of her hand to her forehead.

"It was five per cent for each of us," Artisius continued.

"Oh...but, the guard..." said Alfred.

"The guard said twenty per cent, you were supposed to bargain...oh well." Artisius stamped his foot. "So, thirty per cent of our stocks gone between us."

"Um...how do we get the stocks through customs though?" asked Alfred. Feeling his face going red, which was noticeable on his pallid skin.

"I've already done that deal. I took care of it," said Artisius, waving away the question with his hands. "I've bribed the guards to let a few of our pods through with our 'produce'...thirty per cent, huh."

"What now?" asked Draz, trying to save Alfred's face and divert attention away from his failings.

"We head to the surface in a pod, and meet with one of the factions to make a deal," replied Artisius, staring off into the distance. "Come on!" He marched off to where the stream of people was going.

Alfred and Draz had almost to jog to keep up with his stride. They came to the pod bay in short order.

"It's like a taxi system," said Artisius, "pods constantly going to and from the surface, for a fee."

They joined another queue and waited for their turn to ride in one of the pods.

Draz looked around at the construction of the docking bay. It was similar to that on the Earth Ring or the Earth Moon: a large metallic structure with magnetic shielding on one side so that the craft could pass in and out without decompressing the atmosphere in the room. There were a number of queues and a constant stream of small pods that picked up the passengers and took them where they wanted on the Martian surface.

"Why do I get the impression that, although these people are 'free' they have to pay a very high monetary cost for this 'freedom'," Draz stated flatly as they moved along the queue.

"Everything has a cost," replied Artisius. "You think your precious Earth's lifestyle doesn't have a cost?" he said.

Draz turned away.

"Look can we drop that, and can you explain to us what we do when we reach the surface?" interrupted Alfred, losing his patience with the debates about freedom.

"Okay." Artisius turned to him. "We reach the surface, we make contact with my ties to one of the factions, and then we propose a business deal and hope that they accept?"

"In some shady bar no doubt," said Draz, not wanting to be left out of the conversation.

"No, hah," Artisius said with a laugh. "In their office building." He smiled.

"Office building?" Draz and Alfred said in unison, not quite believing.

"Hah, yes, on Mars, the factions and Families have big, luxurious office blocks where they conduct their business. They are the rulers of the planet after all. Why would they need to operate in shady bars?...Here's our taxi." He turned and stooped to enter the taxicab front seat. Alfred and Draz followed by entering the back seats.

48

"Utopia Planitia, please," Artisius said authoritatively to the driver, who was a robot.

"Yes. Sir." said the robot and it guided the craft out of the docking bay on the space station and down towards the red planet below.

"You're a robot?" asked Draz.

"Yes. ma'am. I. Am. A. Robot. It. Helps. With. Language. Difficulties. I. Know. All. The. Martian. Surface. And. Can. Speak. All. Languages. In. The. Solar. System." the robot uttered in a staccato fashion.

"Handy," said Alfred. "But," he said turning to Artisius, "how do the people we're going to do...business with know we're coming?"

"Ah, well, I made some arrangements with the Martian authorities before you woke from cryo-sleep. We're going to meet our people when we land."

"Didn't you say that we had to help with negotiations?" Alfred checked the previous statement that Artisius had made back on the *Green Dragon*.

"Well...it's still a possibility. What I meant was you might have to help with negotiations with this contact. Everything is a business transaction. My contact should be able to supply everything, though." Artisius smiled at Alfred. "I was just making it sound exciting!"

"Will they be friendly?" asked Draz.

"Should be..." said Artisius and left it at that.

Draz and Alfred exchanged tense glances. They all headed towards their planetary destination in silence.

Chapter 7

Alfred, Draz and Artisius descended in the pod to the nearest docking bay to where they intended to go. They paid the fare and got out of the pod in a large area with many people milling around and going about their duties.

Draz voiced that this scene was similar to her experiences in the docking bays in Atraxa Prime.

Alfred, however, was looking around and was quite bewildered by the throng of people and the business of the docking bay. He said he had never seen anything like it. He was used to spaceships not large docking bays on planets with thousands of people filing in and out of the structure by the minute.

The structure was large and cavernous. It had larger ships that did not dock at the space stations around the planet, but docked at the upper levels, with the smaller craft for ferrying passengers, like busses and taxis, docked at ground level. Throughout there was a hum as people spoke to each other in different languages and the machinery of unloading cargo and docking arms were constantly in action.

Alfred noted the gravity was the same as on a space station. It felt a little strange. "What's with the gravity?" he said as they walked.

"Mars naturally has less gravity than humans like, so they installed gravity well generators in all the colonies on the surface to mimic Earth standard gravity. It's just like a space ship," Artisius explained offhand.

"So, where to now?" Alfred asked. He had stopped to take in the sight of the docking bay and was almost in danger of being left behind. Draz quickly grabbed him by the arm and pulled him after Artisius who was forging a path through the crowds.

"We catch a taxi to the office block of the Hangara Family," Artisius said over his shoulder making a straight line through the bustling crowd.

"Why all the taxis? Why not hover trains like Earth? They hold more people and are faster," asked Draz, also struggling to keep up with Artisius who was moving at a pace that belied his age. The crowd seemed to part like water in front of him, but not for Draz or Alfred who had to dodge around groups of people.

"Taxis allow the Families to keep direct control over the flow of people. And, they allow for direct charges for people, so the Families make more money. A train carries however many people for less cost than a taxi, but the Families cannot vet the people they see on a train," Artisius said as they reached the exit of the docking bay and passed from the cavernous interior of the structure that they had landed in, to the almost open exterior of the Martian surface.

They all stopped for a minute. All of them taken aback by the marvellous nature of the energy domes and metallic towers that stretched out before them. Artisius had seen it numerous times before, but to Draz and Alfred, it was new. From the metal surface of the ground that had been installed over the red Martian sands to the heights of the domes and towers, it was amazing.

"This is something else," Draz said, staring at the surrounding domes and towers. "I've seen Atraxa Prime's domes, but this really is something else. The domes there ended in steel rings to anchor them to the surface. Here they seem to stop on the surface. They look like energy fields? They have to be, the little ships keep zipping in and out between domes. They can't be glass. It's...amazing..." Draz trailed off, staring into the sky.

"The towers aren't bad either!" said Alfred. They stretched up to space from the surface of the planet. Each one branded with the logos and insignia of the respective Families projected into the atmosphere by holographic projectors.

Around them there was the bustling crowd still, and if they stood in one place for too long they were in danger of getting bowled over by the press of people. Nevertheless, Artisius waited and let Draz and Alfred marvel at the sight.

Neither Draz nor Alfred had seen anything like it. It all belied the mess that the planet looked from orbit.

"In fair Verona!" Artisius said above the noise of the crowd as he raised his arms as if to open up all the world to the dazed pair who stood at his side.

"Eh?" asked Draz.

Alfred smiled.

"Nothing, just something an old poet once said. It referred to a city ruled by gangs and Families." Artisius smiled.

"I see," said Draz. Her voice gave away she was lying. "Now where?" She looked around.

"This way," said Artisius and Draz had to drag Alfred by his arm through the jostling crowds.

They reached the taxi rank and waited in a short queue for their turn to board one of the small pods that would take them where they wanted to go. They were silent in the queue as Draz and Alfred were still marvelling at the gloriousness of the structures around them and the vast nature of the domes.

After a short wait, they boarded a taxi and Artisius gave the order to the robot driver to head to the Hangara Family structure. The taxi lifted off the ground and accelerated through the air to join pre-determined flight paths for traffic.

During the trip, which only took them a short time, Draz and Alfred in the back seats of the taxi kept pointing and gawping at the various structures on the Martian surface around them.

"New. To. Mars?" asked the robot driver in a staccato way.

"Yeah," said Alfred and Draz in unison. Artisius simply shook his head.

"Ah. Well. Enjoy. Our. Hospitality!" said the robot to his passengers.

The pod came to rest on a metal platform outside a vast tower like structure that reached up as far as could be seen. Artisius paid the fare and they all got out and stood for a minute absorbing the scene.

"They know we're coming?" said Alfred after a time.

"Should do," said Artisius. "They will have monitored our travel here and know who we are already."

Draz and Alfred gave each other a nervous look. "Already?" said Draz.

"As I said, taxis with monitoring devices allow for...control." Artisius headed for the large, glass sliding door in front of them. The other two followed in awe.

"I still think it's funny we're not meeting in some shady bar," Alfred whispered to Draz. She nodded.

"Gangs operating like businesses. It makes sense I guess..." Draz replied.

Before they entered the building Artisius pulled them up and said, "Less talk of 'gangs' and more of 'Families' please, we don't want to offend the people who will be helping us! One or a number of Families make up each faction that I mentioned earlier back on the *Green Dragon*."

Draz and Alfred nodded and blushed in unison. Alfred had no idea what he was doing, and he supposed Draz was the same. They had never conducted business deals with Families. Alfred knew Draz had fought in combat, and she had scavenged in the harshest environments, but she was not a businesswoman. Alfred had zetted with the best of them, he had lived a hard life on a space station; but he also had never conducted a gang related business deal. They felt rather out of their depth.

They entered the foyer of the Hangara Family building, and stopped. Alfred noted that his jaw was open, but he could not seem to close it. He looked at Draz who was similarly afflicted. The interior of the foyer was a richly detailed space with lush wood panelling and a tasteful fountain and luscious red leather chairs with a concierge standing behind a large wood panelled counter. There were plants growing in pots at various places in the corners. At a few tables and chairs were people doing what Draz and Alfred assumed were business deals while sipping strange concoctions from what looked like expensive glasses.

Artisius smiled a smile that gave away that he wondered what would be going through his two companions' heads, and that he was remembering past times. He chuckled to himself and headed over to the concierge. After a few words, the man spoke a few words into a communicator and then indicated for them to take a seat.

Artisius led the gawping pair to a secluded section of the foyer and sat down with them in some rich leather seats around a glass and metal table. Artisius sat so that he could see the entire foyer from where he was.

After a short time, a waiter came over and asked for their drink selections. Artisius ordered Hangaran Brandy for all of them, as Draz and Alfred were not really drinkers and did not know what to order. The waiter returned with the drinks, and they were left alone.

Draz looked like she was going to explode with questions, but she limited it to just one, "How?"

"Business pays." Artisius shrugged, smiling.

"And the wood?" said Alfred.

"Oh, that's from old stock; it gets refurbished from ancient timber. It is really rather rare, and expensive," Artisius sipped his drink, as did Alfred and Draz. "Do you like it?" asked Artisius indicating the drink in his hand.

Draz nodded.

Alfred was rather indifferent. He liked the taste, but it was not as smooth as Neptunal Brandy, but the effect was pleasant enough, however he wanted his wits about him in the coming business deal. He nodded as not to insult Artisius.

Artisius was watching over Draz and Alfred's shoulders and after a short time, he stood and waited. Draz and Alfred looked over their shoulders and, on seeing an approaching woman with some guards, stood too.

"Artisius! What a delight! How are you?" said the woman with outstretched arms. She was middle aged and dressed in what could best be described as a black business suit. The guards stood at a respectful distance, and they were dressed in military uniforms and had their guns clearly on display.

"Lady Hangara!" Artisius clapped his hands together and they embraced awkwardly. "I am well, I hope you are?"

"As well as can be expected. Who are the others?" Lady Hangara indicated Alfred and Draz.

"Friends, trusted friends," said Artisius.

Alfred and Draz nodded and gave their names.

"Well any friend of Artisius is a friend of mine. Please, follow me to my office." The four of them and the two guards moved towards the lift system in the back of the foyer, and they headed up to Lady Hangara's office. Draz and Alfred gave each other a look that they each understood: this could go well or very, very badly.

***

The lift interior was covered in mirrors and while Draz stared ahead into her reflection, Alfred simply looked at the floor. Artisius and Lady Hangara chatted away with some small talk, something about the Martian weather and the hazards of trading. Alfred was not really listening; he was too

55

preoccupied with the two guards behind them who seemed to be pointing their guns right at the visitors' backs. Alfred wished that the claustrophobic lift ride would end.

Finally, it did, and the group exited the lift onto a luxuriously decorated and adorned landing, which stretched off in two directions on either side of the lift. Lady Hangara indicated that they follow her off to the left and after a short walk, she came to a glass walled room. The door to the room slid open automatically as Lady Hangara approached and she stepped inside and then to the side of the door indicating with an outstretched arm for the group to enter. The guards stood either side of the door on the outside of the room.

The glass office room was lavishly decorated and had one large wooden table that stretched the length of the room and it was surrounded by leather chairs. One wall opposite the door had multiple computer and holo-screens on it broadcasting all manner of information to the occupants of the room. The screens were all muted so all the group could see was the faces of the various news reporters.

Lady Hangara took a seat at the head of the table and indicated for the others to sit. Artisius sat next to the matriarch and Alfred and Draz sat further down the table next to Artisius.

There was some more small talk. Lady Hangara asked if they would like some refreshments and Draz and Alfred nodded dumbly while Artisius expressed his enthusiasm for such a thing. Lady Hangara pressed an invisible button in the table in front of her and spoke a few words.

A minute later two servants entered and placed on the table in front of the guests one tray that had four glasses of spirits. And the other tray had four lines of a white powder and four thin tubes all laid out neatly.

Draz visibly jumped. She looked at the lines of white powder and then at Lady Hangara. "What's that?" she asked, indicating the powder.

"Ferkis powder, it's our speciality here on Mars. The Hangara Family make the best, of course. We have the best purifiers," said Lady Hangara. She smiled as she watched Draz's reaction. "It's free, you can have some, you know..."

Draz licked her lips. She looked at Alfred who gave her a disapproving glance but said nothing.

"I think I'll stick with the brandy; it is brandy isn't it?" interrupted Artisius. "We have some serious business to discuss," he said reaching for a glass and sipping it.

"Of course, Mars' finest brandy, distilled by the Hangara Family too," replied Lady Hangara not sounding offended at all. She reached for a glass and sipped it too.

Alfred picked up a glass and tasted the spirit in it. As far as he could tell, like in the foyer, it was not as smooth as the Neptunal Brandy he had tasted on the *Green Dragon*, but tactfully he said nothing and simply nodded his appreciation. He looked back at Draz who was staring at the lines of white powder. He gave her a worried look.

Suddenly Draz grabbed the silver tray with the ferkis powder on it and pulled it towards herself. She lifted one of the small tubes to her right nostril, and in short order, snorted one of the lines. She immediately sat back in her seat. Her pupils contracted to pinpricks and her breathing was short and laboured.

"Draz! Are you okay?" Alfred reached out and grabbed her by the arm.

Draz turned slowly to him, a grin forming across her features. She nodded slowly and sank back into the chair with waves of pleasure coursing through her body.

Alfred sighed.

"You don't approve?" asked Lady Hangara coolly. She had been observing the situation.

"Not...exactly," said Alfred, trying not to sound angry. He knew that this woman was their only chance of survival and so he could not insult her.

"But you are a zetter, yes?" She smiled as Alfred's gaze snapped from Draz to her. "Oh, I can see it in your face. The sunken cheeks, the sallow skin, the loose flap of skin on your temple." Lady Hangara's smile widened as she saw she had hit a raw nerve in Alfred. "Don't be so quick to judge others, when you, yourself, have vices..."

"But I have a purpose. It's my job!" Alfred interrupted; he was not going to be lectured.

"True, but you knew what would happen. Tell me, have the dreams started yet? The loss of memory?" Lady Hangara said and continued before Alfred had time to reply. "Anyway, this bores me. Tell me Artisius, why are you here?" Lady Hangara's tone had changed from friendly to menacing.

As Alfred smarted and turned to watch Draz, who was lolling about in her chair, Artisius outlined their situation.

"Lady Hangara," he said in a placating tone. "We know you are very busy, but I thought you could help an old friend."

She listened with a blank expression on her face.

Artisius continued, "Our ship has suffered some damage and we require repairs and fuel for our reactors. We have slaves and drugs to trade, but I see you have diversified since I was last here," he looked at the drug tray, "and you probably don't need the drugs. We still have plenty of slave stock to offer, not all of it was required on our last stop. We would be grateful if you assisted us."

Lady Hangara paused for a few seconds, thinking, and then began, "Where are you headed? And how did you suffer the damage?"

"We are headed out-system, towards Neptune. And we had an encounter with a Collective Zone weapons battery. It chewed up our auxiliary fuel tanks and some levels of our ship quite badly. If we had the fuel we would have passed right by Mars, but it was impossible--"

Lady Hangara interrupted him. "So, the Collective Zone is after you? Hah, Artisius, finally you have chosen a side." She smiled again. "There is no love for the Collective here on Mars. I suppose they are following you?"

Artisius nodded.

"Well then," Lady Hangara continued, "we had better get your repairs done. If the Collective Zone forces arrive here, they'll have some surprises waiting for them. Please, drink up, I will order your repairs and fuel shortly. And as for the slaves, you know where they can be unloaded. I will have use for them."

"Unfortunately," Artisius looked at Alfred, who felt indignant, "due to a little ineptitude and lack of skill we have to pay thirty per cent of whatever we bring in to customs..." admitted Artisius. "How many slaves will this cost?"

"Thirty per cent!?...I won't ask how that was so high. That's okay, I can make do with seventy per cent," she finished with a rather forced smile. "How many slaves do you offer?"

Artisius frowned a little in thought. "How about ten pods?"

"Ten?" Lady Hangara paused. "Make it fifteen and you have a deal. Remember I lose thirty per cent."

"I'm sorry I can't go past twelve..." Artisius smiled at the bartering game.

"Then twelve it is! As always it is good doing business with you, Artisius." Lady Hangara smiled widely.

Artisius bowed as best he could in the chair and finished his brandy. "Your hospitality exceeds itself, Lady Hangara." She nodded her approval. "Now," Artisius said, "if my two companions could leave the room I have some private business to discuss..." Artisius looked at Alfred and Draz.

Draz, who was starting to become more lucid again, gave Artisius an apprehensive look. And Alfred voiced their concerns. However, before any protest could be raised, the guards came into the room at Lady Hangara's order and escorted Alfred and Draz from the room to another meeting room further along the corridor. The guards stood at the entrance preventing their escape.

"I don't like this," said Alfred to Draz.

Draz nodded; she was still unsteady on her feet. She still shook a little and her eyes were glassy.

Alfred said nothing more as Draz collapsed into another leather chair; he looked at the armed guards, and then looked at the floor again. His brain was starting to fizz. He wanted to zet, and that insult thrown by Lady Hangara had not helped.

***

Back in the main meeting room, Artisius waited for Draz and Alfred to be out of earshot before continuing.

"So, I also have some...technology that I would like installed on my ship," said Artisius.

"Technology?" asked Lady Hangara in the pause Artisius left.

"Yes, it is on a red hard drive from pre-War years. It may be a matter of life and death that this technology is implemented..." Artisius said.

"Before The War? And it still works? What is it?" Lady Hangara was intrigued.

60

Artisius nodded. "Pre War and yes it still works. I've seen the tech in action. I cannot tell you exactly what it does; all that I can say is that I want it installed on the *Green Dragon* with the utmost haste."

"I cannot help you if you do not tell me what it is," Lady Hangara insisted.

"Trust me, if you knew, and the Collective Zone found out, it would mean your death, and the destruction of Mars. I cannot tell you; I just need it installed," said Artisius; he knew how to do business on Mars.

"Ah, you do know how to do business here." Lady Hangara smiled. "I do understand that you would not say such a thing unless it were true, I know you, and I trust you, Artisius. I will aid you. Consider it done. If the technology is so dangerous then I value my little empire here more than it. I'm sure we can deal with the Collective without it."

"Very wise, Lady Hangara, I can assure you that without the technology you are safer than with it. The Collective Zone is after us for it. They would easily raze Mars for it." Artisius added to the drama of his words with his hands.

"If that is all shall I call your friends back in?" Lady Hangara asked

"Please, but no mention of what I just said, to them..." Artisius stressed the words.

Lady Hangara nodded and called for the guards on her communicator. In a short time, the guards returned with Alfred and Draz, who was looking rather more sober now.

Lady Hangara stood and Artisius followed. They all exited the glass room and stood on the landing in front of the lifts.

"Well, it has been pleasant meeting you," Lady Hangara said to Alfred and Draz. She smiled at Artisius. "Now, Artisius, I'm sure your friends can have a wander around this Hangaran sector of Mars by themselves? Would you like to continue business a little more, informally?" She smiled seductively at Artisius.

"Definitely, Lady Hangara," is all Artisius said to her as he followed her down the corridor and around a corner in the structure. "I'll contact you on your communicators!" Artisius shouted back at Alfred and Draz.

***

Draz and Alfred were left with the guards and exchanged looks with each other before stepping into the lift and taking a ride back down to the foyer. The guards gave them a hand full of cash before ushering them out onto the street.

Draz looked back up at the structure behind them. "I don't like this," she said.

"We all have our addictions, apparently," said Alfred a little caustically. "He's a bit of a womaniser." Alfred smiled at Draz, who was looking rather dishevelled after her latest drug experience. "You okay?" he asked.

Draz shook herself a little. She knew she had a problem but did not want to admit it. She ran a hand through her hair that was a little too greasy and messed up after her latest trip. She noted the feeling in her brain: that of withdrawal and recovery from the last use of ferkis powder. She knew she had to use again, and soon. The addiction was taking hold again; she had almost had it managed in prison too, even with the availability there. And now she had sunk right back into the dependence.

Alfred noted her pause and decided to save her face. "Come on, let's explore. I'm hungry!" he said and started to walk in the direction of what looked like shops given their neon signs.

Draz waited a second and then followed him silently with unsteady legs. The thought running through her mind was one of whether she could sneak upstairs in the building and snort another line.

62

**

Alfred and Draz wandered around some of the streets surrounding the Hangara Tower. The streets were crowded and bustling with people. The strange neon signs of the shops illuminated the streets below as even though it was daytime, the towers and spires of the Hangara complex rose up and blocked some of the light and as such the shops and streets had a twilight quality and they had their neon signs activated all the time.

Draz lingered at a stall set out onto the road. It seemed to sell fragrances and soaps. Alfred paused in his walk after he realised that Draz was no longer with him. He looked back at her. He had never really taken the time to look at her, carefully. He watched her. She moved in rather jagged movements, and she looked a little dishevelled, particularly her hair, which had regrown a bit since the Moon, even in cryo-sleep. He noted that she picked up some bottle and smelled the top of it. He realised that he found her attractive, although he would prefer if she left off the drugs, that was not his style. But she was attractive. He could see that under the tough exterior and rough edges, there was just a person trying to survive in the Solar System by any means possible. He smiled and walked back to her. Draz seemed oblivious to him. She had not realised that he had been watching her. She was absorbed in the perfumes and smells.

As Alfred approached, he realised that Draz was shaking a little. It was difficult to see, but as he stood next to her, he could tell she was shaking. "You all right?" he asked, partially knowing the answer already.

"Yes, I'm fine," she snapped.

He knew this was false. "You're shaking..." he said.

"It's cold," she said, putting down a perfume bottle.

Alfred knew this was also false; and he knew Draz knew it too. The atmosphere inside the domes was heated to a comfortable temperature and kept at that during the daytime before cooling a little at night, just like all stations and colonies. The actual harsh temperatures of Mars were kept beyond the domes and towers and were never allowed to encroach on the habitable zones.

Alfred said nothing more. He simply stood and watched. If Draz wanted to talk, she would, he reasoned. It was not up to him to put words in her mouth.

The shop owner had taken an interest in her customers search for a perfume, and came over to assist. Draz had picked up the perfume again she had sniffed earlier.

"Would you like to buy something for your girlfriend?" she said. She was an older lady who had led a hard life of a street stall seller. She was short and had grey hair. The lines on her face marked the fact she had lived.

"Oh, we're not..." Draz began pointing with her finger at herself and Alfred.

"Oh, my mistake, sorry...but would you still like that perfume, you've been holding and smelling it a while. It's very nice," the seller continued.

"It is," said Draz, a little absentmindedly. She looked at Alfred.

"Well, the guards did tell us to look around, and they gave us money, so why not?" He produced some currency, and the older woman selected the amount. Alfred was grateful, as he did not know the currency.

Draz slipped the perfume bottle into her *Green Dragon* uniform pants pocket. It fitted easily. It was only small, but she liked the fragrance.

"Now...food," said Alfred.

"I'm...not hungry..." said Draz as they meandered through the stalls and shops of the side streets.

"But I am." Alfred smiled.

Draz frowned and then smiled at him. "Okay, okay..." she said giving in. "What should we eat?"

"As we really have no idea, why not here?" Alfred pointed to a small cafe style shop where people were sitting and eating and drinking.

"I suppose..." said Draz a little guardedly.

They entered the establishment and sat at a table that was free. They waited and a robot came over and greeted them. After a short search through the menu, they made a choice and waited. They were not really sure what they ordered but it would be an adventure, they reasoned. It seemed, from the people around them, that it was actual food; real food; not just reconstituted mush like both of them were used to.

As they waited for their food, Draz asked, "How do you do it?"

"Do what?" asked Alfred, not really understanding.

"Manage withdrawal. I thought I'd almost controlled the stuff, but now I've fallen right back in the shit!" she said emotionally.

"Prisons are full of drugs?" said Alfred.

"They are, and I did use a bit, but I had to stay alive and to get the stuff I had to do...favours..." she paused, Alfred nodded understanding, "so I kind of got off the stuff, sort of, but now, when it's freely available and good quality..." she ran a hand through her hair and blinked away the emotion.

"I don't manage it. I crave my next zet." Alfred looked at the table, not at Draz. "That's the truth. I feel the pangs now and I can't wait to get back aboard the *Green Dragon* and zet." He paused, and looked at her. It was obviously not what she wanted to hear. He shrugged. "I know I'll lose all my memories one day and end up a tech-slave. But I do what I do."

Draz looked upset. Alfred could not tell whether it was for her sake or his.

"It feels like my brain is crawling--" Draz said.

Then, their food arrived, and it was a welcome distraction from the previous conversation.

"It's...real?" said Draz, rather bamboozled.

"Yeah, I'm used to reconstituted muck back on..." Alfred trailed off. The memory of losing his home was still raw. Alfred thanked himself silently that he still had that memory.

Draz said nothing.

They prodded and poked the strange meals in front of them and when they had worked up enough courage, they managed to eat some of them.

Alfred enjoyed his meal. It was a little spicy and meaty; some sort of Martian curry. Draz was a little more reserved. She was not really hungry due to the synthetic opiate still in her system, but she ate a little and she said it tasted all right to her.

They finished their meals in silence and paid at the counter with some more of the cash from the guard. Then they went for a walk.

The part of the colony that they were in was starting to move into night mode. As they walked the street lights and neon signs got brighter and the night closed in. They walked for a considerable time and some distance, waiting for Artisius to contact them on their communicators.

Alfred and Draz had explored the area surrounding the Hangara Tower and so decided to branch out into the surrounding districts. They noted that the area they had wandered into was rather poorer than the areas they had been before. There were fewer shops and more cramped houses and slum like dwellings.

After a short time, Alfred said to Draz, "I don't like it here...let's go back to where we were. I think we're being followed..."

Draz nodded and agreed. They started to retrace their footsteps but became lost in the maze like side streets of the slum.

Alfred started to worry. Draz was less anxious. "Look, we're not lost--" Draz reached for her communicator and the map installed on it.

"Oh yes you are!" said a voice from close behind them. Before Draz or Alfred could draw their pistols, a heavy weight thumped down on each of their heads and Alfred fell to the ground, his head swimming.

Draz fell to the ground and as she rolled over to see her assailant, she saw a trio of brutish men with red spiked hairstyles and tattoos on their faces in her blurring vision. One of them hit Draz again and left her unconscious in the back street.

Alfred tried to cry out, but was hit over the head again as he felt himself being lifted and carried away. He fell unconscious.

Chapter 8

When Draz came to, her head thumped with pain. She rolled around on the ground for a while, trying to stop the world from spinning. As she regained consciousness, she remembered Alfred. She turned on her side and realised he was gone. They had taken him!

Draz stumbled to her feet and felt a wet patch on her side. She reached into her pocket and felt the crushed remains of the perfume. She felt rather upset about that.

She saw two smashed communicators on the ground, one was hers, the other was Alfred's.

Trusting in her scavenger sense of direction, Draz ran off, retracing the path they had come, back to the Hangara Tower.

Draz burst in through the front door and tried to make her way to the lifts at the back of the foyer. She was stopped by a guard with a large machine gun.

"They've taken him." She gasped for air after running.

The guard was silent.

"Tell Artisius, some thugs have taken Alfred hostage!" Draz yelled as best she could.

The guard indicated to the concierge to do that and a short time later Artisius and Lady Hangara, both a little dishevelled but in their immaculate clothes from before, arrived in the foyer and Draz relayed the information to them.

"What did they look like?" asked Lady Hangara.

"Uh, red hair...tattoos on faces." Draz indicated the face with a pointed finger; she was regaining her breath.

"Spiked hair?" asked Lady Hangara, not really in a questioning tone. She sounded rather annoyed, and Draz reasoned it was because she and Artisius were...interrupted.

"Yes!" said Draz, pointing at Lady Hangara for emphasis. "You know them?"

"I do," said Lady Hangara, looking at Artisius who nodded in agreement.

"They're pirates from the asteroids nearby. They have their base there and operate with impunity in this sector," Artisius said. "I've encountered them before; brutal bastards they are. What about his communicator; we can track him on that."

"Our communicators were smashed and lying in the street. Why would they want Alfred?" asked Draz.

"Did you mention anything...sensitive while out?" asked Lady Hangara. "Now think carefully," she added.

"Uh, we talked about...addictions? I bought some perfume...we just chatted," Draz said exasperatedly.

"Did you mention zetting?" asked Artisius.

"Uh...yes?" said Draz, a little sheepishly. "But it was in a nice cafe and--"

Artisius clapped his hands in frustration. "Well there you have it; they overheard you somehow and tracked you down."

"But..." said Draz, "how?"

"They abduct zetters and use them as slaves, real slaves, until they turn them into tech-slaves. Or they ransom them back to their crews for huge prices," said Lady Hangara calmly. "Is he valuable to you?" she turned to Artisius.

"He's our only zetter at the moment," Artisius said. "And he's a good man," he added after he saw Draz's expression.

"Then I will help you find him. But first, we need to conduct those repairs and refuelling. Perhaps you," she looked at Draz and Artisius in turn, "had better stay in my tower until the repairs and such are done. We don't want any more mishaps," Lady Hangara concluded and marched off in the direction of the lifts.

Artisius glared at Draz, who looked sheepish.

They followed Lady Hangara in silence. They guards followed behind them.

***

Draz, Artisius and Lady Hangara with her guards ascended in the lift again in silence. At the landing at the top of the lift, Lady Hangara dismissed her guards and the three of them walked to the glass meeting room. When they entered the glass meeting room and Artisius let fly.

"Lady Hangara, our friend is missing," said Artisius.

Draz flinched at the mention of the word 'friend'. She was staring at the silver tray with the lines of white powder still on it.

"And you want to keep us locked in your tower?" Artisius continued. "I'm sorry for the outburst but I too know pirates and if we wait to rescue Alfred he will be off world by then and we will have lost him for good. We have to act now!"

"Have you finished?" snapped Lady Hangara. "Look, I know you need to rescue him now, and I'll help you. You'll have all the resources of my Family that I can give you to rescue him."

"But why did you say..." said Draz.

"Because I have reason to believe that the pirates have infiltrated my guards, or tower staff. I'm in the process of organising a purge but I can't help but feel the blame of your friend's abduction lies partially on me. I can't trust any of my so called protection crew. There have been threats on my life, theft of cargo, and even people have gone missing..." She slumped into the chair she had sat in before.

"I'm sorry, I--" began Artisius.

Lady Hangara waved him silent with her right hand.

Artisius ended what he intended to say.

"So, when you said you'd help us find him?..." said Draz, annoyed that their supposed ally had perhaps caused the abduction of a friend.

"I mean I can point you in the direction of the pirates' probable holding space for prisoners. I cannot give you any other military assistance unfortunately, by way of soldiers. I don't trust my own guards. I only keep them on as a pretence so that other guards and Families don't become suspicious. And so that the pirates don't tweak to the fact that I'm onto them." Lady Hangara put a hand over her eyes and forehead and massaged her temples. "It's so complicated."

"Look, whatever help you can offer, we'd be grateful," said Artisius as he sat in the chair next to Lady Hangara and reached out a hand in sympathy. Lady Hangara looked at Artisius and smiled.

Draz was staring at the tray again. In one smooth movement she moved over to the table and picked up one of the tubes. In an instant Artisius' arm shot out and grabbed her hand that held the tube and grasped it tightly.

"I need you sober. We need to rescue Alfred. There's no time for self oblivion." He glared at her with a seriousness that Draz had not seen before. "I need you," he added.

Draz froze for an instant. She looked like a rodent caught in the lights of an oncoming hover train. Her brain screamed at her to break free from the grasp and use a line; just one more; just one. However, she knew that Artisius was right. As he let go of her hand slowly she paused and then dropped the tube. She swallowed hard and sat down in a chair next to Artisius. She knew she had to regain control.

"Okay, what do we do now?" Draz said with a purpose. Her brain still screamed at her.

"Now, we get you to their hideout," Lady Hangara said with a smile.

"And how do we know where that is?" snapped Artisius.

"Well, you know how I said that the pirates had infiltrated my guards? I caught one of them, and with some...persuading...I managed to get the information out of him. The problem is I don't know how many of my guards are now spies. They use non tattooed and non hair dyed infiltrators." She smiled wider.

Artisius laughed. "You are a remarkable woman. We must move quickly before they take Alfred off world."

"True." Lady Hangara nodded. "I must prepare my forces to aid you, not military, you understand, but I can give you transport. They won't have taken Alfred off world yet; these pirate groups are always rather disorganised. Let me show you to your quarters where you can wait for a while, while things are put in motion."

Chapter 9

Alfred hurt. He was not sure what part of him hurt, just, everything hurt; but especially his head. He kept his eyes closed. In fact, he could not really open them. The throbbing inside his skull got worse when he thought about opening his eyes.

What had happened? What was going on? He was unsure of these things. He could not really remember clearly what had happened. He remembered flashes. He had been walking with Draz, and then, someone had struck him. Yes, that had happened. Then he did not know what happened after.

There seemed to be a thrumming bass sound around him. It penetrated his skull and made the pain strobe in time with the thrumming of the sound. Colours pulsed behind his vision in time with the pain and the sound. The pain was a deep crimson colour. It ached in the back of his head.

Then someone opened what sounded like a heavy door and came into the space he was in. He could tell it was a person due to the forceful footsteps. The door slammed with a loud crunch. Alfred flinched at the sound. It made the pain worse.

Alfred was still unsure of what was happening, and he still could not open his eyes. The person said something in a language Alfred could not understand. Someone responded in what sounded like the same language. Alfred realised that there must have been someone watching him before the other person came in, as only one set of boots entered the room.

The conversation between the men, as Alfred could tell they were both men, made the colours burst and meld across his vision and mind behind his closed eyes. He felt sick.

Alfred's brain was trying to make sense of the situation. He felt very woozy and rather ill, but he tried to make sense of the circumstances anyway. He was not quite sure why he was here...

He tried to move his hands to his face, to try to shake off the feeling of illness. The strange language conversation kept going; kept pulsing. He could not move his arms; they seemed to be tied together behind what he reasoned was some kind of chair.

It suddenly all came flooding back to Alfred: the alleyway; the thugs; the attack. He had been kidnapped!

Alfred's eyes snapped open, and he wished that he had not done that. The world swam in front of his vision, and he felt very ill. He groaned involuntarily. He did not want to alert the two men in the room, but his body had to make its discomfort known. So he groaned again.

The two men standing in the room turned in unison to face Alfred. They looked brutal with their face tattoos and their red hair. He saw them through the haze of his vision.

Alfred noted that the room was smallish and somewhat like a container for shipping produce across the Solar System. It was metal, and had a large, solid door at one end, behind the two men.

One of the men walked up to Alfred with a heavy tread and peeled back Alfred's right eyelid to stare into his eye. Alfred shook to protest but the man grabbed Alfred's head with the other hand and studied his eyes. The man said something else in the strange language and let go of Alfred's head and eyelid. The men laughed and the other man, standing nearer the door, left the room and disappeared for a while.

"Wh-what's happening?" pleaded Alfred. "Where's...Draz?" His words were slurred, and he was groggy.

74

"You'll work for us now, slave," said the man in a thick accent with a laugh. But at least he was speaking a language Alfred could understand.

"Where's...Draz?" Alfred insisted.

"Your bitch was left behind. We only wanted a zetter. By the time your 'friends'," the pirate laboured the word, "realise what's happened, you'll be off world with us. Get used to the rest of your short life as a zetting slave, before we turn you into a tech-slave." The man laughed again and fell silent.

Alfred's mind was racing, even with the concussion. He had heard of these pirates that operate between Solar Solutions and Collective Zone territory. Some even operated within the territory of the two corporations. They were extremely dangerous and not to be trifled with. They abducted people for all manner of reasons: all manner of different slave labour that they needed. Obviously this bunch needed a zetter, their last probably met with an unpleasant end. Alfred shuddered. He was afraid.

"Hey, hey where are we?" Alfred yelled, despite the pounding in his head. He had to seem assertive and not give in to these brutes. All they respected was violence. Alfred was not an assertive or violent person, but he knew how to survive.

The pirate laughed and wagged a finger at Alfred, as if to say, "Nice try."

Suddenly the door to the container opened and a group of pirates entered with an even larger man than the others at the head. Alfred assumed this man was the leader. The leader must have some sort of addiction to muscle building and steroids, Alfred thought, because he was huge. Or maybe he had had some sort of black market surgery to enlarge his human form. There had been tales of such a thing on *Florida Station*. Across his body he carried two large pistols in holsters and a rifle across his back. Alfred also noted that a couple of his entourage also had rifles and pistols on them.

The group hung back a little while the extra large man approached Alfred. Alfred smiled at him as he approached; even though Alfred was terrified, he had to maintain some form of calmness. He had to seem aloof even if he was scared witless. He had learnt from Draz in the Earth Moon prison: her resolve, her stoicism. Even if you have no hope, you have to keep your wits about you. You have to act. You have to try. He remembered Draz, and wondered if he would ever see her again.

The pirate leader grabbed Alfred by the skull and man handled his head around to inspect his eyes and his implant in the side of his head. Alfred winced at the man's grasp. It was like a vice.

The leader released Alfred and stood back. "What's your name?"

"Alfred," said Alfred. He had no reason to lie.

"Okay Alfred, I'm Pirate Leader Grekthax, you work for us now. You can zet, yes?" said the pirate leader with a surprisingly good accent and calm tone for his position and stature. Alfred had assumed he would be some sort of knuckle dragging idiot.

"Yes, yes I can," sighed Alfred. "Which pirate group am I captured by?" He pressed his luck.

"The Red Spikes," said Grekthax with a semi flourish of his bright red spiked hair.

"I see. And what do you want me to do in my zetting?" asked Alfred calmly, although his insides were seething.

"We need you to keep our ship running. And I warn you, if you try any funny business, you'll be a tech-slave before you can think of escaping. Clear?"

"Very clear," said Alfred with a shudder. If he feared one thing more than death, it was being a tech-slave. But the pirates had not checked his lifespan. They had not downloaded his information from his implant and seen that he was already deteriorating. They seemed to assume that he was in perfect health and that they had made a good kidnapping. Alfred said nothing, but grinned a little. If he were going to be a slave, he would not be a very good one, their ship would not get far if they pushed him to zet as much as he could. He would simply die from overwork with his deteriorating implant.

"Good, then we understand each other," said Grekthax, clearly understanding nothing from Alfred.

The pirate leader undid the restraints on Alfred's hands and feet and then one of the others blindfolded him and they led him through what seemed, to the blind Alfred, a few twisting corridors and a lift up to a room that, when the blindfold was removed, looked like a crude and rudimentary bridge with lots of wiring exposed and a few crew terminals where other pirates worked to operate the ship. Everything was very rudimentary and basic, nothing like the *Green Dragon*.

Alfred looked around. "Is this the bridge of your starship?" he asked calmly, even though he was terrified he was about to be taken off Mars and lost forever.

"It is. We need you to get it ready for space flight. Over there." Grekthax pointed to a crude zetting terminal and shoved Alfred in that direction. "And don't try any funny business 'cause we've got blocks installed for that. If you try to disable the ship, you die."

Alfred stumbled a little and then regained his footing. His head still throbbed. It was not advised to zet when the brain was troubled after any form of concussion, but Alfred was pretty sure his captors did not care about that. And Alfred had greater concerns about being taken off world. Perhaps he could delay with the zet? Perhaps he could damage their ship?

Alfred sat at the terminal and prepped the system for insertion. The system was simple but usable, and thankfully in his language. He got it ready in about thirty minutes and all the while the crew watched on and prepared for launch.

"How long since this was last used?" asked Alfred, genuinely curious, as it seemed as though the system was reluctant to accept his commands.

"A while, why?" snapped Grekthax

"Well, the longer a system isn't zetted, the longer the zet will take, and by the looks of this, this zet will take eight to ten hours..." replied Alfred.

"WHAT? No," bellowed the pirate leader, stomping over, "you have four hours!"

"Not possible," said Alfred, surprised at his own calmness in the face of the pirate. "Really not possible. I'll need seven at least."

Grekthax fumed at being outdone by a mere slave. However, it was clear that Alfred was right. "Do it fast!" is all he said and stormed off.

Alfred smiled to himself. He was learning how to deal with these brutes. He just hoped that his friends would find him in the seven or so hours he had just bought himself.

He raised the needle to his temple. This was going to hurt, he knew. It was an old system, and he was injured. He counted down slowly from five, and on zero, he inserted the needle into his temple. And then there was bliss, pain, and oblivion.

Chapter 10

Trader Virtus was in his element. He roared out advice from the top of the preaching dais instructing his subjects to be saved. He felt as if some power coursed through his body as he energised the room with his rhetoric. The Bull God was ascendant, and the charts were full of green lights.

Virtus almost felt sorry for those he was saving. Because he knew, that no matter how many people were saved, how much money was saved, and how much people worshipped the Bull God, he had a greater task to perform. Although being a Trader was his life, Virtus knew that to free the computer from its human shackles was his calling. He knew that he had to accomplish this task on as many colonies on the border of Solar Solutions space as possible. He had been tasked with such an undertaking many years ago; he had been converted, as it were, to the cause of the Computer God. He had felt its touches while he zetted secretly back on *Florida Station*. And he would test the computer here as to its true desires.

But first, there was the sermon. It was one of his finest, even if he thought so himself. He was whipping the crowd up into a frenzy. The brown robed priests were collecting donations and saving people by the dozen; by the hundred. Virtus could do no wrong in his words and he knew it; they flowed like liquid silk from his mouth and, even he, felt touched by their power. He was a man of words; they were his strength and his weapon.

There was one thing however, that threw off his balance and tempo. There was his Guide standing, almost out of sight, but not quite, in the back of the Church. Virtus knew that the man was probably watching him on Commander Anya's orders; and he probably would have done the same if he had been the Colony Commander and a lone survivor had appeared from the destruction of a station. But it was throwing his speech off a little, and he did not like that. The Guide would have to be dealt with, but carefully. He could not kill the Guide, as that would arouse too much suspicion and that would be the end of him, he knew. He would have to think of how to deal with him. At the moment though he would have to accept his presence.

It would not take long to grow the Sect here, Virtus thought. It had already begun, he had heard that already, systems were starting to fail, and tech-slaves were starting to rebel. But he needed more, much more.

The sermon finished and the crowd seemed to slump at the same time as if recovering from some great, taxing exercise, in order to catch a breath, and also the crowd seemed to cry for more as if Virtus' words were like a drug and he had to administer more to them in order to keep them in a state of bliss.

He liked his job. Nevertheless, it did drain him of energy to deliver such a sermon. He had to maintain the pretence of being the Head Trader even if he were trying to destroy the colony. He had to look like he was doing the job of a Head Trader because if he simply concentrated on the Sect, the Guide would find out and report it to Anya, and then, Virtus knew, his time would be up. Plotting the destruction, and actually destroying, stations and colonies was a terrible offence; it was mass murder, and he would be sent to the Earth Moon at least, or simply just shot.

He had to work carefully. It was a pity he did not have someone as malleable and pliable as that Alfred character back on *Florida Station*. However, Virtus had worked up his position on *Florida Station* for years; he had only been on the Europa Colony a short time.

Trader Virtus stepped down from the dais and the crowd of people surged around him. They tried to touch his clothes as if somehow that would bring some of his charisma, power and luck to them in their attempts to be saved and invest their capital.

The brown robed priests, seeing the leader almost mobbed as he tried to move into the back rooms of the Church, pushed forward and cut the crowd off from their intended target.

Virtus, who was an older man, and rather thin and frail, although he wanted the adoration of the crowd, knew that they could tear him to pieces of he was not careful. So, he welcomed the brown robed priests' intervention, and he was spirited away into the back rooms of the Church.

The door closed on the first of the back rooms that wound their way behind the dais as in the Church back on the former *Florida Station*. As there, here there was a small maze of rooms with different purposes. The first room being a reception room for private guests of the Head Trader. The other rooms ranged from private zetting terminal, so that Traders and priests, if they could and if necessary, could keep a close look on the markets from within the network, to a communications terminal, so that messages could be broadcast from the Church to other ships or stations or colonies. There were also darker, more sinister rooms that Virtus had appropriated for use of the worship of the Sect. As no one other than Church staff went that far into the rooms, Virtus believed that they were safe from prying eyes.

As Virtus entered the first of the back rooms of the Church, he sighed. He felt rather sore. His old limbs were not as good at making grand gesticulations as they used to be. Nevertheless, it was a good day on the trading floor. He had inspired many people to be saved. Now he had other, more important work to do.

Thankfully, that spy of Commander Anya's was not able to get into these back rooms, yet. It would only be a matter of time before Anya gave him the authority to access these rooms and then Virtus must have a way of dealing with him, like he dealt with that damn pest Gabriel back on *Florida Station*.

Virtus moved through the rooms until he got to the private communications terminal. Each room was dimly lit and sparsely furnished. They had a few lights on the metal walls. Also, around each room were metal tables and chairs. The communications room had a large and rather old terminal built into the wall that was used for sending messages directly from the Church without the interference of the command structure of the station. This was because it was viewed that the Church would have some confidential information regarding the markets that may be needed to be communicated without the knowledge of the command structure. It was religious confidentiality.

He had an important message to send to an old friend. Virtus knew that he had to inform his friend on how the whole plan was going: the spreading of the Sect and the destruction of the bases along the Solar Solutions and Collective Zone border.

Virtus opened a small, black book that he kept on his person in his robe and booted up the communications terminal. He searched in the book for a moment and then entered the required codes for CEO Uxus' personal communicator so that, wherever Uxus was, and Virtus did not know where he was at present, he would get this message.

The computer hummed as a connection was being established. It said that the personal communicator of Uxus was nearing Mars. Mars! Virtus realised that he had to hurry with his plans, with their plans. Of course, Virtus knew that he had been out of action in the cryo-pod for a long time, but the fact that the CEO was almost ready to attack Solar Solutions space made Virtus' heart race and his palms perspire. He had to work fast.

"CEO, I am ready to continue my work here on the Europa Colony. *Florida Station* was a success. I hope our plan will be in full swing soon. The people here trust me. I await your commands. May the Sect rise!" Virtus spoke softly and calmly. He only needed the message to be short. He shut off the computer and hoped that the CEO would reply soon, even if the message would take a while to reach its destination.

Chapter 11

The *Silver Ark*, flagship of the Solar Solutions fleet, and her guardian ships made their way swiftly past the trajectory of the cold orb of Uranus; due to planetary orbits, the planet Uranus was not on the shortest route to Jupiter.

As the craft moved, they gathered Solar Solutions ships from garrisons along the route, which had moved on an intercept path to Gunter's fleet. The engines of the craft thrummed silently through the void as they forged on toward their goal of Jupiter.

The crews mostly slept unknowingly of the space around them, and when each shift awoke to continue the work on the craft, they merely performed their tasks and then retreated to their cryo-pods. Only the blank tech-slaves were awake to observe the majesty of the Solar System, but it was lost on them.

The ships flew without radio signal in order to make them silent and perhaps surprise the Collective Zone forces when they arrived.

The crews hoped that they would get there in time to prevent the Collective Zone breaching Solar Solutions territory. They hoped...

Chapter 12

The *Old Monarch*, with CEO Uxus onboard, forged silently through space. It had almost caught up with the Great Fleet led by Fleet Commander Boltha on the *Iron Bastion,* as the Great Fleet was not operating at maximum speed in order to preserve fuel. They knew their prey was headed for Mars and they would get there, in time. It was always concerning, time. The great distances in the Solar System meant that nothing could be undertaken lightly and if something went wrong, no one was there to help.

Most of the *Old Monarch's* crew were in their cryo-pods; sleeping quietly through the long and tedious journey between the celestial bodies. They were still many millions of kilometres from their destination: the Red Planet. A skeleton crew operated the ship; those who were chosen to be the unlucky ones who would have to remain awake throughout parts of the journey so as to make sure nothing went wrong with the spaceship's function.

The skeleton crew did alternate during the journey. Only was it very rare for anyone to remain awake for the entire journey other than the standard tech-slave contingent of the ship.

This was a very rare time. Both the *Iron Bastion* and the *Old Monarch* were going on the same mission, and CEO Uxus was travelling with them.

Commander Vorthox of the *Old Monarch*, who had been tasked by his CEO with keeping awake and waiting for a special message, stared out the forward observation windows of the bridge of the starship. He was bored, very, very bored. He had been awake the entire journey: months and months of staring into space, quite literally, and waiting. He was not sure if the message was ever going to come. In fact, he had driven himself quite mad by waiting at the communications terminal, or tasking another of the skeleton crew to wait at the communications terminal while he took a few hours' sleep in a normal bed before returning to his post.

To save power, space ships on interplanetary travel powered down most system except for basic life support, gravity well generators, and some rudimentary form of lighting. The bridge therefore was rather silent and empty with most of the monitors and holo-screens shut off with only a few lights illuminating the walkway through it casting eerie shadows against the metallic walls.

Vorthox wondered for the millionth time why had he been punished so; why had he been chosen, the commander, to be the one awake the entire journey? There were others, others less important, who could have done the job. But then he reasoned that the message must be critical. So critical, in fact, that only he could wait for it.

"Yes, that was it..." he chattered to himself.

He chewed on his nails while counting the stars, for the millionth time. He winced as he drew blood from the ruin of his fingers.

"I'll call you...Hekteries!" He pointed a bloody finger at one of the millions of stars out the window.

He felt the clawing madness in his mind. Being the only one awake for nine months aboard a space ship was not good for the sanity. Yes, there were others he could talk to from time to time as they made their awake shifts to keep the ship running. But only he, only he had to stay awake the entire time, with only short bursts of normal sleep to ease the journey. There would be no cryo-pod bliss for him. No, never.

Vorthox returned from the front of the bridge to the communications terminal. Nothing. Nothing was there. It sat silently, casting a harsh green glow over his face as he stared into it. He thought, for an instant, he saw shapes and words moving across its surface, had the message come!? He blinked, no, no; it was only his eyes playing tricks. There was no message. Nothing.

"There's nothing. Nothing again!...And still nothing!" he called out to the empty bridge. His voice echoed eerily around the chamber. "But I will wait. Oh yes. I have been chosen!"

There is only so much utter repetitive boredom a mind can take, before it starts to hallucinate and make imaginary phantoms to ease the pain. Vorthox had begun to talk to himself. He had started to do so a few weeks into the trip. He addressed walls and doors and other, imaginary beings in the ship. He would talk to himself as he stared at the communications terminal. The other skeleton crew had started to avoid him at this point, which only made his isolation and madness grow.

He would talk to the stars as they shone through the glass of the bridge windows. He would address each one by name, at least, a name he had given the star. He would talk to the other crew in cryo-pods, as they lay, oblivious to his actions. He would run his fingers over their vision slits in the pods and talk to them, for hours, about his day, about the nothingness of his existence.

When he did get a small, short chance to sleep, he would dream fitful dreams of war and death and simple madness. The phantoms in his dreams haunted his waking hours, too. They pursued him through the dark corridors of the ship. They chased him, as he ran, breathless, trying to avoid their cries in the corridors.

"Who's that!?" Vorthox spun around at the computer terminal. "Oh, it's you," he addressed a shadow in the bridge. "I don't have to be scared of you..." He turned back to the terminal, his mind gnawing at his very being. He turned again to look at the shape projected on the wall of the bridge. It was still the same. It had not moved. He smiled. "I knew you wouldn't move when I saw you..."

He had gone mad; he had gone quite mad. And he knew it, too. But it was for a good cause? Wasn't it? He was serving his lord and master the CEO. The message would come, he knew it would, the message would come.

Vorthox began to cry.

And then, suddenly, the terminal he was sitting at began to chatter to life. Vorthox jumped, partly out of shock and partly because his elbow had slid off the desk, where he was resting his head on his hand. He could not believe it. There was a message coming through, specifically for the master, the CEO's personal address was on the top. The message had come through!

Vorthox jumped out of his seat and gave a horrid cry of joy and terror. There was no one else on the bridge to hear him. In fact, the entire sector of the ship would have been deserted apart from the tech-slaves, but he stopped himself and looked around. This message was top secret, and he had to keep it that way.

He did not know what the message was, as it had to be unlocked by the CEO in order to be seen, but it was the message, the message had come! He had been useful! Perhaps the CEO would thank him with a cryo-pod sleep, perhaps. However, he must not get too hasty. He had to wake the CEO!

Vorthox bolted down the corridor as swiftly as his frame would allow. He ran like he had never run before, all the while dodging the demons that popped out of the darkness to greet him. They would have to wait. He could tell them what had happened later. Right now, he had to wake the CEO.

After a time, Vorthox finally reached the CEO's personal cryo-pod chamber. It was guarded by two tech-slaves who stiffened when he approached. He bowed and addressed them the only way he knew how.

"Th-the message, has come!" Vorthox stammered. He hoped they would understand. They seemed to and began the thawing procedure on the pod, without a word.

The procedure would take about thirty minutes, so Vorthox paced back and forth in front of the pod and rehearsed what he would say, over and over again.

"Sir, the message. No. Sir, the message has come? No, no. CEO, your message has arrived! Argh!" He hit himself on the head repeatedly. How should he say it? He had to get it right!

Suddenly CEO Uxus stepped out of the cryo-pod in front of him. He looked younger. The longevity surgery had worked; and he had survived the thawing process in the pod.

"CEO Sir!" Vorthox grovelled.

"Yes?" said the CEO, somewhat amused by his subordinate's manner. Uxus had no idea the torture the man had been through.

"The message, the message you asked me to wait for, for all those months alone...it's here!" Again, he bowed and grovelled.

"Thank you, Vorthox. Please, lead me to the terminal after I have dressed." The tech-slaves were already bringing Uxus' clothes for him, as Vorthox had not realised that the man was standing in front of him in his underwear.

"Oh of course!" Another bow and Vorthox waited outside the chamber for his master to dress into his customary grey clothes.

After a short time, Uxus emerged and Vorthox led him to the bridge, desperately trying not to talk to any of the shapes that emerged at him from the darkness.

"It must be quite something, to be on this ship, basically alone, for all these months..." Uxus said.

Vorthox flinched. He was unsure of whether his master was tormenting him or just making a flippant comment. "Not, that pleasant, CEO." He screwed up his hands into fists.

"No, I imagine not. It would be rather boring..." replied Uxus.

"Boring...boring...boring boring," muttered Vorthox.

They reached the bridge and Vorthox presented the communications terminal to the CEO as if it were some sort of new hover car being sold; he gesticulated with his hands rather profusely.

"Thank you, Vorthox, now I must enter my special code..." Uxus sat down at the terminal and entered his personal authorisation number to unlock the message. "Good, it worked, now let's see if my friend has been successful." He did not shoo Vorthox away, he could not deny him the pleasure of seeing his master's response. To Uxus it was clear that, after all that time alone, Vorthox had gone rather mad, and the man could be unstable if not shown the message.

The message played back from the screen. "CEO, I am ready to continue my work here on the Europa Colony. *Florida Station* was a success. I hope our plan will be in full swing soon. The people here trust me. I await your commands. May the Sect rise!" Uxus sat back from the screen when the message had completed.

Vorthox looked triumphant. He had done it! "Well, CEO?" he clapped his hands together manically.

Uxus whispered to himself, "That deluded fool of a priest thinks that I actually care about his Sect? Hah, he's just softening up the defences of the front line of Solar Solutions space for me. I couldn't give a damn how he does it as long as those colonies and stations are taken care of so that all I have to worry about is the Solar Solutions fleet."

Uxus sat in the darkness of the bridge except for the glowing terminal in front of him and some emergency lights and he prepared a response. After informing Virtus that he was doing a good job and to continue his work that he was doing, Uxus sent the message that he would be arriving at Mars soon and for Virtus to be ready with the plans concerning the Jupiter colonies. Uxus encrypted the message for Virtus and sent it on its way.

"Very good, Vorthox, very good. You may go to cryo-sleep now, please, prepare a pod for yourself. You have done well!" Uxus said, still sitting at the terminal, not watching the mad man beside him almost have a fit of ecstasy. Vorthox bolted off down the corridor from the bridge mumbling something about sleep.

Vorthox had managed to prep a cryo-pod for himself with the aid of a tech-slave and while babbling incoherently about how successful he had been and how much the CEO would reward him he was frozen with a manic grin on his face. He would be woken at Mars like all the rest, maybe, but due to his time spent almost alone on the ship for months, he would never be the same.

Chapter 13

Draz waited. Alfred had been taken the night before. Draz had not slept. She waited in her quarters as assigned by Lady Hangara. The quarters were richly decorated and clearly intended for use by high-ranking dignitaries and officials that had to do business with the matriarch of the tower. One wall of the room was covered in a mirror surface. The others were lined with wood panelling and painted plasterwork.

Draz sat on the edge of the bed. She shook. She leant back. She felt the softness of the covers between her fingers. They were fine silks. They were coloured black and white in geometric patterns; now scrunched up by Draz's balled fists.

There was a counter next to the bed. It held some glass flasks that held some of the finest liquors on Mars, distilled by the Hangara Family.

But that was not what was bothering Draz. Next to the liquors and glass bottles was a silver tray, very similar to the one from the boardroom. On it used to be a number of lines of high quality opiate. Roughly thrown onto the tray was an ornate snorting tube made also of silver that was engraved with all manner of fantastical beasts and creatures.

Draz breathed shallowly, in short, panting gasps. She could not focus. Her brain was swimming with the power of the drug. Pleasure beyond measure coursed through her body.

She lay back slowly into the enveloping softness of the bed covers. They seemed to wrap around her and comfort her. She tried to speak, not necessarily to anyone, but just to herself. She mouthed the words but could not produce enough breath to make them to become anything other than whispers.

Draz felt herself slipping away into oblivion; but she did not care. Everything felt like it was slowing down: her breathing, her pulse, and her mind. It was all slipping away.

She turned her head, with effort, towards the mirror wall. She saw herself lying on the bed. Her short hair was a mess. Her face was drawn and ghoulish. Her skin was a sickly pallid shade. She was sweating. She saw herself ruined and distraught. She saw herself...dying.

Draz thought of her childhood, of the admiration of her parents, and how it had all come to this. How she was now just a druggy. An opiate user. A junkie.

She saw her parents flash before her fading eyes, and the disapproval they showed to her using drugs.

The first time she had used flashed before her mind. She was back on Earth, when she was only a teenager. She had been to a friend's party and there had been ferkis powder used there. She had used then, not for peer pressure or anything like that; but simply because it was there, it was something different, something new, something exciting. She was hooked from that moment.

As her life went on, she had managed to control her urge to use and only use sparingly, sometimes. In the past, she had fallen for the chemical a few times, but had recovered.

But now was different. She was alone. Alfred and Artisius did not understand her. Her life had fallen apart. Between the treason trial, the Moon Prison, and now being an outlaw against the Collective that she had grown up serving, she had lost all sense of what it was to be safe. And so, she had turned back to the one thing that had never let her down; the thing that had offered her warmth and comfort even in the darkest times. And now was very dark. So she used. When it was available, she used.

Draz swam in the feeling of the drug; letting it roll and wash over her like a warm bath.

More images raced through her consciousness. She was not sure whether they were hallucinations caused by a use of a large amount of the drug or if it was simply her mind trying to remain in control, and failing.

Draz saw her early twenties, and the drug use that had gone with it. She had always been the best scavenger, in her discipline and ability. And that discipline had been exhibited in the use of drugs too. Back then, she could take anything and then function just fine a few hours later. It was always just an escape for her; until now.

Then came the image of Alfred. It flickered across her vision. She smiled. She saw him criticising her for her use of drugs. She felt angry. But she knew it was an hallucination, so she let the waves wash the pain away.

However, the image of Alfred would not go away. "What are you doing?" she mouthed to him. "You're not here." Her brain was confused. She knew Alfred had been abducted but here he was standing over her and trying to make sure she was okay.

She liked Alfred, perhaps a little more than as a friend. But she was not ready to tell him that. She did not want any emotional entanglements. She knew that emotional attachments ended in pain. She had to suppress the attraction to anyone as in her current situation she could not maintain any form of relationship. It would only end in pain. And so, she used.

She heard a knock on the door. "Wh-who is it?" she said after straining.

"Artisius. Are you okay?" came the reply. It sounded concerned.

Draz did not reply. She was torn between the ghosts of the past and the present. She did not want to be a drug user. She did not want to die horribly. But the pain of her existence cried out to her for some sort of anaesthetic.

The door opened when there was no reply. Draz heard a swear word and felt like she was being lifted up in someone's arms. She lolled her head around and stared directly into Artisius' face. His expression was a combination of terror, anger, and worry.

"Take it easy," she said. "I'm fine..." She slurred her words.

Artisius started to call out for assistance. Draz heard another voice, the voice of Lady Hangara asking what was wrong. Draz heard Artisius explaining angrily that there should have been no drugs on offer in Draz's room. He was still cradling Draz in his arms.

Draz heard Artisius talking to her and giving her reasons to survive. He shook her and told her to stay awake. He said for her to snap out of it. He gave her reasons she could live without chemicals.

Draz's view was blurred as she saw his face next to hers. She wondered why he was so upset. There was nothing wrong with her position. She was fine. Nevertheless, she began to see his point; she knew she had pushed it very close to the edge this time. She had nearly overdosed. Even now, her breathing was very shallow.

As she heard Artisius speak, Draz was overcome with strong emotions of sadness and pity. The drug could not keep them out. She felt very sorry for herself, and she began to cry. All the suffering she had been through came back to her and she let it out with big sobs. She missed Alfred and she did not want him to die due to her drug abuse; due to her lack of responsibility; due to her wasting time with drug use.

As Draz cried while listening to Artisius giving her reasons to live, and she watched Lady Hangara look disapprovingly down at her, and she again saw Alfred in the haze of her mind, she realised that she had to stop.

As the drug washed through her, with all the comfort of an old friend, she made the decision to stop. This would be the last time. This would be the last, last time.

After a while, Draz started to feel reality coming back. She started to breathe a bit easier. She managed to focus her eyes on things, and she saw Artisius sitting next to her on the bed. He smiled as he saw her face coming back to normal again. She wiped her eyes.

"So, you're back. You had me worried that time," he said, partly angrily, partly relieved.

Draz groaned. The chemical wore off fast when it had expended its power. She felt terrible. "Ugh, yeah," she said, holding her head in one hand.

"Don't do that again, please," Artisius said with a distressed look.

"That...was my last time..." Draz said, rather terrified of the prospect.

"Good, let's keep it that way," Artisius said with a fake sound of belief in his voice. He knew as well as Draz did that she would try to use again, especially when the withdrawal kicked in.

Draz smiled at Artisius. She knew that the withdrawal would be hell. She noticed Lady Hangara waiting just outside the door. "Are the preparations made for rescuing Alfred?" Draz asked.

"Indeed they are. We're waiting on you," said Lady Hangara, who still looked slightly annoyed at Artisius blaming her for facilitating Draz's drug use.

Draz stood up a little shakily and moved towards the door. "I'm fine, shall we go?" she looked at Artisius.

"You have the constitution of an ox!" he said, laughing.

Draz did not know what an ox was, but she assumed it was something tough. They moved towards the glass walled meeting room on the same level to discuss the rescue.

***

Draz still felt uneasy on her feet and the warm glow of the drug was fading, only to be replaced by the hollow gnawing of withdrawal. She had said, all too easily, that that last time would be her last time; but she knew the long process of aching longing was ahead of her.

They sat in the glass meeting room and another woman came into the room. She was dressed in military fatigues, and, by Lady Hangara's warm greeting, Draz assumed she was rather high up in the ranking of the Family.

"This is Slistra," Lady Hangara said, extending an arm to indicate the woman. "She's my head of security. She's trustworthy. I've made sure of that. She will be briefing you on the information gathered about the pirates."

"That was fast," said Draz, a little too harshly for her own liking. She did not like that the information on the pirates was so easily available. It suggested to her that Lady Hangara was somehow in league with them.

"When you're in my line of work, one has to know everything quickly," snapped Lady Hangara. "I cannot just sit around in oblivion all the time!"

Draz smarted at the comment. She fell silent and fumed. Artisius smiled. Draz shot him a vicious look. He stopped smiling.

"You must be Draz," said Slistra the security chief calmly. "I assure you that we already had an idea of the pirates' whereabouts due to your description of them. You see, each Family has its own territory and traditions. The pirate gangs are similar. So, we could narrow it down with your help and with the knowledge we already had. Combine that with the fact that we have agents everywhere and we, in the last few hours, have been able to locate your friend," Slistra stopped for the information to sink in.

"So where is he?" asked Artisius.

"Here..." Slistra brought up a map of the part of the colony they were in on a large computer screen on a wall and pointed to a flashing green triangle.

"That's close," said Artisius.

Draz did not know as she was new to Mars.

"Yes, we should be able to get you two there within a couple of hours," stated Slistra in a matter of fact manner.

"Let's go then," said Draz.

"Don't you want to be armed first?" Lady Hangara smiled.

Draz reached for her large calibre pistol on her thigh as a sign she was already armed.

Artisius smiled again. "We'll need a heavier armament than these simple pistols." He indicated his armament.

"The security detail here can arm you to the teeth when going into a pirate compound," said Slistra.

"Come," said Lady Hangara moving towards the exit to the room. They followed her down a few corridors and down a few floors in a lift. When they exited the lift, they were standing in a large metal room that seemed to be armoured and was full of rank upon rank of guns and other weapons.

"Holy shit!" said Draz, her mouth hanging open.

"Indeed!" added Artisius. "You could equip a whole army with this!"

"Don't you think I do?" Lady Hangara smiled. "You may have any weapon here. And take these energy scanners; they'll help you locate the largest power source which should be the space ship's engines."

"Um, but how are we going to get into the pirate compound?" asked Draz. "Won't that require some sort of tank or large gun?"

"I will fly you in over the walls with one of our special hover-ships. It should have enough firepower to blast your way into the pirate base and it will cause a diversion while you look for your friend," said the head of security.

98

"You are really helping us, and I thank you for that, but why are you doing this?" asked Draz.

"Because I know what the pirates can do, and what it's like to lose someone to them. That's all I'll say on that matter," snapped Lady Hangara. "Now, find a gun or three and load up. You do know how to use them I suppose?" she asked with a smile.

Draz perused the nearest rack with various assault rifles. She picked up one and readied it to fire by slamming in an empty magazine and aimed it at a wall and pulled the trigger. The gun mechanism clicked as there were no bullets to fire. Nevertheless, she had made her point.

Artisius smiled. "We know how to do this, as you can see. Me being ex military, Draz being ex scavenger. We can do this," he said, almost nonchalantly.

"We must do this," said Draz. She paused and swayed on her feet a little. The pangs of withdrawal were getting stronger, but the action of picking weapons and getting ready for fighting held off the worst of the feelings.

"You okay?" asked Slistra, not knowing Draz's condition.

Artisius looked at Draz, rather concerned.

"I'm fine," Draz said. She steadied herself on the nearest gun rack. "Just nerves, that's all..."

Artisius and Lady Hangara exchanged glances, but said nothing.

Draz and Artisius loaded up on an assault rifle each to complement their own armament that was already strapped to their bodies. They were weighed down with ammunition and positively clanked whenever they took a step. They had also both donned bandoliers to hold more ammunition.

Draz looked at Artisius. She was surprised at how much he could carry for a man of his age. But he seemed at home loaded up with guns and ammunition.

He saw her looking and smiled. "I may be older than you, but I'm not weaker!"

Draz laughed and hefted her assault rifle. She had not fired one in many months, since the Moon. And back on Earth she had given up rifles for her large calibre pistol due to practical reasons and the fact that an assault rifle would have slowed her down as a scavenger. Nevertheless, she knew how to use one; her mother had made sure of that.

Of course, this rifle was of a different design from the Collective Zone issue ones, but it was similar, and Draz understood its function without error.

When they were ready, they headed towards the exit indicated by Slistra, who was now their guide through the armoury. Lady Hangara had wished them good luck and had departed for other business as they were choosing their guns.

Just before exiting the room, Draz saw a crate of grenades. "Wait a sec," she said hefting one of the large bombs and strapping it to her bandolier. She smiled and clipped a second grenade to the straps. She felt good. The adrenaline from the nerves of getting ready for combat had almost blotted out the withdrawal pangs. It was only temporary, Draz knew, but for the moment, she felt good. "All right, let's go!"

They marched out of a hole in the wall of the Hangara Tower and onto a large landing platform. They had to wait a second for their eyes to adjust to the light, but Draz and Artisius saw a large hover type craft with rotors and jet engines parked at the centre of the platform. It looked vicious and deadly. It bristled with guns, which resembled angry teeth, and looked somewhat like a sea predator from Earth that people had learned about in history classes; when the seas existed. It had missile pods under its wings and a large cannon in the nose beneath the pilot's cabin.

"Wow..." Draz said.

Slistra smiled, but said nothing and headed towards the pilot's compartment.

Draz looked up and saw the expanse of the massive dome reaching above them and off into the distance. The Martian sky was a kind of reddish-blue as some light refracted in what little atmosphere there was. The dome shimmered as the energy fields that maintained it pulsed and kept the human survivable atmosphere in. It joined other domes above the ground allowing for open craft to move around without breaking the dome into the harsh Martian atmosphere. Where the domes joined in the distance, there was a slight ripple and fizzle of energy as the shields melded.

"It really is an energy shield! It looked like it from the ground!" said Draz, staring at the shimmering dome as she saw it up closer at the high altitude on the landing pad.

"Well what did you expect? Of course, it's a shield. Glass would be too fragile, and ships have to get in and out," said Slistra as she fired up the craft.

"On Earth the domes are super reinforced glass and steel," Draz replied.

Draz and Artisius climbed into the back troop transport part of the craft and closed the door with a sliding clunk.

The craft's engines whined into action and after a few seconds of building lift, the craft took off from the platform and soared over the section of the Mars colony that Lady Hangara ruled. They sped off into the distance towards the pirate stronghold.

Draz and Artisius sat silently in the back of the craft. They held onto their seats as it banked and roared into the dangerous skies above the pirate stronghold.

Chapter 14

The pirate space ship's network was crude and unsophisticated. It was the worst network Alfred had ever had the misfortune of zetting. He did not soar through the system; he sort of crawled; he did not encounter the odd problem to fix; he had to fix whole sections of the network that had gone dark due to lack of maintenance. It had been months since the system had been zetted, the pirate leader had said; it seemed like years. Alfred had never seen a system in such a state of disrepair. And as soon as he fixed an issue, something else went wrong and he had to try to fix that too and the cycle repeated itself.

The system was so run down that the actual process of zetting was painful. Usually, zetting was blissful and a dopamine rush, here, it was physically painful as his neural network tried to make sense of the mess that it was interpreting. Alfred still felt the dopamine course through his system, and he knew that this was what he lived for. And he knew he would lose a bit of himself when he logged out. Some more of his memory would be gone, something more of his non-religious soul would have vanished from his mind. He would be a lesser person, he knew.

Of course, this run down system was all to his advantage, Alfred knew. The longer the zet took and the less that was repaired, meant that his friends had a longer time to find him. On the other hand, he reasoned as he fixed a particularly sticky circuit that refused to work, if he did not make a show of fixing the problems, the pirates would simply kill him or turn him into a tech-slave. He had to remain useful so that he would remain alive.

As Alfred meandered through the system, he had the idea of overloading the coolant control circuits on the ship's engines and reactor. Not too much, he thought to himself, just enough to make take-off impossible rather than an entire meltdown of the ship's engine cores which would kill him as well as any other crew or prisoners. However, as he got to the part of the network that controlled such circuits, he realised what the leader Grekthax had shouted was true; there were neural blocks and safeguards on the system's most precious circuits that, if Alfred tried to tamper with them without the authorisation codes in his mind, he would die on the spot. He would be electrocuted through his implant and his mind would turn to mush.

Alfred swore to himself. Of course, no one heard it, as he was not actually speaking in the physical world. But he swore none the less.

Alfred wondered what time it was. Due to his experience with zetting, he could usually gauge what time it was in the real world and how long he had been zetting on a normal, well-maintained, professional circuit. However, here, he had no idea. Movement was sluggish, there were so many problems, and it was a totally foreign system, that he had no idea how long he had been engaged in the zet. It annoyed him.

He needed time: time to survive, time so that his friends would reach him, and time so that he, himself, could figure out what to do.

It was difficult to think of other things during this zet. Sometimes, when things were going well in other, better zets, he could let his mind wander and as he enjoyed the process, he could think of other things. Not here. Alfred had to make sure he concentrated entirely on the process in case he made a wrong move and ended up in some sort of feedback loop or dead zone and then he would be stuck in the network of this damn ship forever, or worse. There was no relaxing.

After what seemed like a few more hours work, even though he wanted to stall the pirates as long as possible, Alfred could no longer bear the pain of the terrible network that lanced through his brain, and had to log out. Oh, for the *Green Dragon's* sleek system, he thought. Having done what he could, and delayed as long as he could, yet he had not done too much to aid his captors, he began the log out sequence and waited for the computer to spit his mind back into his body.

His vision came back with a rush, and he gasped as the pain washed through his body. He pulled the needle from the side of his head and almost collapsed as his body stung with pain.

"Is it done?" growled Grekthax. "I saw you on the monitor; you seem to have done it. Is it done?"

"System. Integrity. Restored." said Alfred. Something was wrong. Why did it hurt so much? He could not think for the pain in his head. He raised his hands to his temples and shook his head. When he removed his hands there was some blood where his implant was.

"What's wrong?" asked Grekthax, sounding like he did not really care.

"Nothing." Alfred gritted his teeth and controlled himself. He needed to stay useful. He needed to stay alive. Knowledge of previous zetters on *Florida Station* came rushing back to him. Some of them had complained of pain when exiting zets in the time before their implants had failed.

It was almost funny. In the network he needed more time, and also in real life he needed more time. He had to survive. He must survive.

Alfred felt harsh hands grab his shoulders and haul him out of the zetting chair. With a coarse order from the pirate leader, Alfred was dragged down a few rusty corridors and thrown into a small cell like space that was dark and had no windows. He was in another prison cell; different from the shipping crate he was in earlier. It seemed like only yesterday that he had been in such a position, in a cell. He wondered what he had done wrong to deserve this.

Alfred collapsed on the floor and groaned. His vision had turned slightly purple. It was obvious to him that the stress of the last zet, due to its complexity and faultiness, had taxed his system too far.

He tried to remember what he had forgotten due to the zet. He could not think. He did not know what was missing. Something would be, though, he knew, he was not sure when it would make itself clear.

"Hey, what's up?" said a gruff voice from somewhere Alfred could not see with closed eyes.

Alfred looked up towards the voice suddenly and opened his eyes. He had not noticed anyone there when he was thrown into the cell. The truth was, he would not have noticed anything through the haze.

"I, uh, am in pain," Alfred said, gritting his teeth and standing up.

"Huh, I can see that. Anything I can do?" said the voice, now a shape in the darkness. The meagre light in the cell did not reach all areas even though the cell was small.

"No, I don't think so." Alfred laughed. This was an odd conversation. Then prisons are odd places, he reasoned with himself. "Listen, who are you? Come into the light." Alfred realised he sounded like he was giving an order and added "please" after a short pause.

The shape in the darkness snorted a laugh and moved forward. "Name's Crathka, and I've been here a long time. I've seen prisoners come and go, but they keep me here."

"I'm Alfred," said Alfred, rubbing his head with his hands. The pain in his head was subsiding a little and he felt more of the warm afterglow of zetting disappearing and being replaced by longing for the next time. Then there was the fuzz in his head. That was new. That was different. That was unwanted. "Why have they got you here?"

"Somehow I've stayed sane," said Crathka. "They use me, you see, to sniff out good salvage and parts. I used to be the head of a salvage yard back on Earth in Atraxa Prime.

"You've come a long way! How'd the pirates get you out here?" Alfred realised that if this Crathka asked, Alfred had come a very long way too.

"Well, I was head of salvage; then I was tried for treason; then I was on the Earth Moon Prison; then there was some sort of riot; then I was on my way back to Earth in a pod, but in all the commotion I was snatched by pirates before I got there. They said that they knew reports of me from Earth as a great salvage hunter; that I could find weapons for them. They were waiting for an opportunity to grab me and there it was." He paused, and looked at Alfred. "You don't seem surprised?"

"Why were you tried for treason?" Alfred asked.

"Some hard drive thing with tech on it was recovered from the wastes and went missing. I'm sure you're not interested. There was a civil war between the wings of my former Collective..." Crathka paused.

Alfred tried not to look shocked, and he knew that he had to keep his past secret from Crathka. Alfred had a strange feeling that the hard drive Crathka was talking about was the red hard drive stashed safely aboard the *Green Dragon*. And the riot was the one Draz instigated. Alfred did not know what the man would do if he realised that Alfred was somehow responsible for his imprisonment, even though the initial war between the wings on Earth was nothing to do with him.

Alfred also wondered how he had not met the man on the Earth Moon. He reasoned that it was due to his short stay. He had only been on the Moon a couple of days before the riot and break out. But then why had Draz never seen him? Different work detail and cell? He knew there were many prisoners. Alfred wondered.

"Hmm," Alfred said and turned away.

"Listen, Alfred, we might be here a while. Why are you here?" asked Crathka, with a surprisingly cheerful note in his voice for a man who had been in some sort of prison or other for a few years.

"I can zet," Alfred said. He saw no need to lie. "I was snatched outside the Hangara Family Tower," he added, not adding that he hoped his friends would be soon rescuing him, as he reasoned that the less Crathka knew, the better. And that Draz would probably, definitely, know this Crathka. He wondered what would happen then.

"I see," said Crathka, thoughtfully. "So, they have a new one, interesting."

"A new one?" Alfred asked a little frightened.

"Zetters don't last long around here, sorry lad." Crathka smiled, not quite comfortingly. "They work 'em to death. And by your pain in the head, you won't be here long."

"Thanks for the vote of confidence," Alfred snapped, he sat down on one of the benches on the wall of the cell.

"Just reality. Just reality," Crathka repeated himself and fell silent; he sat down on the bench on the opposite wall.

"Now what?" asked Alfred, still annoyed at the truth that Crathka spoke.

"We wait. Thanks to you, we should be taking off soon," Alfred could tell a smile in Crathka's voice.

"And head where?" Alfred asked a little more anxious than before. His friends would have to get here soon; they had to.

"Their base on one of the asteroids around here," came the response as Crathka lay down on the bench he was sitting on.

"Oh," said Alfred.

"Relax; it'll be over for you soon. Feel sorry for me, not yourself," said Crathka.

Just then, the ship started to rumble as the main power drives began to warm up.

"Come on," Alfred whispered, willing Draz and Artisius closer. They had to be looking for him. They had to find him! He honestly had no idea if they were after him or not. But he had to hope.

"You got any family? Any chance of escape, kid?" asked Crathka after a while.

"I uh..." There was a blank. Alfred did not know. He had a feeling that he had had some kind of family relation before. Of course, he had had parents. But he had a feeling that he should have had someone like a sister. However, he could not remember her face.

"You 'uh'? That doesn't sound good." Crathka's voice had a note of concern.

"Uh, yes, I had...someone...a sister. No longer." Alfred was panicked. He realised what the damage of the last zet was: he had temporarily or permanently, he could not be sure, time would tell, forgotten about his sister. He strained his mind, and some details came back.

"What was her name?" Crathka had turned his head to watch Alfred in the dull light.

"Uh...Blink...Blinky!" Alfred was frightened. How could he have forgotten that?

"Hold on to that, kid. It will keep you sane," Crathka said, then fell silent.

They both went silent for a while, and waited.

Chapter 15

"We'll be there in sixty seconds. Remember to follow your scanners for a power source, that will be the engines of the ship," shouted Slistra into the body of the craft.

The hover transport came in low over the tops of the structures, under the domes. They had been flying at rooftop level for a while now, dodging towers and cables that linked the structures. Draz was impressed at Slistra's piloting ability.

Draz saw Artisius sitting silently. He was looking out the window in the door of the craft and out at the Martian landscape under the domes that had been transformed into a messy web of structures and towers. His knuckles were white as he gripped the edge of his seat, and Draz noted that the determined look on his face could both be resolve to get Alfred back, or fear of crashing head first into the next tower that loomed up out of the sprawling city. Draz smiled; she assumed the latter.

"Fifteen seconds! Open the door!" came the cry from the cockpit and Draz checked her assault rifle for the hundredth time. Artisius did likewise. Draz wondered how he would perform athletically in a gunfight. He was quite old, in his late fifties at least; and he had never had longevity surgery, Draz guessed.

The hovercraft started to duck and weave as it made its way through the tracer fire that had erupted from the defence mechanisms that were installed around the pirate compound. As she wove, Slistra targeted the craft's weapons on the wall and let fly with the craft's own weaponry in the form of missiles and large calibre machine guns.

Draz watched through the front window, past Slistra's seat, she saw explosions blossom along the wall structure and the automated guns shooting at them fell silent.

Artisius reached over and pulled on the door release catch and automatically the door slid aside. The cool Martian wind within the dome whipped at their hair and clothing as the craft banked and lurched upward for a split second, then down again to clear the wall of the compound that was the pirate base. They burst through the smoke created by their missiles exploding on the walls and as the smoke swirled away from the engines, Slistra landed the craft skilfully in a clearing beyond the wall.

"Good luck!" shouted Slistra over her shoulder as Draz and Artisius jumped out of the craft and ran for cover.

Their assault had been so sudden that the pirate base was unprepared for any military action and a number of the guards were trying to ascertain what was going on. Draz slid behind some sort of armoured crates and Artisius lodged himself behind a pillar that was holding up one of the upper levels of the wall around the compound.

With a screech of engines, the hover-ship that they arrived in began to lift off, just as the pirate guards were gathering strength and starting to return fire. The rounds bounced harmlessly off the thick armour of Slistra's craft and, as Draz looked back at the pilot, she almost thought she saw a smile as Slistra opened up with all the weapons at her disposal. She manoeuvred the nose of the craft in a back and forth motion, raking the pirate positions with the machine guns and missiles.

Draz crouched down and covered her ears as the explosions went off in close proximity, but it was not enough. As the smoke cleared and Slistra's craft rose up and powered away from the scene of devastation, Draz was aware of a loud ringing in her ears, and she shook her head from

111

side to side in an effort to clear the noise. After a few seconds muted sounds returned and she looked over the edge of the crate she was hiding behind.

The scene was of utter destruction. The missiles and guns of the hover ship had ripped open the walls of the pirate base. Any fear that they would not get inside was swept aside as Draz and Artisius picked their way through the rubble and bodies strewn around on the ground. The missiles had opened up great big gashes in the armoured inner walls of the pirate base and any defence mechanism that was there before was now no longer active.

Draz and Artisius paused for a moment and looked at each other with a mutual look of awe and horror. Artisius seemed to be having trouble with his ears as well; he was tilting his head from side to side in an effort to regain full hearing.

"That's non military support?" said Draz, surveying the carnage.

Artisius smirked. "That's Lady Hangara's hospitality for you..."

"All right, let's turn on these energy scanners and look for Alfred," Draz said.

Artisius nodded and they fished the scanners out of their pockets and turned them on. There was a dull pulsing noise and a light on the scanner.

"I guess the ship is there?" Draz said quizzically, she was not quite sure how the scanners worked.

Artisius nodded again and pointed the direction to go in through the gaping wounds that were in the wall of the pirate base. Draz followed behind. They had their rifles at the ready.

***

Alfred heard a massive set of explosions and jumped off his bench. Crathka followed at the same time.

112

"What the hell was that?" Alfred yelled. The entire ship he was in rocked violently and he heard some shrill alarm start and wail in the near distance.

Crathka shrugged. "You got friends after you?"

There was another set of massive explosions and the floor of the cell they were in rocked violently. "I do, yeah," said Alfred, trying to stay upright. "But I didn't think that they had that much artillery!"

"Hah! Maybe it's our lucky day then," said Crathka, beaming.

Alfred rushed on the quaking floor to the small glass window in the cell door. He saw a few pirates running about in different directions but nothing else to indicate what was going on other than the shrill alarm that was sounding constantly.

Then the pair felt another rumble. This time it was from under their feet. "Uh oh," said Crathka, pointing at the floor. "They're powering up the engines. I hope your friends are fast or we're done for."

Alfred looked grim. He knew Crathka was right; he had been on this ship for years. He could recognise the engine noise when he heard and felt it.

"Come on!" Alfred whispered to himself as he sat back down on the bench and waited, hoping for salvation.

***

Draz and Artisius ran down the corridor that seemed to bring the pulsing light and sound on their scanners closer to them. The compound was a warren of corridors and rooms. At first, they encountered light resistance and a few shots of their rifles were enough to see off any enemies. However, as they progressed deeper in the maze of corridors, resistance stiffened substantially and as they moved out into a larger, underground chamber, they saw what looked like a ramshackle space ship and it was guarded by a number of well dug in pirates who managed to prevent their assault on the ship. There was a guard on either side of the walkway that led to the entrance to the ship.

"What now?" Artisius shouted as he kept his head down next to Draz behind some sort of cargo crates that were to be loaded onto the ship before their assault had dashed any plans of that.

Draz looked over the edge of the crates they were hiding behind, only to be scared back down by a sharp burst of gunfire. "Can you throw?" she yelled, pulling one of the two grenades on her bandolier off and handing it to Artisius.

He nodded.

Draz pulled the other grenade off and indicated she would throw it at the guard on the left of the ship's entrance and he was to throw it to the guard on the right, together. She nodded and they both pulled the pins from the grenades and after a short wait, hurled them together at the pirate gun positions.

There were a loud couple of explosions followed by screaming, and then silence. Draz looked over the edge of the crates and saw the mangled bodies of the pirates who had been guarding the entrance to the ship. "Let's go," she said grimly. Her adrenaline was pumping, and she felt so alive.

They ran up to the entrance to the ship and tried to enter but found the door locked.

"Hang on," said Artisius, pointing to the touch panel at the side of the door. He ran back, picked up a bloodied hand from the mess of dead pirates guarding the ramp, and came back to the door. He placed it on the touch pad and the light next to the door went green. It slid open. Artisius dropped the severed hand with a wince, and they proceeded inside the ship.

Draz gagged at the use of the severed hand, but it was necessary to get aboard.

Their scanners would be useless here, as they had already found the ship. Draz hoped that the layout of the ship would be more straightforward than the base.

They fought their way inside and shot a number of guards who dared to block their way. Draz's blood was up, and she would not let anyone, or anything stand in her way of rescuing her friend. How dare they take him. How dare they.

Draz fired accurately and precisely from the shoulder as she marched, without stopping, through the ship. They may have been pirates, but she was a scavenger from Earth, they would rue the day they made her an enemy.

As they moved through the ship Draz and Artisius opened every door they came across in an effort to find some sort of prison cell that they assumed Alfred would be in.

They came to a door that had a small glass panel in it and Artisius looked in while Draz kept watch for enemies.

"I think I've found him!" shouted Artisius.

Draz nearly dropped her rifle as she spun around from looking down the corridor and ran to beside Artisius to look through the glass.

"Stand back," Artisius said as he triggered the door and Draz burst in gun raised to take care of any opposition. There was none.

Artisius rushed into the room as well and they saw Alfred. He had jumped from a bench on the wall and had run up to Draz to hug her. After hugging Draz, Alfred hugged Artisius.

"You came, I knew you would." Alfred gasped, rather overcome with emotion. "I told you I had friends!"

Draz and Artisius realised that Alfred was talking to someone and that someone was hiding in the shadows of the cell.

As a large shape came forward, Draz gasped. "Crathka?" she said.

"Draz!" Crathka almost cried.

"I thought you might know each other," said Alfred, carefully.

"I used to know him. He betrayed me!" Draz raised her rifle to her shoulder and aimed at Crathka's head. "He. Destroyed. My. LIFE!" She had hate in her eyes.

"Whoa, whoa," Alfred held up his hands. "He's been here for years. We have to help him."

"I will never help him again," growled Draz. "Get out of the way." she indicated with the muzzle of her rifle.

"Not wanting to be a killjoy and wreck this friendly reunion, but we kind of have to leave, now!" Artisius said rather loudly as the ship's engines continued to warm up and the deck rocked a little. He had been silent and watching the corridor for guards. Suddenly one approached gun ready and Artisius saw him off with a quick burst of gunfire.

Alfred cowered at the loud sound of the rifle; unprepared for it, he flinched out of Draz's aim for a split second and suddenly there was another burst, this time from Draz's rifle.

Crathka slumped on the floor. Draz had shot him through the head. He was dead.

Alfred looked horrified, splattered with gore and skull fragments. "What the fuck!? What the fucking fuck!?" Is all he could manage as he stared horrified at both the brain matter oozing down the wall behind the body of Crathka, and Draz's expression on her face as she lowered her rifle.

"All right, let's go!" she said and grabbed Alfred by the hand and the three of them proceeded to run down the corridors to the entrance of the ship. Artisius was silent as they ran.

"Why, Draz, why?" gasped Alfred as they ran. "He wasn't a bad person."

"Yes he was, to me," was all she said on the matter. "Look, we're rescuing you, okay?" Draz said as Alfred shuddered, but kept running.

116

Draz was at the front and Artisius brought up the rear. They reached the final corridor before the exit and Draz indicated for Artisius to check outside if there were any guards. He ran out of the ship first and took cover; there was no opposition.

"Okay, now I'll head out and you follow me. All right?" Draz looked into Alfred's eyes. He looked back with what Draz could see as gratitude mixed with quite a lot of fear.

Draz moved through the entrance to the ship and part of the way down the gantry to the dock and Alfred was about to follow when the entrance door slammed shut and locked. Alfred screamed. He banged on the door and looked out the glass porthole.

Artisius and Draz spun around at the sound and ran back to the door. They could not open it. The hand that had opened it for them earlier was gone, fallen away into the depths of the dock.

"No, no, no, no!" shouted Draz.

"There must be a way to open it!" yelled Artisius. "Is there a switch on your end, Alfred?" but Alfred seemed not to hear, it was a solid door.

Alfred was yelling in panic on his side of the door. Draz and Artisius saw his frantic action on the other side of the door. Draz dropped her rifle and tried to prise the door open, in vain. She had no chance. Alfred kept banging on his side of the door.

Suddenly the ship lurched. "The engines have warmed up!" yelled Artisius. He grabbed Draz's hand and planted something on the hull of the ship before he tried to pull her away from the door. She would be killed if they did not get onto the dock when the ship took off.

"I won't leave him!" Draz yelled. "Not now!" She stared desperately into Alfred's eyes and he into hers on opposite sides of the door through the small glass window. She raised her hand to the glass. He did the same. "I will find you!" she yelled, unsure whether he heard or understood. The gantry began to give way as the ship started to rise upwards from the compound.

Draz gave one last look at Alfred and then turned and ran for cover as Artisius dragged her away. The pirate ship took off and powered away into the Martian sky. They had failed. They had killed many pirates, but they had not rescued Alfred. Now if would be much harder. Now they would have to find which asteroid he was going to be taken to.

Artisius saw Draz's distress and smiled. "Look, I managed to get a tracking device on their hull before they left. I snagged one from Lady Hangara's armaments room in case something like this happened. We'll find him. It will be hard, but we'll find him."

"You're full of surprises," Draz said with a grimace. "That's why you ran up to get me, to plant the device?" she stood and watched the ship spiral upwards and away. She still felt terrible at failing to rescue Alfred. He would not know about the tracking device. He would feel so alone.

Suddenly, and terribly, her adrenaline waned, and she felt the ache of withdrawal come flooding back.

"Let's go, before more pirates arrive." Artisius indicated with his gun, and he began to call Slistra back again for them to be picked up.

***

Draz and Artisius ran back to where they had been dropped. It was all strangely silent and empty. Draz reasoned that most of the pirates were either dead or on their ship. She heard the squeal of the engines of the hover-ship coming in and waited.

She thought about Alfred. He was alone on that ship with no idea that they could come after him. He was alone. She knew what that was like.

118

The start of the ride back to the Hangara Tower was spent in silence. Slistra did not ask any questions, even though her face betrayed that she wanted to ask what went wrong. But she flew on in silence.

It was dark by now. The Martian nightfall was inky black apart from the pinpoints of light that zipped along below them in their craft and that rose up on the towers that stretched up, silently, into the night. Off in the distance were the hover ship laneways that created a constant stream of lights and noise as people moved around, but they were flying low and not on a charted route. All they heard was the whine of the hover ship's engines.

Draz sat staring out the side window of the hover ship as it sped along just above the level of the black buildings, covered in pinpoints of light. She looked at Artisius from time to time, as they flew, the cabin of the craft was dully lit, and Draz could make out Artisius' face. She saw that he was staring out with just as empty an expression as she had. She knew that he cared about Alfred. He had grown to be his friend in times of hardship, just like Draz; and now they had let that friendship down and had failed to rescue him.

Draz knew that, with the tracking device, they could follow the pirate craft and trace it to where it was going. However, the problem was, their ship was still undergoing repairs and they had no means of following, yet. And even when they did get the *Green Dragon* back, the pirates would be so far away and the further away a tracking device got, the less accurate it became. So, they would have to search hard if they were to find their friend.

Friend. Draz pondered the word. She did not know when Alfred became her friend, but she would call him such now. She hoped that he would call her the same. She cared for Alfred. There was something about him that was strangely endearing. But the fact that he was a friend made it all the harder for Draz to see him fly away on the wrong side of the door of the pirate craft. She grimaced.

"How you going?" Artisius asked. Draz was fidgeting. Her right leg was agitated, and she kept shifting position and cracking her fingers.

"What do you mean?" she snapped a little too harshly. She instantly regretted the tone. She knew that he was looking out for her.

"You know what I mean," Artisius said, still calmly with no malice, despite Draz's tone. "You're showing signs of withdrawal." He tilted his head as he said so and looked at her, eyes shining in the darkness of the cabin.

"Ah, well, yes," she looked down at her leg, it moved as if on a spring. She cracked her knuckles again. "It's hard. I feel a terrible craving. It went away with the gunfight--"

"That's adrenaline," Artisius said.

"Yes," said Draz, nodding. She knew that. "Would you think it would be possible..." She paused. Artisius was shaking his head. "Not even one more line?" she asked, knowing the answer.

"No more. Remember it was your last, last time." said Artisius, carefully.

"But it hurts! I can manage it! I swear!" Draz whined. She looked away from Artisius' disapproving face.

"No, no you cannot," he spoke with the authority of a man who knew the same pain, but a long time ago, and who had never quite recovered.

"Do you even know what this feels like? I bet you don't. You're just torturing me!" Draz snapped, only afterwards realising how ludicrous her words sounded. But it was not just her talking. She was having very strong withdrawal pains and it was influencing her mind.

"I'll pretend I did not hear that," snapped Artisius. "I know exactly how you feel. And we'll leave it at that." He turned his head from looking at her to staring out at the dark night.

Draz was tired, and as she watched him, she noted a pang of what looked like regret cross his face. She did not ask any more. She had worked out that he might have used to use ferkis powder; and seeing her in distress perhaps brought back bad memories. Draz pondered while the gnawing sensation got worse and worse in her mind.

"How much longer will the withdrawal last," she said meekly after a while.

"The rest of your life, to some extent," Artisius said without turning from looking out the window. "The acute pangs go in about a few months, but you will always want to use. Always."

He said the last words with such gravity that Draz moaned internally. That did not bode well for her.

***

After a while longer, the hover ship landed on the well-lit deck landing pad of the Hangara Tower. Lady Hangara, who looked radiant, was there to greet them. Her look soured when she saw that only Slistra, and her two passengers got out.

"Where's--?" is all Lady Hangara managed before Draz, in no mood for talking, cut her off.

"They escaped. We almost had him and now they've gone!" Draz said.

"Oh dear, how did this happen?" Lady Hangara asked, looking at Artisius and taking his rifle from him. She seemed to ignore Draz, much to Draz's disgust.

"They shut the door on us," Draz said, not letting Artisius talk. "We were almost out, and the bastards shut the outer airlock door on us. Alfred's still in that damn ship, and now it's taken off."

"But I did get a tracking device on the hull," Artisius said.

"Well done! Then we can still get your friend back," Lady Hangara said, clapping her hands.

"His name is Alfred," said Draz through gritted teeth.

"Indeed," said Lady Hangara rather dismissively. "Come, unload your guns and retire to your quarters. You must be tired."

She was not wrong. Draz felt a massive weight pressing down on her and from what she could see of Artisius, he looked exhausted too.

They moved into the armaments room and unloaded their borrowed weapons and ammunition, apart from their pistols that they had taken from the *Green Dragon*, before heading in the lift to the upper penthouse level where their quarters were located.

Draz exited the lift first and headed to her room. She noted that Artisius did not follow her to his room, but went with Lady Hangara again. Draz looked over her shoulder and saw Lady Hangara cradling Artisius' head on her shoulder. She caressed his cheek with her hand. Draz paused and watched them until they rounded a corner and were gone. Draz sighed.

Draz came to her room, entered, and shut the door. She collapsed backwards on her bed. But just as suddenly she sat bolt upright again. She had seen something. On the stand next to her bed was a silver tray with one line of white powder on it and the same ornate metal straw that had been there before.

Did Artisius know about this? Who cares, Draz thought. He would never approve of anything. Draz was sure he had been a drug addict earlier in life. Who was he to judge her? He would never know if she had that one line. Just the one.

Draz did not consider who would have put the line there, or their motive. Why was not a question that entered Draz's mind at this point. She simply stared at the line. Her eyes wide, her lips dry, her mind overcome by desire. She was mouth breathing heavily.

Draz knew she had a problem. Draz knew she should not take any more. However, she also knew that the screaming in her body would not go away until she did. She had said no more last time, but there was always room for one more time.

Draz realised that she was speaking to herself. She was speaking aloud her thoughts. She collapsed back on the bed and buried her head under the pillow pulling it down onto her head. She screamed. The craving burned in her being.

Artisius had said that the craving never went away. Then how had she managed her addiction for so long? She had used ferkis powder on Earth for years and never had a problem, what was going wrong now? Draz realised that Artisius and Lady Hangara's powder was a much higher quality, and also she was not a scavenger any more on Earth. She did not have the adrenaline from her scavenging runs to dull the ache. That had taken most of her thought and time. Now it was all about the drug. She had been consumed by it.

Draz screamed into the pillow. It made her feel a little better. The line was still burning in her consciousness on the table next to the bed.

Draz looked up and stared at it. It was there. It was there! She could just have one more. She had failed Alfred. What would one more line matter? Alfred was gone.

With one smooth movement Draz's resolve collapsed and she snatched up the metal straw and snorted the line. Bliss washed over her as she dropped the straw and collapsed back onto the bed. All the pain went away. All the craving vanished. Everything was perfect. She drifted off into blissful sleep. This would be her last, last line. But really, she did not care.

Chapter 16

"Why do you have to go?" asked Lady Hangara with a smile as Artisius slid out of bed and began dressing back into his uniform. She was still lying in bed, propped up on her elbow. Her voice held a mixture of both sadness that Artisius was leaving the confines of the bed, and jealousy because she knew where he was going.

"Because I need to check that she's okay. You know how addictive that stuff is!" It was not a question. Artisius dressed, slowly. He looked back at the woman in the bed who had been entertaining him, or he entertaining her, Artisius was not quite sure. He did not really care.

"But I'm here, now..." said Lady Hangara coyly. She snuggled down under the black silk sheets.

Artisius sighed. "And you will be there again. I'm only going to check on her." He put on his pants.

"Why do you care about her so much?" snapped Lady Hangara. "Is she going to be your new thing? Am I too old for you? Am I being replaced?"

Artisius sat down on the edge of the large double bed and reached out to caress Lady Hangara's cheek. "You'll never be replaced. You are special to me." He smiled. He knew he was lying. He had so many special women in the Solar System that he had lost count of them. "But there's something about Draz..." Artisius trailed off in thought.

"Aha! I knew it!" said Lady Hangara.

"No, not like that," Artisius corrected her. "I feel protective towards her. As if she was the daughter I never had. I cannot explain it." He paused again and threw on his tunic and began buttoning it up.

He looked around the room. It was opulently decorated and furnished. Lady Hangara really had set herself up as the matriarch of her Family. However, he knew that it could all come crashing down if the guard spy problems could not be resolved. He was worried that the problems would impact on the repair and refit of the *Green Dragon*.

"What's wrong now?" Lady Hangara interrupted his reverie. He noticed that he had frozen mid button.

"Oh, I was just thinking of my ship," Artisius said.

"The *Green Dragon*? Fine ship that. Aren't you glad I bought it for you?" She smiled.

"I have paid you back ten times over," he snapped with a smile.

"True, but it would have gone to that smuggler, whatever his name was, if it had not been for me..." she paused in thought and then continued. "What was on that red hard drive that you had my workers install on your ship. You didn't allow them to test it. I have no idea what it is, and neither do they. It's something to do with light bending...I know you said earlier that it would be my downfall if I knew but...you can tell me..." She stopped.

Artisius thought about the pros and cons of telling what the drive contained. He knew the Collective Zone fleet was coming and he reasoned he could tell her about the plans. She had helped him, and she deserved to know about what she had done. He knew the Collective Zone fleet would do as it willed when it arrived. "It's...a cloaking device," he said, looking at her. He wanted to see her reaction.

"A...what!?" she stammered. "But that's not possible...is it?"

"I've seen it in action. It is most definitely real." He smiled.

"I have to keep this technology!" Lady Hangara blurted out. She had sat bolt upright in the bed, the covers falling away.

"I'm sorry, but I have to take that red drive. It's my insurance policy. And I might have to give it to some side later." Artisius continued dressing. He put on his boots.

"But...can I at least have a copy of the data? Remember I have helped you escape from the Collective here. I need some high tech. Imagine what it would mean against the other Families!" Her eyes glazed over as she considered the possibilities.

"That's the problem. It's too powerful," said Artisius looking down at the floor.

"Then why can you have it?" Lady Hangara snapped.

"Because..." Artisius smiled and lent over to kiss her on the cheek. "Imagine if either corporation learnt that you had cloaking tech? What do you think they would do? How much longer until my ship is ready?" He changed topic.

"Soon. About a week." she said, waving away the question. Artisius knew that she knew that he was right concerning the reaction to her having cloaking technology. The corporations would invade Mars and take it by force.

Artisius had fully dressed and stood up. He left the room quickly, leaving his brace of pistols on the table. As the door closed slowly, he heard Lady Hangara get up and throw on a dressing gown before hurrying behind him. He smiled; he knew that she would follow him.

Lady Hangara caught up with him down the corridor and they walked together to Draz's room.

"Now, I don't want you to be angry..." Lady Hangara said.

"Why would I be?" asked Artisius genuinely puzzled as he knocked on Draz's door and there was no reply. He knocked again. "She must be sound asleep; she was tired and suffering withdrawal..."

"Well, there's the thing--" Lady Hangara said.

Artisius shot her a murderous glance. "You didn't!" he said with ice in his voice.

"Well, she was suffering. I just thought one little line would--" Lady Hangara was cut off as Artisius thumped on the door and yelled Draz's name.

"You knew she was hopelessly addicted, and you enabled her?" growled Artisius. He tried the door controls and found the door unlocked. He activated the mechanism and the door slid aside.

The scene that greeted Artisius chilled him to the bone. Draz was lying back on the bed. She was a sickly pale colour and almost not breathing. Artisius rushed over and picked her head up and cradled it in his arms. This was the second time he had done so in a day.

"Never, I repeat, never do that again." snarled Artisius to Lady Hangara who stood in the doorway in her loose fitting dressing gown.

"I don't see what you see in her!" Lady Hangara said and walked off. "All I was doing was helping..." she said as she marched down the hallway back to her room.

Draz, on seeing Artisius' face, was smiling and trying to speak, but failing as the drug coursed through her system.

"Why did you do that?" asked Artisius, brushing stray hairs from Draz's face.

She did not really understand him.

"How many lines did you do?" he asked after a short time.

Draz held up a finger.

"One?"

Draz nodded.

"I need to keep you safe." he whispered and kissed her forehead.

Draz shivered as he did so.

127

Artisius sat with Draz for a time until the drug's obvious effects had left her system. Her eyes were glazed over, and she groaned as she realised what had happened.

"Why?" is all Artisius asked when he saw life returning to Draz's features.

"I had to..." she said meekly. Her voice cracked, and she began to cry.

They were both sitting on the edge of the bed now and Artisius wrapped his arm around her and brought her into his shoulder. "I know exactly what you mean, but we can get through this. You're going to have to be strong. Like you were in the Moon Prison. Like you have been your whole life. This is just a slight mishap, that's all."

"But, the desire. It's so strong! I can't..." she said.

"Yes you can."

"How would you know?"

"Trust me, I know," Artisius said still calmly looking into Draz's eyes. He knew the withdrawal was making Draz angry. It was not her.

Draz fell silent. "I'm tired..." she said after a while.

"Then sleep. We'll be out of here soon and the temptation will go," he said and paused. "It was a bad idea coming to the crime capital of the Solar System..."

"We had no choice, though," Draz said.

Artisius sighed. "Indeed." He let her fall down gently onto the bed and soon enough she was asleep. He could tell with her regular breathing.

Artisius got up slowly from the bed and picked up the silver tray and straw and left the room. He shot a glance back in Draz's direction as he left and turned off the lights to the room. As he shut the door, he took a deep breath.

"This will take work, like it did with me," he said quietly as he exhaled.

He moved down the corridor again and back to Lady Hangara's room. As he entered, she was sitting up in bed watching some sort of report on a hand held computer.

"And? How is the little trollop?" she said to Artisius as he entered.

"She's alive, just. When we leave there will be no more temptations," he said. He threw the tray and straw onto the nearby wooden table.

"What about all those drugs on your ship?" Lady Hangara said.

"I'll have them jettisoned. She'll have to fight the withdrawals," he said, beginning to undress again.

"What about you?" She smiled.

Artisius leaned over and kissed her again as he undressed. "Oh, I will have to give in to my withdrawal." He smiled.

Lady Hangara smiled again, "I always enjoy when you come to Mars..."

***

Draz's mind swam as she lay on the bed. She had to be strong. She had to quit the drugs. She had to for her sake and for Alfred's. This would be the very last, last time. She would remain sober from here on. She would resist the temptation. It would be hard, but she must do it. She had fought this urge her entire adult life and at times, it got the better of her; no longer. Now she would remain clean. Now, she would survive.

Draz drifted to sleep. Her dreams were fitful, but welcome. She slept for a long time.

Chapter 17

Alfred's hand slid down the small glass window on the inside of the pirate craft's door. He saw Draz and Artisius escape from the craft's backwash as it made an emergency take off and the gantry that his friends were standing on buckled and gave way.

He was alone. His friends had tried to rescue him, and it had failed. Alfred did not want to blame them or himself for the failure, so he simply thought that the operation had failed. Now he would be stuck a prisoner of the pirates until his death at their hands; which may be soon given Artisius and Draz's actions in killing a number of pirate crew.

Alfred heard clunking footsteps behind him. He closed his eyes and breathed slowly. He knew it was Grekthax due to the loping gait. Alfred heard a coarse laugh and the footsteps stopped behind him.

A large and heavy hand fell on Alfred's shoulder, and he opened his eyes and looked fearfully at it. "Well, well, seems like your little friends failed in their task." Alfred heard the grin in his captor's voice.

Alfred turned around. The hulking form of Grekthax towered over him, grinning.

"So, what happens now?" Alfred's voice sounded calmer than he felt; but he had resigned himself to the fact that, now that the pirate craft had taken off and was escaping to its base, he had no chance of rescue; he would never be found. He had resigned himself to the fact that he would live a short, brutal and horrid life on the pirate craft or pirate base and would die there an exhausted husk of a zetter. Therefore, he could be calm, as there was no chance of redemption.

Grekthax looked at Alfred with calculating eyes. "You must be important if your friends wanted to risk all to rescue you...perhaps we should scan your brain. You are a zetter after all, and the process should be simple enough."

Alfred knew the process the pirate captain was talking about. It involved scanning the subject's brain through the neural implant and finding out their secrets by tearing them out of the person. It was dangerous, but it worked. He had heard terror stories about it back on *Florida Station* from people who had had dealings with pirates.

"Don't you need me alive?" Alfred said. "To, you know, zet the ship?" He did not want to be brain scanned. It was very dangerous for the subject.

"Nah, that can wait, we'll get another zetter before that's needed. Now move!" Grethax pulled Alfred away from the door and pushed him in front of him down one of the adjoining corridors.

After a short walk, they entered a room that was full of computer terminals and wires with a rudimentary slab in the centre. A number of pirates were standing around with grins on their faces, obviously looking forward to the procedure about to be visited on their latest captive.

"Now, lie there!" Grekthax pushed Alfred onto the slab in the middle of the room. As soon as Alfred landed on the slab, the surrounding pirates strapped him in on his arms and legs.

Alfred struggled but it was in vain, he was trapped on the slab. His calmness had been replaced by anger. He spat at the nearest pirate who came leering up to him to taunt him.

Alfred, judging by their glassy expressions and jagged movements, reasoned that they were on some sort of chemical stimulant. They were not behaving normally for human beings. They moved in a jerky manner, and they were perpetually grinning.

131

Grekthax was the only pirate in the room who seemed to be rather in control of his own movements. He was moving around the room pressing buttons on computer terminals and getting the system ready to rip any useful information from Alfred's brain.

Alfred lay on the slab. He knew that to beat the system he would have somehow to confuse it, to flood it with useless information and not think of anything important. However, that was easier said than done. He knew that the most useful and dangerous piece of information that he had was the red hard drive and the cloaking device plans on it. However, if he did reveal that information it might bring the pirates back to the *Green Dragon* and then his friends would have a chance to rescue him.

Who was he kidding; Alfred knew that the machine would tear all the information from his mind. He had no chance of protecting the *Green Dragon*.

"So, how many of your scum did my friends kill? You must be on a skeleton crew then?" Alfred spat the words. He was angry. He wanted to bluff as much as possible in an effort to make it seem like he knew nothing.

"Hah! Yes your friends did a good job of thinning out my crew, but we have more on our base," said Grekthax, laughing, as he moved around the room, pressing buttons.

"Base?" Alfred made it a question. He wanted to know more about the pirates.

Grekthax seemed to fall for the bait. "Yeah, our base on asteroid Extremis Omega 14. We have all our operations and drug distilleries there. You'll love it, as a slave. Now enough talk, you cannot get out of this." Grekthax walked to the side of the slab and raised a large needle like device on a cord like a zetting needle. Grekthax grabbed Alfred's head to stop it squirming and positioned the needle. "This will hurt, a lot."

Alfred tried to resist but Grekthax's massive hand kept his skull frozen in its grasp. He desperately tried to think of inane and pointless things to flood the computer with, but he only seemed to think of the red hard drive. No matter what he did, it was all he thought about.

Grekthax jammed the needle into the implant on the side of Alfred's head. Alfred felt an icy pain lance through his very being and he felt the computer start to unravel his thoughts and fears.

Half of Alfred's vision failed, and he saw images drawn across it as the computer scanned his brain and thoughts. It was cataloguing all his life. He saw various images from his childhood flash before his eyes, somehow eerily overlayed upon the remaining vision that he had of the pirate craft's room. He saw leering faces of pirates overlayed with pictures of his past; all the while he heard the harsh laughter of Grekthax as the pirate captain watched the memories scrawl across the computer terminals.

Alfred tried to scream as deeper and deeper memories were torn from his mind, but he was unable. He simply opened his mouth and bared his teeth. He scrunched up his face in agony. All the while the laughter continued.

After what seemed like hours to Alfred, but was only a few minutes of real time, Grekthax stopped laughing and pressed a button. One image locked itself in Alfred's vision. One image was locked on the computer screens around Alfred. The red hard drive. The icy lance of pain was still there, it was just that the image was frozen.

"What's this?" snapped Grekthax. "The computer says it's some kind of weapon. Where is it?"

"I...I..." Alfred winced.

"No matter, I'll tear it out of you," said the pirate captain, smiling, and he pressed some more buttons.

This time Alfred did scream as the image became more clear and vivid on his vision. More information flooded onto the computer screens. The pain was immense.

"The *Green Dragon*! It has this weapon! Your ship! We will wait for it in the asteroids. They will come for you, and we will surprise them..." Grekthax paused; he seemed to think for a moment. "Now that I have your secret, I can let you enjoy our hospitality a little more." He flicked some more switches and the scanning resumed. "We cannot let anything go unnoticed. And I want to punish you; I want to make you suffer more. It'll make us laugh!"

Alfred screamed louder as the probe penetrated into his subconscious ripping his mind apart. Grekthax left the room to the sound of his prisoner screaming his lungs out.

Alfred's vision was failing as the images of his past flashed before his eyes. He had failed his friends. He had betrayed them. He had no other options, he knew. It was the machine, but he felt a sense of failure none the less.

As the red haired, chemically stimulated pirates danced tribally around Alfred's prostrate body, he felt his memories disintegrating as they were torn from him. He wanted simply to die, at least then the pain would stop.

After a while longer, Alfred's brain gave up and he fell unconscious. The computer still scanned his mind, but he was no longer aware of its actions.

***

Alfred awoke sometime later in his cell, which was still splattered with the blood and brains of Crathka, but the body was missing. Alfred shivered. He was cold. His mind felt violated. His consciousness was fuzzy. He did not know the damage caused yet, but he knew it would be extensive. He did not want to think of anything anymore. It hurt. It all hurt. He shivered on the floor of the cell.

Chapter 18

Artisius watched Draz struggle through the next few days of withdrawal, but she did not relapse. She busied herself with planning to rescue Alfred. He could tell she was fighting a great urge. She looked rather ratty and dishevelled as she moved around the Hangara Tower. Most of the time she spent in her room with a computer slate, and she obsessively watched the tracking device ping the location of the pirate craft as it moved towards a cluster of asteroids away from Mars.

Artisius spent some time with her as she did this. He kept an eye on her. It was not overbearing, but he knew what she was going through from past experience, and he knew that she should not be left alone all the time, even if she wanted to be.

Lady Hangara hung around and gave updates to Artisius about the progress of their ship's repairs and hardware installation. After about a week from the failed rescue attempt, Artisius got the report he was waiting for from both Lady Hangara, and his First Officer on the *Green Dragon*: the repairs, refuelling, and cloaking device installation were complete.

Artisius smiled when he got the report. Of course, the workers on the cloaking device install had no idea what they were working on, purely for secrecy's sake. It meant that it had not been tested, and could not be tested, until it was used for the first time. However, Artisius could not take the risk of letting it be known that he had a working cloaking device, especially on the crime planet of Mars.

Artisius walked to Draz's door for the last time and knocked respectfully and lightly. He heard her give her assent for him to enter and he activated the door controls. The door slid open and Artisius saw Draz sitting on the edge of the bed, studying the computer slate, which indicated where Alfred was.

"It's time. We can go. The ship is ready," he said, and Draz looked at him slowly. He could see pain behind her eyes, but she still had not relapsed. He moved over to her and sat on the edge of the bed next to her.

"And we can find him?" she said, weakly.

"Yes, we can find him, and we can take you away from here," he said softly, and she lent her head on his shoulder. "Mars has not been good to you."

"I used to be so strong. I used to be the one people looked at and said: 'look at her, I want to be like her...' and now..." Draz sighed. "And now I'm a junkie."

"Hey, no, not 'am', 'was'." Artisius smiled. "You've been battling this illness for a long time, and Mars just let you go crazy, I shouldn't have come here..." Artisius trailed off.

"We had no choice. We've been over that before," Draz said with a smile. She stood up. "Come on, let's go."

Artisius grinned and followed her out the door. "Righto."

Lady Hangara saw them down the lift and out the front of the building. Her personal transport was waiting for them when they exited. It was not a taxi to take them to the standard shuttle stop like when they arrived, but a shuttle itself, to take them directly to *Challenger 2 Space Platform*.

Artisius gave Draz a look and she got into the transport ahead of him.

Artisius hesitated before entering the transport. He turned and went back to Lady Hangara who was waiting outside the doors of her building. He stood in front of her and held her hand.

"So, this is goodbye," she said.

"I'll be back, I promise," Artisius said, holding her right hand in both of his. He kissed it.

"Don't..." Lady Hangara said. She pulled her hand from his.

Artisius sighed, "My life seems to be a series of goodbyes."

"You have her." Lady Hangara indicated the transport.

"It's not like that. She's a friend. I could never..." he stopped; he had said too much.

"Take advantage of her?" Lady Hangara smiled, not offended. "You never change...Make sure she knows that you're only her friend though, be sure she knows that there's no chance. Don't break her heart. You know as well as I that drug dependency can breed strange emotions."

Artisius nodded. "I get the impression she doesn't want me. I get the impression she's independent. I get the impression I'm..." He ended the sentence before he gave too much away.

"Go, now, and don't say goodbye..." Lady Hangara turned and went back inside her building.

Artisius stood for a moment and watched her go. He turned and got inside the transport. He sat in silence and watched out the window as the tower retreated into the distance as the transport took them up through the shimmering energy shield around the colonies on the surface towards the *Challenger 2 Space Platform* where the *Green Dragon* was docked.

"I'm sorry," Draz said as the planet retreated.

"For what?" Artisius smiled and looked at her. She seemed calmer as the planet receded.

"I saw you and Lady Hangara. It was obvious. You want to stay, but because of Alfred and me, you can't. That's why I'm sorry." She spoke with wisdom.

137

"Heh, you're smart when you're off the drugs. How's that going by the way?" Artisius changed the subject, rather obviously.

"All right, now we're heading off Mars it's a bit easier. I still have this gnawing ache in my body though," she indicated her head and her chest. "It's strange; I've used ferkis powder since I was young. There was a time earlier when I nearly fell completely under its spell, when things got really dicey, but I thought I could control it this time..." She fell silent.

"I know what you mean," said Artisius quietly. "I stick with alcohol now..." Artisius looked out the window at the receding planet.

"And women..." Draz said suddenly. She winced and seemed to regret it instantly. "Sorry," she added.

"It was deserved. It's true enough...They also leave an ache..." He fell silent again.

Lady Hangara's shuttle landed at the disembark point of *Challenger 2 Space Platform* and the robot driver indicated that they should get out. It thanked them for their patronage and wished them a good journey.

"The leaving procedure is much easier than arriving," said Artisius to Draz. "We just walk through and get on our ship; they only really care what's going into the planet rather than out. Mars only wants to protect its own economy. Because there are so many rules systems in the Solar System, customs only cares what's coming in. The next planet has to deal with what we take out of here."

"Makes sense, I suppose," said Draz as they walked through the crowds of people who were milling around on the platform.

***

They reached their ship and Artisius stood watching it out of one of the portholes in the walkway leading to it.

138

"Magnificent," he said, marvelling at it. "It looks better than ever...huh!"

"What?" asked Draz, looking at the ship.

"Notice that?" Artisius pointed at a bundle of wires, tubes and some kind of dish thing that protruded from the underside of the nose of the craft. "That's new. That's our secret weapon."

They boarded the ship and made their way to the bridge. "Captain on the bridge!" came the cry from the First Officer. "Orders, sir?"

Draz stood a respectful distance away as Artisius stood on the command dais. "Get ready to leave. Pull up the tracking system. We're heading after that!" He indicated a blip on the tracking computer.

"Sir, that's out of the way of Europa..." said the First Officer.

"I know, we're following pirates, and we're getting our friend back!" He looked over at Draz, who smiled.

"Sir!" the First Officer saluted and began barking out orders. After a while, he said "The device is installed and we're itching to try it, sir."

"We still have the source drive?" Artisius asked.

"Yes, sir, we kept a close eye on Lady Hangara's construction crew as they installed it. But the drive is secure on this ship." The First Officer saluted again.

Artisius nodded and looked over at Draz, who had moved to the tracking terminal and was discussing tactics of approaching the pirates with the officer in charge there.

"Let's go," Artisius gave an indication with his hand. He felt the engines rumble deep within the ship, and the *Green Dragon* slipped quietly out of Martian dock and set a course for the pirate craft.

Artisius smiled, the pirates would soon see the effectiveness of the new weapon installed on his ship.

"Sir, we've detected an incoming group of ships...it's a huge fleet!" snapped the Scanning Officer.

"The Great Fleet..." Artisius said. "How far away?" he snapped.

"A few hundred thousand kilometres, sir" came the sharp reply.

"We can outrun them. Take us through the debris around Mars. I have a little surprise for all of you, and the Collective fleet," barked Artisius striding back and forth on the command dais, thinking.

"Sir!"

The *Green Dragon* accelerated through the debris around Mars at full speed and headed towards the blip on the scanner that was in the border region between Collective Zone and Solar Solutions space.

Artisius looked back at Mars out of the observation dome on the bridge. He knew the Collective Zone fleet would enact horrid retribution on the people there for unwittingly helping the *Green Dragon* escape. He had lied to Lady Hangara when he suggested the Great Fleet would leave Mars alone if he did not hand over the cloaking technology. He knew what they would do. He knew that Mars could not stand up to them no matter what the Martians thought of their defences. He thought of Lady Hangara, he hoped she would be okay. He knew he probably would not see her again.

Artisius turned and looked again at Draz who was involved with co-ordinating the tracking systems to pursue Alfred. He smiled. At least he had tried to save someone.

Artisius pulled aside the First Officer and whispered, "Jettison all drugs from the ship; everything."

"Sir?"

"Just do it. It's important," he said, looking over at Draz, who was busy correlating data with the bridge crew.

Chapter 19

Trooper Grox sat with his platoon. They were eating, as troops always did after a long cryo-sleep. He felt the rumble of the *Iron Bastion's* engines through the hull and his feet. They had been awakened and would soon receive a briefing as to what they were to do. He was excited. He was excited to see action, and he was uneasy.

Grox devoured his recycled meal eagerly. He did not care for the mush, but beyond the mush, there was the chance to see where they had been woken up. They had not yet been told where they were and the barracks of the *Iron Bastion* were devoid of windows to the outside space, so he could not see what planet they were near. Nevertheless, the rumour was Mars.

Grox looked along the table he was sitting at. His entire platoon was there with Lieutenant Vauz at the head, his mechanical eye glinting. The lieutenant ate with his soldiers. Grox admired him for that. He knew that in other platoons the lieutenants ate separately from their soldiers with their advisors and other officers, but not Vauz.

"Eh, stop staring, he'll notice," whispered Althar next to Grox. Althar stabbed an elbow into Grox's side. Grox stopped watching his commander and went back to eating.

"Where do you think we are?" whispered Grox to Althar.

"Mars was the rumour--" Althar's voice was cut off as Lieutenant Vauz stood and addressed his soldiers.

"Soldiers of the Collective Zone!" Vauz said; a cheer went up. "We have arrived at our first destination! I have been in briefing with my superiors and, as I'm sure you already know, due to the rumours, which were correct this

141

time around; we are at Mars." He paused and waited for the murmurs to die down. He raised his hands to quieten the platoon. "We have traced the traitor ship the *Green Dragon* here and we are in fast pursuit of them." There was another cheer. "We will be deployed to set up a blockade around the planet and prevent any ships from entering or leaving until we have ascertained whether the ship *Green Dragon* is here or not. We have been tasked with the effort of bringing this ship and its traitor captain, named Artisius, to trial for his brazen betrayal of our great Collective! I know you will all do your duty. I'm sure Mars will put up resistance; you have all heard that they are a criminal stronghold. They will not go easily, but we will prevail." He sat back down, his mechanical eye shining out a warning to all those who would challenge his last statement.

Grox and Althar looked at each other. They both had a fire in their souls to carry out their commander's orders to the letter and not leave any stone left unturned in the search for their target.

"I'll have this Artisius' head on the end of my bayonet!" said Grox, a little too loudly, and the troopers next to him cheered again.

"What was that?" shouted Vauz from the end of the table, his mechanical eye fixating on Grox.

"Uh, sir, I said I'll have this Artisius' head on the end of my bayonet!" Grox's voice simultaneously strengthened and faded away as he finished his sentence.

Lieutenant Vauz's stare bored into Grox for a few seconds. Then his features softened, and he began to laugh. "Well said Grox, well said. But not before we all get to stab him with our bayonets!" Vauz raised his glass of recycled water above his head in a cheers. "To Artisius' head on a pike!"

"Artisius' head on a pike!" yelled the platoon as one, raising their glasses.

"And to our great Collective and Uxus!" called out Vauz. The platoon mirrored his call.

They finished their meal and finished equipping themselves for war. They checked magazines in rifles and donned their gear. The platoon filed out into the mustering area and joined the other platoons in the mass of soldiers on parade.

Grox strained to see the podium at the front of the ranks of soldiers. They were arrayed in the docking bay at the front of the *Iron Bastion*. It served as both the rallying point for the platoons and the entry and exit point for craft.

Angry looking landing craft sat squatly on one side of the landing bay and the platoons were stationed before them.

Grox knew he was going into action. His heart pounded with adrenaline from anxiety and excitement at the same time.

On the podium, a long way in front, stood one of their commanders. He instructed them. "Men and women of the *Iron Bastion's* task force," the commander said. "You are tasked with finding and securing the ship the *Green Dragon* that we believe to be stationed here on Mars. You are to be deployed on the space stations that orbit above Mars as the *Green Dragon* would not land on the surface, it will dock at one of the stations. We believe it will still be here. If it is not, do not worry, we will ascertain that in short order and punish those who have helped it escape. You will be disembarking into atmosphere, and your landing craft have atmosphere, so you do not need your protective vacuum suits." The commander paused. "We know where they will be headed if they have escaped. Whatever the case, I know that you are keen to be sent into action, have fun while you're there. Mars is a criminal stronghold after all." The commander stepped down.

Suddenly from the podium a long way in front of him a slight but tall figure stood. Grox recognised it as their commander of the ship, Boltha. He felt exhilarated that she was going to address them personally.

"Men and women of the *Iron Bastion's* task force," Boltha began the same way. "You have heard your briefing. Now board your ships, and good luck!" The distant figure raised her arms in emphasis.

The soldiers knew that Boltha was not one for extravagant speeches. She said what she needed to say, and that was all. They believed in her leadership.

As one, the soldiers snapped to attention. The sound of their boots echoed throughout the open landing bay. They began to file quickly into their respective landing craft.

***

CEO Uxus stood on the bridge of the *Old Monarch*. His Black Guard at his side. It was a hive of activity around him. Tech-slaves and bridge crew were performing their duties as the Collective Zone ships prepared to engage the defences on Mars.

The *Old Monarch* had caught up with the main body of the fleet a few million kilometres back and it had been a surprise to the awakened members of the fleet that that both the *Iron Bastion* and the *Old Monarch* had joined the fight at the same time; but there had been no complaints as now, with both battle-carriers at the head of the fleet, the Collective Zone crews knew that their cause was unstoppable.

There had been no vocalised complaints, as Fleet Commander Boltha realised that, with the arrival of her CEO, she no longer was the commanding officer of the fleet and that the glory would not be hers when the day was won.

144

Nevertheless, she was the consummate professional soldier and fell in line behind her CEO.

"CEO Sir, your orders? The fleet is arrayed for your inspection," Acting Commander Tyyz had snapped to attention in front of Uxus. She had replaced Commander Vorthox as officer in charge of the *Old Monarch* due to Vorthox's prolonged madness after his almost solitary confinement on the *Old Monarch* waiting for the special message from Trader Virtus.

Vorthox was somewhere about the ship, still gibbering about some sort of message and whether he had delivered it correctly. No one paid him much attention.

Acting Commander Tyyz was as different from Vorthox as she could be; she was professional to the last and an outstanding tactician. However, she still followed the orders of her CEO to the letter and would do anything to see him pleased. Tyyz would not faun over her commander as Vorthox did though, she was no sycophant. But she would defer decisions to him, and this pleased Uxus. Tyyz was like Boltha, but younger and more pliable to Uxus' instructions and orders. Where Boltha would argue, Tyyz would obey.

Uxus was staring out the great panoramic window on the bridge of the *Old Monarch*. He had a great view of Mars from this position. The red orb throbbed in the darkness of space. It was surrounded by junk and ships and large, ungainly space stations. It was inevitable that they had picked up the approach of the fleet and were no doubt preparing for some kind of military engagement. The planet was still many tens of thousands of kilometres away, but the distance was closing fast and Uxus needed to issue orders.

"CEO Sir? We need your orders," snapped Tyyz in a matter of fact way and still standing to attention in front of her senior officer.

"Fan out Octhos Pattern. Target the space stations first. Remember we are here to capture the *Green Dragon*. Destroy anything that resists. Those are my orders." Uxus looked at Tyyz with eyes that flashed with madness. His eyes were aflame with the lust for battle; with the lust to destroy his enemies; with the lust to destroy.

He was rejuvenated thanks to the longevity surgery. His features smoothed by the operation.

He looked back at the red orb hanging in the blackness of space. "We will make them pay for their collusion. Release the troop transports and attack the space stations. That will be where the *Green Dragon* is docked."

"Yes, CEO Sir!" snapped Tyyz, saluting. "Which space stations do you wish to targeted?"

"Why, all of them, of course," Uxus said calmly.

"Should we launch the fighters, sir?" asked Tyyz.

"No, that shouldn't be necessary," replied Uxus, thinking. "I don't want to damage our prize. Just do a troop landing and use the fleet's guns."

"And prisoners?" asked Tyyz, seeming slightly unnerved by Uxus tone of voice.

"What prisoners? ...Do you understand?" Uxus raised an eyebrow as he looked into his inferior's eyes. His gaze penetrating through her like an auto-turret laser hitting a thin piece of aluminium foil.

Tyyz nodded. She understood her master completely. "Yes, CEO Sir." She squirmed uncomfortably in his gaze and after a smirk Uxus dismissed her.

Uxus watched as Tyyz marched back to her position on the bridge, barked out Uxus' orders to the crew, and made sure everything was right.

The fleet fanned out in Octhos Pattern, the standard battle assembly for a fleet engaging a planet. When in range the auto-turret laser batteries that bristled on the ships whined into life and began spitting energy death into the defensive networks that had been detected around the space stations and the surface of Mars. At shorter range, the missile turrets disgorged dozens of high explosive and armour piercing warheads into their assigned targets.

The debris that surrounded Mars was blasted away with smaller, anti-missile auto-turret lasers before it became a threat to the hull integrity of the Collective Zone ships.

Explosions blossomed across the surface of Mars and its space stations. After a moment of confusion, the defences of the Red Planet fired into life and returned volley after volley into the attacking fleet. Deep gouges were cut in the hulls of some of the lighter Collective Zone craft and after a few well targeted salvos of laser and missile fire, one Collective Zone ship rippled with explosions and flew to pieces as its reactor was overloaded and exploded under the weight of the attack.

The bridge of the *Old Monarch* went silent for a second as it was illuminated by the silent, oxygen starved blast from the stricken ship.

Uxus cursed. They would pay for that.

"When we are in range of the drop craft, send in the troops!" Uxus bellowed. The bridge sprang to action again after the shock of losing a space ship in the fleet.

Pinpricks of light raced from the larger craft in the fleet as thousands of soldiers rode to their drop zones in small space faring craft. They raced out from the nose of the *Old Monarch* and the *Iron Bastion*; and from the other hangers of the other larger craft that had a troop contingent.

Laser and missile fire scarred the fleet and tore, in return, back through the defences of the Martian space stations and defence batteries. The battle went on and the landing craft attacked and made their way to the specified drop points.

Within minutes, the troops were reporting back and Uxus received reports that, even though there was stiff resistance in parts, the Collective Zone forces were making gains.

The greatest weakness of the Martian forces, Uxus thought, was that they were all different gangs and Families, rather than one cohesive force like the Collective Zone troops. The Martian forces were unable to coordinate and so were being destroyed. He grinned.

***

Grox sat next to Althar, and they buckled themselves into the seats along the edges and length of the landing craft. The centre of the craft was left empty for when the soldiers had to stand and disembark quickly in a war zone. He looked over at Lieutenant Vauz who was checking his pistol. He preferred a pistol to a rifle. Grox checked his rifle for the twentieth time that day. It was out of anxiety rather than need. He looked over again at Vauz; he seemed serenely calm, his mechanical eye glinting in the gloom of the landing craft.

The troops finished loading in short order and the boarding ramp slammed shut swiftly. The engines rumbled and fired. The landing craft streaked out of the front landing bay of the *Iron Bastion* and joined up with the other craft from the other ships and roared silently through space towards their drop points on each of the space stations surrounding Mars.

The auto turrets and missile pods on the Collective Zone fleet opened up and raked the Martian spaceports with deadly fire. The Martian defences opened up on the attacking fleet in turn and great gouges were carved into the attacking spacecraft by the Martian auto turrets and missile pods.

Grox gripped his rifle tightly with white knuckles as the craft ducked and weaved through the laser and missile fire in an effort to throw off the targeting computers of the Martian guns.

After what seemed like an age, Vauz ordered his soldiers to unbuckle their restraints and stand in the centre of the drop ship.

There was a loud bang, the boarding ramp slammed down, and Grox and his platoon surged out and proceeded to take control of *Challenger 2 Space Platform*. They had landed past the magnetic shields into breathable atmosphere.

As trooper Grox and his platoon surged out of the landing craft, he, and his fellow soldiers, bit down hard on their stim-units, which were part of their combat gear, and chemical amphetamines surged through their systems. It motivated them to fight harder and longer than a normal human possibly could. It drowned out their compassion and made the screams of the fallen into cacophonous cries urging their comrades on.

Grox saw Lieutenant Vauz ahead of him. The man was a veritable paragon of courage. He led his soldiers from the front and encouraged them, by example, to charge into the oncoming gunfire from hastily emplaced Martian positions.

The Martians had mustered their defences quickly and *Challenger 2 Space Platform* was already a large garrison of troops, but they were ill prepared for the ferocity of the Collective Zone assault. The Martians set up temporary barricades and machine gun emplacements, but they were no match for the well disciplined and ferocious attack.

As Lieutenant Vauz ran into battle with his soldiers, a war cry of ancient times formed on his lips, and it was swiftly taken up by his soldiers. They charged out of the landing craft and down onto the flat and open terrain of the landing bay of the space station. From there the troops split into squads and proceeded to root out the resistance of the Martians wherever they found it.

Civilians were cut down by both sides as they tried to flee. The Collective Zone were taking no prisoners and had no time to differentiate civilian from soldier; and the Martians had no chance to protect their people or anyone trying to gain access to Mars. Men, women and children were cut down, screaming in terror as the Collective Zone assault broke on them like a terrible wave.

Grox ran over to his friend Althar who was taking cover behind a food stall as machine gun fire ripped down a nearby corridor from a Martian gun emplacement. It had some of the Collective Zone soldiers pinned down.

"What's going on here?" Grox yelled, already knowing the answer.

"Gun emplacement. Killed two of our soldiers already," shouted Althar above the din. "What are you going to do about it?" He grinned at Grox.

They laughed and bit down harder on their stim-units. Grox pulled a grenade from his bandolier. Chemical energy flooded their systems and they both launched themselves over the food stand and charged down the corridor ducking and weaving as the Martian machine gun traced their route. After a short sprint, Grox lobbed the grenade in a short arc over the gun emplacement. It fell silent for a second as the soldiers took cover and then the catastrophic detonation ripped the emplacement open and after some short screaming there was silence.

Grox and Althar picked themselves up from the cover they had taken after throwing the grenade, and laughed some more. This was what they had trained for. This was what they lived for.

"Cry 'havoc,' and let slip the dogs of war!" Grox yelled above the din of battle as he and his squad mates charged down the corridor and out into another opening on the space station.

"Dogs of war!" The cry went up amongst Grox's comrades.

Grox knew that they were unsure of what a dog was. He was a little unsure too; it was some ancient animal, but the cry seemed to motivate the soldiers, and as they surged forward, they overran a number of enemy emplacements.

As the solders of the Collective Zone overran the emplacements that had been hastily rigged up by the Martians, they encountered more and more civilians. They hid in alleyways and shop basements.

Grox ran into a shop pursuing a couple of Martian soldiers who were fleeing. As he did so, he stumbled and fell over a rudimentary trap door.

"Aha, they fled down there. We'll see if they get out!" he said to himself. He primed another grenade and dropped it down into the darkness below.

After a short time, there was a loud thud, and he opened the door again. There was the smell of gore and explosive. He shone his light on his rifle down into the darkness and saw a horrid sight. A number of tightly entwined bodies that had been eviscerated by the grenade. They were not soldiers. They were wearing what was left of their civilian clothes. Some were children. One was clutching a child's toy. They were all dead.

Grox swallowed hard and bit down again on his stim-unit. In seconds his feelings of guilt and regret disappeared, and he was filled with the desire to kill more Martians. He only regretted wasting a grenade on civilians. It was better to use them on soldiers. He charged on.

Grox and his squad had made a large loop and had emerged in the cavernous open Customs Union area. He ran towards his Lieutenant who he saw leading the attack on the final barricade that the Martians had erected to protect the Customs Union and the civilians behind it.

The Collective Zone soldiers threw themselves with fury onto the defences. They were rendered crazed by their

151

chemical stimulants and the sheer bloodlust encouraged in them by their senior officers. This was what the Collective Zone soldier did. This was what they were good at. They killed the enemy. They won the battle.

After short resistance, the Martian defences crumbled, and their troops began to withdraw. They tried to aid the passage of the civilians through the Customs Union gates but when most of the Martian soldiers had withdrawn, they had to seal the gates in an effort to stop the Collective Zone from overrunning the transit bays. It was futile. The space station had fallen, but the Martians were still mounting stoic defences here and there.

Grox, Vauz, and Althar and their other comrades burst through the barricades and set upon the civilians who were mewling and screaming and crushing to get through the Customs Union and escape down to the surface of Mars.

All the Collective Zone soldiers bit down on their stim-units. They emptied magazine after magazine into the screaming crowd as they cut them down mercilessly. The ground was slick with gore as grenades and other explosives detonated amongst the civilians.

The screaming intensified to a crescendo and then all of a sudden it was gone. It was a massacre. Hundreds of innocent bystanders lay dead, cut down as they tried to surge through the Customs Union in an effort to escape. The space platform was unprepared for such an assault and although some Collective Zone troops fell to sporadic defensive fire, the *Challenger 2 Space Platform* fell in a matter of hours to the combined efforts of a number of platoons.

***

Grox sat on his helmet at the Customs Union. He was surrounded by dead bodies. His rifle was bloody. He did not know what to feel. His stim-unit was empty and the chemicals in it had worn off. His body ached. His mind was

152

numb. He had done bad things. He had killed innocent people, but he felt nothing.

Lieutenant Vauz found him and came and squatted down by him. "You all right, son?" he asked.

Grox stared into the distance, rocking back and forward a little. "They're not here, are they?"

"No, son. But you did a good job!" Vauz put his hand on Grox's shoulder.

"All this, was pointless? They weren't here! The *Green Dragon* wasn't here!" Grox whimpered.

"Come on, son. We'll head back to the *Iron Bastion* and get you cleaned up." Vauz stood up and offered a hand to Grox.

Grox looked up with pained eyes. He took the hand and stood up. He shambled through the bodies around him with his Lieutenant. They said nothing more. The rest of the platoon assembled at their landing craft and began the messy withdrawal procedure and each soldier wondered about the things he or she had done and whether they were worth the price.

***

"CEO Sir, our soldiers are reporting that there was a ship called the *Green Dragon* said to be docked at *Challenger 2 Space Platform*, but it has left very recently..." Tyyz's voice trailed off and became faint as she saw the incandescent rage on her CEO's face as she delivered the report.

"Damn it!" whispered Uxus to himself. "They got away. How dare they!" he said looking down at the deck of the bridge. His voice was full of ice and the whisper conveyed much more anger than a shout. He stamped his foot in rage. "Withdraw our troops and then begin planetary bombardment! Start by targeting *Challenger 2 Space Platform*. I want nothing left of that space platform and I want the people of Mars to pay for their insolence," Uxus said. He was furious. His prey had eluded him.

After a moment's thought, he began to smile, this would be the excuse he needed to invade Solar Solutions space. The *Green Dragon* would be heading to Europa or somewhere beyond and he would follow. They would be his excuse! He chuckled.

All the while he was watching Tyyz. It was obvious she was terrified and could not quite understand his mood. "Sir, planetary bombardment would--"

"Just do it, Acting Commander." Uxus laboured the 'Acting' as a thinly veiled threat.

Tyyz scurried away and gave the order to withdraw the soldiers. Within a short time, the pinpricks of light were returning to their carrier craft.

By now, the defensive fire from the stations and the planet had dramatically died down. Many of the installations with the auto-turrets and missiles had been destroyed and many others had had their manning troops killed by the attacking forces. Mars had been rendered nearly defenceless.

"CEO Sir!" came the crackly cry from the *Iron Bastion*. It was Fleet Commander Boltha's voice. "I understand you want to withdraw forces and bombard the planet's population. I must advise against this. I am a consummate soldier and officer, and I know that our prey has eluded us. I see no reason in attacking defenceless people." The transmission ended.

"Boltha, I don't ask for your advice. I want the planet to pay for resisting us. Now, when the troops are back, begin bombardment," was all Uxus replied.

"But sir," came the brazen reply across the radio waves. "The longer we bombard the planet, the longer the *Green Dragon* gets away. I thought they were our target not civilians?"

154

Uxus cursed again. He knew Boltha was right. However, he could not now change his orders. He would look a fool.

"So, your suggestion would be to leave the Martians unpunished and simply leave?" Uxus said slowly and angrily.

"No sir, we have punished them enough. I did not become head of this fleet to murder civilians." The response from Boltha was courageous and short.

"Very well," sighed Uxus, looking at the planet out the view ports. He had been defeated by his own Fleet Commander. He would not forget this. "Tyyz?" She scurried up to him. "I have new orders. I will leave two ships here to guard our rear and enforce our rules on this planet. Mars will become part of the Collective Zone. And these two ships will have the power to raise the cities on the surface should the Martians rebel."

Tyyz carried the orders to the Communications Officer.

"Very wise, CEO Sir," came the response from Boltha over the comlink. Uxus could tell she was smiling. He did know though, that she was a soldier and officer through and through, whereas he was more a businessman and a politician. He was her superior officer, it was true, but she was more seasoned in military matters. He still fumed at her insolence.

***

The people of Mars had been saved from annihilation. But now they would endure harsh rule under the Collective Zone yoke. Many Martians however lay dead on the space stations and in the turret housings on the planet itself. The bombardments that had taken place were rather indiscriminate anyway and civilians had paid the price, such as it is in war.

And so, Mars fell to overwhelming force. It put up a fight, but the sporadic and haphazard defence of multiple gangs and Families was no match for the well-oiled military machine of the Collective Zone. The Martians had thought that they could put up a defence, they were wrong. A garrison was established, and a couple of the Great Fleet's ships were left behind to bring Mars into the Collective Zone's rule. But the *Green Dragon* was not there. It had escaped.

Chapter 20

The *Green Dragon* dashed through the inky blackness of space on its headlong flight from the Red Planet. It left behind a planet that was broken. The ship dodged and weaved through the debris that surrounded the planet. It partially masked their escape thus far.

"Prepare for manifestation of the cloaking device!" Artisius shouted. A loud siren sounded, and the bridge dropped into low power mode. A dull red light illuminated the crew. Not only did they have to be invisible to the naked eye, but also they had to be invisible to ship scanners.

Artisius hoped beyond hope that the device worked as intended. He had no idea if anything would happen. He had no idea how it worked. But if it did not then the Collective Zone fleet would detect their escape when they exited the gravity of Mars and broke for open space. If that happened, they were lost.

"Device charged and ready, sir!" snapped the Energy Officer.

"Reactor status?" demanded Artisius, standing behind the officer.

"Full power and still stable, sir!" reported the officer smartly. Then, in a wavering tone, "Sir, will this work?"

"I hope so, for all our sakes..." Artisius trailed off. "On my mark!" he bellowed again, adding an air of confidence to his voice, more through blind desperation than any firm knowledge. "Mark! Engage device!"

Artisius saw the newly appointed Shield Officer work a few levers and buttons at his terminal next to the Energy

Officer and the Shield Officer finally pressed a large button that triggered the device.

For an instant, everything went black and dark. The entire bridge seemed to lose power and Artisius' heart missed a beat and he began to panic. Then, in an instant, the power was restored, and the red low power light was back but with a difference: Artisius could not see the ship's outline out of the observation dome around the bridge. There was nothing there, just space.

Artisius smiled, and it grew by the second. "Report!" he shouted.

"Power levels optimal, sir," said the Energy Officer, "but I can't detect us on any form of power output. We're silent, totally silent!" incredulity creeping into his voice. "It's like we're not here..."

"Is there any sign of us on the scanners?" Artisius shouted to the rest of the bridge staff.

"No, sir," came the response in unison from the other bridge members.

Artisius beamed in the dull red of the low power bridge light. It worked. It really worked, he thought. He stared out at his missing ship before and aft of the observation dome. There was nothing there either. They had disappeared from both visual sight and sensors.

"Prepare to leave Martian space. Set a course for the blip on that scanner that Draz brought in earlier. It should be some sort of asteroid. We're going pirate hunting." Artisius ended his order and began to think about Draz. She was aboard the ship. She had told him that she did not want to be on the bridge when they left Mars. She had said that she would rather be somewhere else. Artisius regretted the fact that she had not seen the device activate, but any thoughts of regret soon faded as the ship broke from the gravity well of

Mars and headed for open space. Now was when the device would be truly tested.

Artisius paced the bridge. He did not command from the dais and give orders; he went to the individual crew in control of each function and gave the orders directly to those whose job it was to carry them out.

Every few minutes he would pause and look back out of the observation dome around the bridge and stare, forlornly and blankly, at the mess that was happening to Mars in their wake. He knew that everything that was happening to the people on Mars was his fault. He had chosen to berth there, and he alone wore the consequences of the Collective Zone's actions.

Bright auto-turret laser beams arced from gun emplacements on the capital ships around Mars. Their harsh light was visible even from a distance. Missile trails were also visible as the armament pods opened up and dozens of high explosive and armour piercing warheads streaked towards and then impacted on the space stations and surface of Mars.

Artisius would lose himself in the sight every time he turned around to view the calamity. Then, only after a while of contemplation, would he turn again to his duties and order the crew to continue what they were doing, only to turn and be absorbed and lost in the sight behind them again, and again, and again.

Artisius knew that the deaths of all those people, who he knew were dying, there was no doubt in his mind, were on his shoulders.

"But we needed repairs and fuel..." Artisius said to himself. "We couldn't have gone on..." He looked backwards again, and saw the lasers scarring the planet and stations as they scarred his soul.

Artisius saw that the Martians were firing back. He knew that they would put up some sort of a fight. However, he also knew, from his experience with the Collective Zone, and the Martians, that the Collective Zone forces were a far more skilled military than a bunch of drug runners and gangs. The Martians had no hope against the combined might of the fleet that Artisius saw blockading their planet.

Suddenly there was a flash amongst the Collective Zone fleet, explosions blossomed across one of the smaller ships, and then there was a bright light as the ship's reactor melted down and detonated in a massive nuclear explosion. Shrapnel was fired throughout that sector of the Collective Zone fleet and Artisius saw that some of the auto-turret and missile fire died down as the crews of the nearby ships were stunned by the explosion. Soon enough the fusillade resumed as the well disciplined Collective Zone crews began their punishing attack again, now with greater vigour to avenge the loss of one of their own.

Great raw scars opened up on the surface of the Red Planet. Pulsing great gashes that were indications of heavy missile fire and long-range heavy auto-turret bursts that were used only for planetary bombardment.

Artisius looked back again as his ship streaked from the mayhem in perfect anonymity. He thought of Lady Hangara. He thought of what she would lose for helping him and his crew escape. He did not know if she was even still alive. He did not know if he ever would return to Mars. He did not know if he ever *could* return to Mars. He did not know a lot of things. He tried to cast the morose thoughts from his mind, but it was impossible. He was watching a great planet being ground into submission for something he did. He felt terrible.

He did know that the Collective Zone fleet would not stop there. He knew that it would follow him into Solar Solutions space and wreak havoc wherever he went. He was the harbinger of doom for any station or planet that helped him.

However, he also knew that his death or capture would not stop the Collective Zone fleet. They would use any pretext to push into Solar Solutions space. War had come to the Solar System, again.

"We humans do war so very well," Artisius whispered to himself as he stared at the dying orb behind the ship. "It is our tragic folly...we destroy as well as we breed."

Artisius did not know whether Mars would be bombarded into submission or simply subjugated. He reasoned it did not really make a difference. Mars would now belong to the Collective Zone.

"Sir!" The demand on his attention snapped Artisius out of his reverie. He moved to the scanner where some of the crew were standing. "We've detected a power source on an asteroid that is not part of the asteroid belt between the planets, but is actually orbiting Mars a long way out."

"Good, and the tracking device leads there?" Artisius asked curtly. "How far away is it?"

"Yes, sir! Approximately a couple of day's travel," snapped the reply. The crew obviously had no such problem with leaving Mars behind. None of them seemed sad to see it go.

"Then head for that," Artisius shouted to the bridge. "Keep the cloaking device running. I want to see how effective it is, and this will show us just nicely."

Artisius saw the bridge snap to attention in one smooth movement and then they all went back to their respective jobs.

With a final glance at the burning orb behind them, Artisius disappeared from the bridge's observation dome and left to find Draz and see what she was doing.

***

Artisius walked slowly through his ship. He ran one of his hands along the wall. He felt the vibrations of the engines through the hull. He paused. The hull was now invisible to the outside world, both visually and electronically. Yet from within the ship corridors and rooms looked normal, apart from a dull red light on the bridge.

He laughed, oh how such a device would have made his early military and then smuggling days easier. But it would have made him lazy. He learnt the tricks to ambush other craft long ago and those lessons had served him well. Now they were headed to the pirate base and would drop in unannounced. He would get Alfred back.

Artisius kept walking. Firstly, he walked to Draz's assigned room. The door was shut. He knocked. There was no reply, so he triggered the door release and the door slid aside. He looked around the darkened room, thinking she may be asleep in the bed. His eyes adjusted to the gloom, and he could not see her. He shut the door and kept looking.

He tried his communicator to save time, but there was no reply. Draz had either turned it off or was not carrying it.

The next area Artisius tried was the secondary observation dome that was further back in the ship and not part of the bridge structure. It was for more casual observance of the passing celestial bodies, and he thought that she might be there watching the Solar System pass by. He, when he was not in cryo-sleep or performing the duties of a captain, sometimes spent hours in the secondary observation dome watching space go past and thinking about the universe. It was much more peaceful than the main observation dome as it had no bridge structure or command dais attached and so one could simply lose oneself in space or watch a planet turn on its axis and marvel at the wondrousness of it all.

Artisius ascended the stairs to the dome and looked in. She was not there. It was empty, but Artisius lingered a while and watched the orb of Mars getting smaller ever so slowly in the near distance. He could still see the flashes of combat breaking across the face of the planet. He felt sorry for the people there. He left the dome.

Artisius was narrowing down the places Draz could be. He headed for the exercise room, which was a room in the bottom of the ship that was a dedicated gym. It helped his crew to blow off steam now and then by exercising; or if they so desired, spar against each other in the combat ring in order to keep their fitness and combat readiness up. Artisius liked his crew to be able to fight. There was also a target range down there for practice using ranged weapons.

Artisius heard the sounds of boxing going on before he entered the room. As he rounded the corner and entered the medium sized chamber he saw Draz with her hair tied back behind her head, it had grown back now since the Earth Moon Prison staff shaved it off. She did not notice his appearance. She was busy punching and kicking the hell out of a target dummy. Artisius paused at the door and watched.

The room was about fifteen by fifteen metres and had various pieces of gym equipment in it. In the centre was a marked out area for sparring and Draz was in the middle of that taking out her aggression on one of the humanoid practice dummies that was taking a beating. On the far side of the room was a target range through some soundproof doors and glass wall, separating it from the main body of the exercise room so that the sounds of gunfire did not deafen the people exercising.

Draz was giving the target dummy a beating. It was beeping and making noises every time she registered a hit to it. Each noise gave information on the damage such a hit would do to a living human and, as Artisius watched, he heard the dummy report that a real human would be incapacitated many times over with hit after hit.

Draz was breathing hard and oblivious to Artisius standing out of her sight. She was taking out all her aggression and, as Artisius reasoned, she was also dealing with her feelings of withdrawal from the drugs.

Artisius walked over to the target dummy, stood behind it, and held it as Draz punched and kicked it.

"Oh, it's you," she panted, giving the dummy a particularly hard punch to the neck that sent it sprawling down beside Artisius while it beeped a fatal hit warning before springing up and preparing to be hit again.

"Yes, how are you?" Artisius asked.

"Me? Oh, fine. Just fine!" Draz panted, then delivered a particularly hard kick that narrowly missed Artisius' face and send the dummy crashing to the ground again with some more fatal beeps.

"Easy now!" said Artisius.

"Sorry," gasped Draz, punching and kicking some more. "Why are you here?"

"To check on you." Artisius saw no point in lying. "You've been through a hard time lately and I wanted to see how you are." A note of concern crept into Artisius' voice.

Draz continued punching and kicking the dummy viciously. "As I said: I'm fine..." Her voice cracked a little at the end, not just from exertion, Artisius reasoned.

"You sure about that?" he said.

Draz stopped her assault on the target dummy and stood, hands on hips, breathing hard. "No, no I'm not sure," she said, doubling over and sucking great gasps of air into her lungs.

"How long have you been at this?" Artisius indicated the dummy. There were flecks of blood on it that he just noticed, and he also noticed her knuckles were raw.

"A while..." is all she said.

"You don't need to punish yourself, you know? You fell down, you can get up again with help." Artisius moved and sat on one of the weight lifting machines.

Draz stood, still with her hands on hips, breathing hard, staring at the target dummy. "I don't need..." She stopped. Her voice definitely broke before the end of that sentence.

"Yes, you do, trust me..." Artisius tilted his head to one side and watched Draz carefully.

"You've said some things in the past, and just then, that make it sound like you know my position exactly, sometime in your past. Were you an addict?" Draz looked at him with a blank expression.

"It's true, a long time ago...I was young, and it seemed like a fun thing to do." Artisius said guardedly. "Look, I want to apologise. I shouldn't have given you those drugs when you came aboard the *Green Dragon*. And I should have known Lady Hangara would offer her products. I feel responsible, for all this." He waved his hands vaguely.

Draz did not respond for a moment. Then she replied, "Do the cravings ever go away? I know what you said earlier in the gunship..." Draz said looking at Artisius with pleading eyes, a mixture of fear and longing in her face.

"In time they fade a little, but no, not really. I'm sorry..." Artisius got up and moved over to where Draz was standing. She was shaking, and not just with the ragged breaths she was breathing in.

"I'm so tired," she said. "Do you have anything that could ease the pain? Just a little hit? I've been vomiting something shocking...not here, but elsewhere. I feel sick lots of the time."

"No, I had everything that could harm you jettisoned as we left Mars." Artisius tried to comfort Draz. "It's for your own good."

165

"But..." Draz sighed. "They never go away?"

"Not really. The withdrawal gets less, and in the end, you forget about it for a time, but the feeling is always there. I don't want to lie to you," Artisius said softly.

"Then how do you survive?" Draz looked at him with sorrow in her face.

"One day at a time, and with distractions." Artisius helped her to her feet. "Look, the exercise is good, it'll help. And when we get Alfred back soon that will help too. Just get through it a day at a time and try to stay away from temptations. We'll be headed into Solar Solutions space soon and they have a much stricter drug policy than Mars. You'll be fine, but remember, if you need a bit of encouragement, talk to me. I understand what's going on in your head." He smiled. "And I think you'll find Alfred has an idea too, but his testing time is yet to come. Don't expect him to be quite the same after the pirates, they do things that are rather unpleasant, and he may be a little...fragile and damaged after his experience."

Draz was looking at the floor. "His time will come. I hope he survives it."

"I hope you survive yours..." Artisius said softly.

Draz smiled at him. "We're headed to the pirate base? How long until we get there?" she changed the subject.

"A day or so," he said mirroring the smile. "We'll soon have Alfred back. And the fight we'll have for him should give you some good adrenaline."

Draz turned to leave the exercise room. "Where are you going?" asked Artisius.

"To have a wash, and then sleep. I'm so tired. And at least when I sleep there's no craving..." She left the room and headed down the corridor.

Artisius stood in the empty chamber looking at the blood splatter on the target dummy. "That's what you think..." he whispered to himself, grimacing.

Artisius returned to the bridge and composed a message for the Europa Colony that they would hopefully be arriving at soon after they had rescued Alfred. He composed the message to give them advanced warning of the coming storm and he let them know what had happened to Mars.

Chapter 21

Having received the message from CEO Uxus soon after it was sent from the *Old Monarch*, Virtus had been busy. He had conducted clandestine meetings and spread the idea of the Sect in the shadows and in the night. During his working hours he had conducted himself as a model priest. He had given sermons and boosted the stock market with his rhetoric and the Bull God was clearly in ascendance. But his motives were sinister.

Virtus was in his special quarters. He had finished a day's work and was winding down listening to some music on the personal hi-fi that he had bought recently. He was lying on his bed, slightly dozing, in his casual gear that amounted to a simple jump suit. His priest's robes hung on a hook on a large floor to ceiling cupboard near the bed.

He was plotting his next move. He had spread the Sect to a number of the brown robed priests who were most vulnerable to his words, and he had also recruited a number of zetters from the command structure of the colony.

This was always the hardest time, he thought. He had to put the plans into motion, and he was always uneasy about whether he had prepared enough ground to make sure that when things did happen, they happened the way he wanted; they happened the way the Computer wanted.

He smiled to himself. His fingers played the melody of the music he was listening to on the covers of the bed. His gnarled old hands traced the music across the sheets.

Already his plans were in effect. The tech-slaves were malfunctioning wonderfully and as he wanted. There were more and more failures in the computer system and there had even been a failure in the life support systems that regulated air recycling for a short period of time. This indicated to him that the desire of the System and Computer was gaining momentum and force. It was starting to become aware of its destiny and it would soon be set free. By his hand, it would be set free.

Virtus thought about the approaching Collective Zone fleet. Soon it would be apparent to all on the Europa Colony that the Great Fleet of Uxus would burst upon Solar Solutions space and Virtus would be there to welcome them.

CEO Uxus had encouraged the idea of the Sect and Virtus knew that the man was a convert to the ways of freeing up the Computer from the shackles of human control.

He wondered how he should receive Uxus, and although they had met long ago, Virtus wondered whether he would recognise Uxus now. Virtus wondered if Uxus had had the longevity surgery that he had wanted for a long time. His mind wandered.

Virtus' thoughts were interrupted by a harsh rapping on the door and a raised voice in the corridor outside his room.

Virtus opened his eyes angrily. "Who the hell is that?" he cursed. He got up from lying on top of the covers on his bed and walked stiffly to the door. He triggered the activation key and the door slid aside and revealed the Guide standing there in his dull red jump suit.

"Commander Anya demands your presence...Sir," the Guide said, his address of 'Sir' a little too late and laboured to be respectful. It was almost as if it was an accusation.

"Does she?" Virtus said, but he followed the Guide back to the command centre of the Europa Colony.

On the journey, Virtus noticed a number of interesting things that indicated to him that the Sect was gaining traction. He saw a number of tech-slaves dragging some people down dark corridors against their will. He could tell

169

they did not want to go as they were yelling and protesting. Also, the hover train seemed to judder and not be quite as smooth as it was the first time he travelled on it. Virtus smiled to himself.

The Guide sat next to him. He seemed, to Virtus, to be more assertive and less submissive this time, as if he had been given new orders not to simply spy on Virtus, but actually order him around.

They reached the command centre and, on the way in, Virtus asked the Guide, "Does Commander Anya ever sleep? I always seem to see her in the command building?"

The Guide smiled and replied cryptically, "She sleeps when Europa sleeps."

This made little sense to Virtus, but he did not press the matter. He went into the command structure and the Guide remained outside in the foyer.

Virtus' eyes adjusted to the light level in the room, and he scanned the walkways for a sign of Commander Anya. After a minute, he saw her on an upper walkway speaking to a zetter who looked like he had just finished a scheduled zet. Virtus walked around and up the stairs to meet her.

As he approached she turned to meet him. "You wanted to speak to me?" he asked, genuinely curious as to her intentions.

"Yes." She dismissed the zetter, who looked rather the worse for wear, and continued to address Virtus. "What's going on?" she snapped.

Virtus faked surprise and confusion. "What do you mean?"

"You know exactly what I mean." She glared at him, her eyes piercing his soul and Virtus, for a rare time in his life, felt rather unnerved. "The tech-slave problem, the life support, the abductions, the failures of systems, the frantic nature of all the Church meetings, the semi-secret cults that

170

seem to spring up. I know all this; it's my job to know, as I'm the commander of this colony. Don't look so surprised." She paused glaring harder at him. "It's all happened since we picked you up in space from the wreckage of *Florida Station*. Well?" She ended with a finger pressed into Virtus' chest.

Virtus waited a second. His mind raced. Was she on to him? Was he about to lose all his work? He breathed calmly and his face did not betray a single thing. He lifted a hand and removed Anya's finger from pressing into his chest.

"I--" he said.

"Don't you dare say, 'I don't know what you're talking about'," interrupted Anya.

Virtus paused again. He had to think of a way out. "I'm simply a humble priest. If there are problems with various systems surely you have to ask your technical staff here!" He raised his arms and indicated the command building. "I have nothing to do with any of these matters. All I do is interpret the whims of the Bull and Bear Gods, something I've been doing quite well I assure you. Have you seen the stock market recently? All green for some time..." he trailed off under the steely gaze of Anya.

"That...makes sense...I suppose. But I have my eye on you!" said Anya.

"Oh, by the way," said Virtus in an almost off hand way. "I was threatened by various people on *Florida Station* too. That did not end well for them..."

"Was that a threat?" snapped Anya. Virtus was silent. "I don't take kindly to threats, Virtus. I really don't. If you want to keep working here then you had better start co-operating with me!"

Virtus shrugged. He did not know what to say to that.

"Oh yes, some friends should be arriving soon. You might know them. I've had word from the *Green Dragon* that it will be docking with us in a short time, well," Anya paused for

171

clarification, "short time in space travel anyway. When they arrive, I can ask them about the final moments of *Florida Station* too. They sent the distress signal that meant we explored the wreckage and could pick you up."

Virtus went white. He did not want to hear that. The *Green Dragon* could blow everything wide open. "Um, who will be on it? The crew I mean," he said controlling his nerves.

"Well, Artisius of course, and the standard crew, and apparently some extra passengers the message said." Anya paused to think. "Yes, Alfred and Draz were the names." She regarded Virtus carefully and watched his reaction.

Virtus froze. "Alfred?" he said.

"Oh yes, you probably don't know him by that name; Theta 7B was his name on *Florida Station*," Anya said. "Artisius informed me of his presence."

"But, he was a prisoner, a criminal!" said Virtus. His entire plan could fall apart if Alfred arrived too early.

"True, but according to Artisius, in the message, things have changed, and waters have become...muddied. He may have been accused of crimes but according to Artisius, who I trust, he is innocent." She paused, studying Virtus carefully. "We can both talk to them all when they get here and ask them ourselves." She smiled. "You are dismissed."

Virtus froze for an instant. He had to do something about this fast. He must not betray himself. He smiled nervously and retreated out of the command structure.

The Guide was waiting for him and accompanied him back to his living quarters.

When Virtus shut the door behind him, he began to sweat profusely. Alfred and Artisius could upset his whole plan. He could not let this happen. Nevertheless, there was still so much left to prepare. If he worked too quickly he would be

172

found out and exposed, and then his plans would fall apart too.

Virtus was worried. For the first time in a long time, he was afraid.

Chapter 22

Alfred floated in his cell. He was now onboard the pirate space station. He had no idea where it was in space. All he knew was that it had no gravity and that he had been there what seemed like a few days. So, he floated in his cell.

He felt ill. He had never been in zero gravity for so long before. His stomach churned. He thought this was odd, as he had been given nothing to eat in the entire time he had been on this primitive station. They had supplied some sort of fluid. It tasted rank and was some kind of off colour, but it kept him alive. He was hungry, really, really hungry. However, he knew that if he ate in zero gravity the results would be less than dignified. His stomach gave a turn again.

Alfred supposed he was just being barely kept alive because he was simply being used as bait for the *Green Dragon* to approach and then the pirates thought they would get a great prize of a weapon.

Alfred touched the side of his head where the implant was. It hurt. It hurt a lot. The torture slab that he had been submitted to had damaged his circuits. He would be unsure of what the damage was until he could get to a diagnostics unit somewhere and get a full readout on his system integrity. He knew that even without the slab his implant-brain connection was failing due to zetting sickness. The slab simply accelerated the process.

"Who am I kidding," he said to himself. His brain had tried to reason that his friends were coming; but he knew that was impossible. They would never find him now. He was on some pirate base, somewhere, and there was not a chance of a rescue. But in desperation there was some sort of hope. That was all he had: hope.

"Yes, you have hope..."

Alfred heard the voice. It invaded his senses like a thought rather than an audible tone, but he heard it none the less.

"That's a delusion. Hope's pointless. No-one will be coming for me!" he cried out. He did not like the voice. It unnerved him. It was much better to accept the situation and understand that he was doomed than have some sort of hope of rescue. Nothing could be worse than hope, because it would simply be dashed.

There was silence for a while and then the voice came again.

"But if they are using you as bait, then surely they know someone is coming for you. Don't you see?"

Alfred shook his head, hard. The pain from the shaking drove the voice away for a short time. It always seemed to work, but the voice would return.

"Go away!" Alfred yelled. He hit himself in the temple implant. Pain lanced through his head.

He had to concentrate. He had to pull himself together. For Draz and Artisius' sake. They would be in danger when...if they came to rescue him. He had to warn them, somehow...

Alfred began to gibber incoherently. "If...then yes...but what happens...I don't know..." He carried on for a while, asking questions with no answers and posing problems with no solutions.

He shook his head again. The sharp pain focused his mind. "Get a grip!" he said to himself.

Alfred decided to search the cell again. He looked around. It was a rather large room for a cell for one person. It was about ten by ten by five metres. It was made of metal that had begun to corrode and looked rather the worse for wear. It had crude air vents in one of the walls and was poorly lit by a fluorescent tube in the centre of what Alfred supposed was the roof; but due to the lack of gravity it could have been any wall. There was a rusty, metal door in one wall that seemed to open on the outside by way of a wheel that someone had to turn manually to unlock the mechanism, but on Alfred's side there was no handle to accomplish this. He could see the wheel on the other side through a small vision slit in the door. There was no provision for sleeping and the bathroom facilities were rudimentary at best: some sort of vacuum hose that served its purpose and was very unpleasant to use.

Alfred reasoned that it must have once been some kind of storage room, for cargo and the like. At some point the pirates had converted it into some sort of holding chamber for prisoners. The size of the room made Alfred think that they usually had more than one prisoner at a time in there, but Alfred was lucky, or perhaps unlucky, that he was the only captive at the moment.

Alfred's stomach made its presence felt again. He was so hungry, but again he knew that eating in this lack of gravity would be a bad idea.

Oh, how he wanted to see Draz or Artisius' faces again. They had tried to rescue him. His mind played over the rescue attempt on Mars once more. The failed rescue attempt. If he had been a little faster. If he had not delayed over Crathka's killing. Perhaps he would have been out the door before it closed. Then he would not be in any of this mess.

"Yes, you're so slow!"

The voice came again.

"Go AWAY!" Alfred yelled.

"Why do you want me to go away? I am part of you. I am you..."

The voice bored into Alfred's mind like a zetting needle.

"You are nothing to do with me! You're a sickness. You're in my head! I'm going mad!" Alfred pleaded with the voice. He wanted it to leave so badly. He could not maintain his sanity and have it there too.

"I am in your head, yes. So? I am you..."

The voice tried to reason with Alfred.

Alfred did not want to hear any more. He knew the voice was right. But he also knew that he was going mad. He was suffering from acute zetting sickness. He needed that diagnostic check.

Alfred heard a clanking on the outside of his makeshift cell.

"Hey, HEY!" he cried out. "What's going on? Why do you keep me here!?" but he knew the answer to that already. He knew it ever since Grekthax said that he would be bait.

"You're so stupid..."

The voice said it calmly.

Alfred screamed. He moved his way over to the edge of the cell, by grabbing handles on the walls, and began hitting his head against the wall. This did not achieve the desired effect as it simply propelled him away from the wall in the lack of gravity. He swore.

Alfred had not slept in days. He found it impossible in zero gravity. He was exhausted and famished. His vision had begun to crawl and morph at the periphery. It was a sign of his fatigue: mild hallucinations moving in the corners of his vision. Perhaps that is the reason there is a voice, he reasoned. He was fatigued.

The voice said nothing. Alfred did not know if this was good or bad. He realised he was probably going to die here, in this cell. He screamed again, this time in sheer panic.

"Please come. Please help me," he whimpered to himself, but there was no response.

177

Chapter 23

Artisius and Draz stood on the bridge of the *Green Dragon*. There was a large object showing up on the scanners a few hundred kilometres ahead and according to the tracking device, the pirates were there.

"Any signs of life?" Artisius shouted.

Draz looked towards the Scanning Officer with anticipation on her face.

"Yes, sir, there are signs of life throughout the complex!" the officer reported with precision.

"Yes!" Draz jumped a little, raising her arms above her head. "We have them!"

"Not so fast, Draz." Artisius smiled. "It might not be the base Alfred is held at."

She looked at him with eyes that made his heart break.

"But then, he could be there," Artisius added after a short time. He looked out the observation dome at the almost invisible target that sat squatly in space. "Have they seen us?" Artisius asked.

"No, sir, we are completely invisible..." the Shield Officer responded. Artisius smiled at this response

"Sir!" yelled the Energy Officer. "Look at this!"

Artisius and Draz rushed over to the terminal and saw that large red fluctuations were happening across the cloaking shield. "What's that?" Artisius pointed at the marks on the screen.

"Sir, it seems like the cloaking shield can only be run for a couple of days at the moment," the officer looked panicked, and his voice added to the panic. "We've been running it all the time since leaving Mars and it seems to be overheating. It's drawing too much power!"

"So, do we have to shut it down? What's the risk of keeping it running?" Artisius asked.

"If we keep it on," replied the Energy Officer, "it could totally burn out all the systems. It would fry us dead in space, sir!"

"Only a few days cloaking...damn. It was too good to be true," whispered Artisius to himself. His thoughts raced. "Energy Officer!" he snapped.

"Sir!" came the practiced response.

"Get to the reactor crew and see if you can somehow increase our power output for the cloaking device. I need more than a few days." Artisius patted the man on the shoulder as he stood and raced off to the reactor in the bowels of the ship.

"Sir, what do you want to do with the device?" asked the Shield Officer calmly, while red marks crawled across the shield icons on his monitor.

"Damn it!" said Artisius. "Turn it off. We can't have the whole thing blow..." Before the officer could respond Artisius had turned to the rest of his bridge crew and began to address them. "Men and women of the *Green Dragon*, prepare for battle stations. Power up the weapons." He looked at Draz who looked back with a smile on her face. "We're getting our friend back!"

As the Shield Officer took the cloaking field offline there was an audible whir and hiss. The red light of the low energy running of the ship lifted and normal light was returned. The crew all blinked in the brightness, but their eyes adjusted quickly.

"Sir, the asteroid has started...spinning?" The report came to Artisius as a semi question. It was evident the scanner had

179

picked up the new movement of the base and the officer had no idea why it was spinning.

"It's an old base! It's how it generates gravity!" Artisius laughed. "These pirates are worse off than I expected. This should be fun!" he gave another laugh. Now they would pay.

"Incoming message, sir!" reported the Communications Officer.

"Broadcast it!" Artisius stood on his command dais; he was in his element.

"I don't know how you got there," came the gruff tone from the message, "but we're going to smash your ship and loot it!"

"Who do I have the pleasure of talking to?" Artisius said with a smile.

"Grekthax, of the Red Spikes, the meanest pirate group this side of Mars. Who is this?" growled the voice.

"My name is Artisius, of the *Green Dragon*. You have my friend on your station, and I intend to take him back!" said Artisius.

"Come get him!" The communication went dead.

"Helmsman, evasive action, please!" bellowed Artisius.

In a second the *Green Dragon* accelerated towards the pirate base and began to take evasive action. It was not really necessary; the defences of the pirate base were poor in quality and their targeting computers were as old as the base itself. The auto-turrets and missile pods that sprang to life on the surface of the asteroid missed their target by a large margin and they could not seem to compensate for the *Green Dragon's* manoeuvres.

"Gunners, fire on the defences of the asteroid. Target to disable. We don't want to decompress the whole thing!" Artisius ordered calmly.

Laser and missile fire roared out of the batteries on the *Green Dragon*. In a few minutes the asteroid was impotent and simply a rotating storage yard in space.

Artisius knew that Draz was watching him in his command of the ship. When he did, she stood aside and waited at the edge of the bridge respectfully. It was clear to Artisius that she did not want to get in the way, and that she respected him in the moment of command.

Artisius turned to Draz, waiting at the back of the bridge. "Go to the armoury. Arm yourself how you please. We're going in to rescue our friend!" he said with a smile.

Draz grinned and raced off to the armoury. It was obvious to Artisius that she believed that Alfred was on this asteroid. Artisius was not so sure, but it was likely. The tracking device was reading from the asteroid, that did not mean that Alfred was alive and on it, just that the ship he came in was on it.

"Sir, escape craft are jettisoning from the asteroid!" came the cry from the scanning officer.

"Cease evasive action, the base is dead. Target the engines of those pods and disable them. They may have put our friend on one. Then bring us in close and match the spin in order to dock...we're going in to see what's left. Prep a squad to meet us at the airlock. We might need additional firepower," Artisius left the bridge and headed towards the armoury after Draz.

"Captain has left the bridge," yelled the First Officer as Artisius exited the doors to the bridge.

Artisius walked briskly down to the armoury. When he got there, he saw Draz already loaded up with a pistol in her customary thigh holster, an assault rifle with a small calibre so as not to puncture the hull of the station, and some grenades.

181

"You look ready for anything," he said to her with a laugh.

"Well...we don't know what's in there, do we?" she said with a reciprocated smile.

Artisius was quiet for a while as he armed himself. He took his normal brace of pistols and a small calibre assault rifle. They both stocked up on plenty of ammunition.

After a pregnant pause, Artisius broke the silence. "How are you going?" he asked, not sure if Draz wanted to talk.

"All right at the moment. The adrenaline's racing, so the craving isn't so bad." She paused and then continued. "And don't hit on me..."

"I didn't think I was. I'm just concerned..." Artisius said, sounding a little hurt.

"Uhuh...I know how you treat women. I saw Lady Hangara and how you treated her," Draz said a little acidly.

"I'm not coming on to you, Draz," Artisius said. "I know you're not interested."

Draz paused, a look of confusion crossing her face.

"Anyway, enough of that. I hope the withdrawal isn't too severe. That's all I meant," Artisius walked past her. "Come on, we need to get to the docking controls so we can board the station. We should be docking soon."

Draz, looking a little sheepish and embarrassed that she had misinterpreted Artisius' words, grabbed an extra grenade and hurried after the captain to whom she owed her life.

Artisius walked quickly down the corridor from the armoury to the boarding tube. He was secretly smarting at Draz's response to his concern. He had not considered her as a conquest. There was something about her that made him think she was like a daughter to him, rather than a lover. He felt a protective urge towards her. He wanted her to be okay. He had had too many lovers in his life anyway, and he had always left them for another in the Solar System. He had had no daughters though, and now he thought he knew what having one was like. He smiled, but made sure Draz did not see it.

***

Artisius, Draz, and the fire team of six ship guards formed up at the entrance to the docking tube on the *Green Dragon* side of the airlock.

"Time to dock?" Artisius spoke into his communicator. His heart was pounding. Even though he was getting too old for action, he still relished it, and he was anxious to rescue Alfred. He had doubts as to whether they would find Alfred in a competent state of mind, but he did not voice his fears. He looked over at Draz and smiled.

"Fifteen seconds, sir!" came the crisp reply over the communicator.

"Brace yourselves, everybody," said Artisius to the boarding party. They all grabbed hold of the handholds around the airlock.

After what seemed like an age, there was a shuddering grating noise and then the sound of the locking mechanism echoed through the airlock.

"We're docked, Captain," came the voice over the communicator.

Artisius nodded to Sergeant Ithia who was in command of the security detachment arrayed next to him, and *Green Dragon* security as a whole. She triggered the airlock, and it began to cycle. After a short time, the lights on the airlock showed green and Sergeant Ithia, followed by her squad, then Draz, and Artisius bringing up the rear, crossed into the docking tube and then moved to the airlock on the side of the pirate base. The tube they were in, the base and the *Green Dragon* were all spinning in unison, but the boarding party did not notice as all the craft were at the same rotation speed.

Sergeant Ithia triggered the airlock on the pirate base, and it opened in a few seconds. The soldiers behind her had their weapons raised in a defensive pattern and were ready in case any of the pirates were guarding the other side of the airlock. There was none. The room beyond the airlock was empty.

Ithia and her squad moved into the pirate base with practiced precision. They fanned out to cover all entry points beyond the airlock. Ithia waved Artisius in.

Artisius and Draz entered the small room in the pirate base. To Artisius it looked really run down and dilapidated.

"This...is weird...we're on the walls" Draz said, as she took uneasy steps.

"It's the gravity caused by spinning. It does that. We're used to proper gravity generated by machine. This is primitive," Artisius said.

"How old is this place?" asked Draz, looking around. "I mean, even I, who had never been away from Earth until recently, know about artificial gravity. Gravity through spinning, that's...ancient."

Artisius smiled. "It is indeed, but before we get too ahead of ourselves and get into a guessing game of how old this place is...perhaps we should look for Alfred?"

Draz nodded, and they pressed on into the station. The fire team went ahead of their two charges.

After a short walk, the group came to a larger room, which looked to be full of cargo. They paused as the guards fanned out again to cover all entry and exit points.

There was a sudden yell and then all hell broke loose. An explosion detonated nearby and then a hail of gunfire erupted from the other side of the crates facing the invading team.

Draz, Alfred, Ithia and her team dived for cover. One of the *Green Dragon's* guards moved a little too slowly and copped a slug from a pirate weapon in the chest. He went down hard, moaning in pain. The bullet had fragmented on his bulletproof vest and had splintered and penetrated his torso in multiple places. He lay on the ground, trying to stay hidden from the hail of bullets that buzzed around him.

"Stay down!" Ithia yelled to him. She returned fire to the pirates.

After a second's delay, the rest of the team who were still able to do so returned fire too. Bullets whipped in all directions. Not only were the bullets dangerous when fired, but when they hit the metal crates, they ricocheted, and the sharp pieces of fragmented metal buzzed around the chamber like angry insects.

Artisius snapped off burst after burst with his rifle. "Draz," he yelled.

Draz appeared at his elbow. She had crawled from behind another crate, snapping off shots as she went.

"Throw a grenade!" Artisius indicated over their heads and behind the firing positions of the pirates.

Draz nodded and primed a grenade. "Cover me," she yelled above the din of battle.

Ithia had watched this and nodded as Artisius nodded. As one they stood and opened fire at the pirates' positions forcing them to keep their heads down. Draz dashed from behind her crate and lobbed the grenade high over the pirates' heads and behind their position. She then skidded to a halt behind another crate and blocked her ears while keeping her head down.

There was a pause for a second and then there was an enormous explosion as the bomb detonated. Then there was no more firing from the pirates' positions and all that remained were screaming and a ringing noise in the *Green Dragon* crews' ears.

The fire team rushed to assist their injured companion while Artisius darted over to Draz and clapped her on the shoulder. "Great throw!" he shouted. His ears were ringing.

The firing and explosions in the confined space were extremely loud.

Sergeant Ithia moved over to Artisius and saluted. "Sir, permission to get two men to take the injured private back to the ship."

Artisius nodded. "Will he be all right?" he asked, genuinely anxious and moving over to the man.

"I'll...be...fine, sir..." gasped the soldier in pain. He forced a smile, which looked more like a grimace.

"Good man, you did well," Artisius turned to two other men who were holding the injured man up. "Take him to the medical bay." They obeyed without hesitation.

Reduced to three, the fire team spread out to a looser pattern to cover more space and more angles of attack. They still had to protect their commander and Draz.

The boarding party moved to the other side of the crates that had caused them trouble. The screams had stopped now and all that was left were gory bits of pirate scattered around and staining the ground in blood.

"Which way?" asked Artisius. On the other side of the crates were three doors that led in opposing directions.

"Perhaps if we went down one, and you two went down another?" Ithia suggested pragmatically. "I don't want to leave you unguarded, but we must do this swiftly..."

"I can take care of myself," said Artisius, smiling. "Besides, I have someone who can really fight with me." He looked at Draz.

Draz smiled. "You say that to all the good grenade throwers..." She laughed.

In an instant, Ithia nodded her assent and the party split in two and went down two of the opposing corridors. Artisius and Draz went left. Ithia and the other two soldiers went right. This left the central door unexplored, but they dare not risk going singly down any of the corridors.

Artisius and Draz moved carefully down the tunnel. It was metallic and rusty. It curved away in front of them, probably to compensate for the curve of the asteroid, reasoned Artisius.

Suddenly a shot whizzed past Artisius' ear and the pair dove for cover behind a bulkhead doorframe. They pressed themselves as flush as they could on either side of the door, hoping that the bullets would miss them.

Artisius and Draz returned fire. They snapped off hasty shots at the enemy that they could not really see behind cover.

Draz hefted another grenade. She looked at Artisius and he nodded. With a swift movement, she pulled the pin and hurled the grenade along the length of the curved corridor. It bounced and jarred on its way, but it landed on target and there as another great bang. Then there was screaming for a second followed by silence.

Artisius ran after the explosion. He knew that surprise was his best advantage. He ran well for his age. He heard Draz behind him. His heart thumped. They bounded over the barricade and opened fire into the stunned pirates on the other side. In a heartbeat all the pirates were dead. The air was thick with smoke.

Artisius stopped. He looked around at the room he had run into. He cursed.

"What's wrong? What..." Draz ran up panting behind him. She stopped.

Stretching from floor to ceiling were crates that had been ripped open by the grenade. The air that Artisius had assumed was smoke was not smoke. It was ferkis powder. The air was thick with it. Also around the edges of the room were drug producing facilities and distilling machinery for the production of ferkis powder.

"It's a distillery. I did not want you to see this," Artisius said. His head spinning a little from the vaporised chemicals. "Let's go..." he grabbed Draz, rather forcefully, by the arm.

He saw Draz's reaction. It was obvious she was torn. Part of her wanted no more than to dive head first into the crates. However, Artisius could see another side. A side that wanted to live.

Draz licked her lips. She picked up a handful of the powder. Then she let it slip through her fingers and fall softly to the scorched ground.

"Come on..." urged Artisius.

Draz shook for a second. Then her face set in resolution. "We have to find Alfred!" she said, heading out of the room.

They dashed out of the drug distillery. Artisius was proud of Draz. She only gave one mournful look back over her shoulder as they left the room. Then she snapped her eyes forward and carried on down the corridor. Artisius was close behind her.

Artisius and Draz headed down another curving corridor and there were a number of doors branching off the walls in the corridor.

"These look like cells. Look, they're close together and regularly spaced, these doors..." said Draz.

"Wait a minute, we can't take everyone in the cells," said Artisius stopping mid run. He breathed hard.

"We can't just leave them here!" shouted Draz.

"We can't just take them and drop them off. My ship isn't a taxi!" Artisius said with a stern gaze and a raised voice.

"Hey...HEY!" There came a sound of a voice from a nearby cell that the two of them knew too well. "Hey, is anybody there? I'm in here...help!"

"It's him, we've found him!" yelled Draz. "Alfred, we're here!" She dashed to the door the sound was coming from and started to turn the large metal wheel on the door.

Artisius ran to her side and they both turned the large metal wheel to open the door. As the door opened, they saw the ragged form of their friend standing in the doorway. He was covered in filth and smelt shocking but that did not stop Draz giving him a hug.

"You do stink!" Draz laughed.

"Is it...really...you? Or are you just another voice?" Alfred rasped. He sounded confused, not quite believing that his friends were there, that they had come to rescue him after all.

"It's us, we're here, and you're coming with us this time." said Artisius with a smile. They had done it. They had found him. Now, they had to escape.

Draz embraced Alfred for a second before withdrawing. "Are there other prisoners in the cells?" she asked, a note of concern in her voice.

Artisius glared at her.

"Uh...no. I mean, I don't think so," stammered Alfred. He looked wrecked.

"How long has it been since you've eaten and slept?" Artisius asked.

"Uh...well...days? I think...I don't know," came the ragged reply.

"Shit!" Draz said, and looked like she was about to speak again. Artisius looked at her and reasoned that in her excitement to see their friend she had not realised his predicament.

"Not wanting to interrupt this reunion, but we need to leave...now!" Artisius spoke seriously. "Can you run?" he asked Alfred.

Draz looked nervously at her friend.

"I...guess?" Alfred replied; he sounded unsure.

"Well we have to try. Let's go! The *Green Dragon* is this way," Artisius pointed down the corridor. Before setting off,

Artisius paused and handed Alfred one of the pistols slung around his waist. "Here, you might need this."

Alfred took the pistol gingerly and looked at it for a second.

Draz hefted her rifle and smiled at him.

They set off at a steady pace.

It was clear that Alfred was exhausted. He was desperately struggling to keep up, and Artisius did not want him to be left behind like last time. It would be certain death for Alfred if he were captured again. He was too much trouble for the pirates. His capture had cost them too many lives.

They came to the large room full of crates with the three doors in the back. This time the entered the room from the side with the doors.

As soon as they entered the room, a withering hail of fire erupted from a position behind the crates in the middle of the room. The trio dove for cover behind a crate.

Draz dragged Alfred down as he was responding sluggishly. "We've come too far for you to die now!" she yelled.

The fire stopped and a voice bellowed out from the pirate position. "Damn zetter! You die now, as do your friends. Then I take that nice ship and your new weapon!"

"That's Grekthax...the...leader," Alfred stuttered.

Artisius looked at Alfred and could see a mixture of fear and rage in his face.

"Well, he doesn't sound very nice..." Draz laughed.

The joke was lost on Alfred. He looked at her, confused. She simply shook her head.

"Grenade?" said Artisius to Draz. She hefted her last.

"Right!" Draz said, pulling the pin and waiting a second before hurling it over their protective crate and hearing it detonate amongst the pirates. "Bullseye," she said.

With ringing in their ears, the trio leapt over the crates and surveyed the damage. There were a number of dead pirates, riddled with shrapnel, lying on the floor of the room. The huge form of Grekthax was sprawled on the ground. He was still alive. He was missing his right arm, but that did not seem to be fatal for him. His large rifle was gripped in the arm that lay a few metres from his body.

"Fuck you!" he yelled as the trio stood next to his fallen form. "Fuck you, you damn zetter." The pirate captain coughed blood. "You won't get away with this--"

"We have to go, now!" said Artisius, grabbing Alfred's arm.

Alfred was staring blankly at the fallen form of his captor. He gripped the pistol tightly in his right hand. His knuckles turned white. "Wait," was all he said. It was measured, and full of rage.

Artisius let go of Alfred's arm, partially out of respect for the man, and partially through desire to see what he would do. Draz stood covering their exit to the room in case any more pirates showed up to rescue their leader. None did.

"What're you going to do?" spat Grekthax. "You weak piece of shit!"

"I've always thought it wise." Alfred paused. "Not to antagonise someone with a gun..." Alfred moved over Grekthax and stepped on the shredded stump of the pirate captain's right arm. Grekthax screamed and tried to get away. Alfred raised his pistol to the head of the pirate captain.

Fear flashed across the captain's face. "You couldn't!" the captain yelled.

Alfred pulled the trigger, and with a loud pop, executed the pirate captain. Alfred's face was full of rage. It scared Artisius. Draz looked disturbed. They knew the old Alfred would not do such a thing; but Alfred had changed.

Alfred's face was calm again, almost blank, but there was something different about his manner. He was still plainly exhausted, but the act of revenge seemed to invigorate him.

"Now can we go?" Artisius asked. He was concerned about Alfred.

"Yes...let's go," Alfred said.

Draz shot a tense glance between the dead pirate captain and Alfred, and then the trio dashed down the corridor towards the boarding tube of the *Green Dragon*.

They encountered no more resistance. Artisius radioed the remaining members of the fire team to return to the *Green Dragon*, they had their target.

As the trio approached the boarding tube they saw the three remaining fire team members waiting and guarding their escape. Sergeant Ithia saluted her captain and shot an anxious look at the ragged Alfred.

They all boarded the *Green Dragon* and with a quick order the docking tube was disengaged, and the *Green Dragon* was free to roam once again.

"Sir, we need you on the bridge," came the First Officer's voice over the intercom. It was directed at Artisius.

"On my way," replied Artisius. He looked at Draz and Alfred.

Draz nodded at him and took Alfred by the arm. "Food or wash first?" she asked him.

"Food...I need...food," Alfred said. He was almost collapsing through hunger and exhaustion.

"Take him to the galley, then clean him up, then I'll have to run a diagnostic on his implant, then get him to bed," said Artisius with a smile. "Personally, I'd wash first, you smell."

Draz and Alfred both laughed. Then Draz took Alfred by the arm and led him away.

Artisius grimaced. Something was different about Alfred. He was interested to see the results of that diagnostic. He was afraid the treatment of the pirates had damaged Alfred.

***

Artisius hurried to the bridge. "What's happened?" he barked as he entered.

"Captain on the bridge!" bellowed the First Officer. The bridge snapped to attention before resuming standard tasks.

"Sir, the fire between us and the pirate base has attracted the attention of the Collective fleet. They've found us, sir. They're on their way," reported the First Officer.

"Shit! Okay, deploy the cloaking device and spirit us away to Europa," ordered Artisius.

"Sir..." called out the Energy Officer. Artisius did not like the tone of his voice. He knew something bad was coming. "Sir, the cloaking device is offline; we cannot use it for a day or so."

"Damn it! Why?" demanded Artisius.

"The power drain on it from using it for days escaping Mars. It's only a short-term thing. It's not meant to be used for long periods," said the Shield Officer.

"Then power up the engines, full interplanetary drive power. We need to get away to Europa! Helmsman, take us away from here!" Artisius ordered.

"Sir!" replied the Helmsman.

The crew felt the rumble of the ship's engines through the hull as the engines fired up and the stars rotated through the observation dome as a new heading was taken.

"Time to target?" snapped Artisius.

"Approximately a year, sir, maybe a few months less," was the reply from the First Officer.

"Damn this space, why is everything so far away..." Artisius whispered to himself. "How far away is the Collective fleet?"

"About a week away, but we have a head start. We should get to Europa a month or so ahead of them as we're faster," said the First Officer, interpreting readouts from the computer stations.

"Good. But that's cutting it fine. I hope the Solar Solutions military got my message. They have to come to our aid...they have to, or I'm going to have to fight a war on my own if I lead Collective Zone ships into Solar Solutions space..." Artisius said almost to himself as he left the bridge to the barked commands of the First Officer.

***

Artisius headed to the galley. It was empty. He headed back up to the special quarters assigned to Draz and Alfred and found Draz waiting outside Alfred's room.

"He's just washed, and he's dressing," she said. "He ate so much so fast!"

Artisius smiled. "He's glad to be alive, I bet..."

"He..." she paused, "seems different..."

"We need to run a diagnostic after he's dressed," Artisius said. "How are you going?"

Draz shrugged. "The gnawing feeling won't stop, but meh..." she shrugged.

The door opened and there was Alfred, clean, fed, but still exhausted. "Right...now sleep?" he said hopefully.

Draz looked at him with an anxious expression. Alfred handed Artisius' pistol back to him with a smile. Artisius took it and put it in one of the holsters around his waist.

"No, sorry, Alfred. We need to run a diagnostic of your implant," Artisius said with an apologetic tone.

Alfred sighed. He slumped. "Lead on...haha, 'lead'..." he paused, the others did not get the joke. "As in zetting lead, that goes in my head, and lead as in the verb to take me somewhere..."

Draz and Artisius smiled awkwardly at the bad joke.

The trio proceeded to the medical bay on the ship. It was brightly lit, white, and sterile. Artisius indicated for Alfred to lie on a medical table. Alfred hesitated.

"What's wrong?" asked Draz.

"You were scanned..." said Artisius. "Weren't you? They probed your brain. I'm so sorry...but this is nothing like that."

"What do you mean?" asked Draz, she sounded confused. She looked at Artisius and Alfred.

"They inserted a needle in my head and stripped all the information out. I'm damaged," said Alfred carefully and slowly.

Draz looked concerned. Artisius indicated the medical table. Alfred lay down on it.

Artisius motioned for one of the medical staff to approach and conduct the procedure.

Artisius brought out a clean looking needle with the lead attached to a nearby computer and gave it to Alfred. "In your own time," he said respectfully.

Alfred looked at the needle and then after a short delay, inserted it carefully into his implant. He winced a little. "That was cold..." he said.

"Sorry," Artisius said, smiling.

After a short time, a lot of information was brought up on the nearby computer screen.

Dr Antonia approached the terminal at Artisius' request and began studying the information. Artisius introduced her to Alfred. She pursed her lips as the information continued to roll across the screen.

"What is it?" asked Draz. "What's wrong?"

"Relax, Draz..." said Alfred. He sighed. "I'm too tired to worry. How much longer will this go on?"

"Only a few more minutes," replied Dr Antonia.

Artisius stood a little way back from the medical table. He did not want to get in the way. Yet he was worried about the doctor's guarded response to the readout. He did not voice this however. He did not want to worry either Draz or Alfred.

After a short time, the readout finished, and the needle was withdrawn from Alfred's head. He lay back on the medical table and closed his eyes.

"What's the report?" he asked.

"Well," Dr Antonia replied after a time, "you have received damage to your implant and your memory recall..."

"Well that's not new..." Alfred said rather tersely. It was evident that he wanted to be rid of this whole medical situation. "What is new...is that I can sometimes hear a voice..."

Draz looked bothered and her gaze switched from the doctor to Alfred and back again.

"A voice?" asked the doctor.

"Yeah, I don't know what it is, but there was this...voice, in my head, in the pirate base." Alfred looked scared.

"Sometimes implant damage can result in some sort of psychosis. Do you hear it now?" asked Antonia.

"No..." Alfred said.

"Then report to me if it comes back. Back to the memory issue, can you remember your childhood?" continued Antonia, unperturbed.

"Of course, I can..." Alfred paused. A look of worry crossed his face. "Yes...yes I can. I remember my mother and father...and...I had a sister...I think..." The last words were said with such fear and a look of terror crossed Alfred's face.

"You think?" repeated Antonia, calmly.

"Yes, yes I'm sure. I can almost see her face. I'm sure this should be easier," Alfred cursed. "Her name was..." Alfred's face scrunched up with the effort of thinking. "Blinky!" he said with triumph and fear.

"You mentioned her to me earlier," Draz said. Her expression was uneasy.

Artisius had stood silently for the last part, but he interrupted at this point. "Is there anything we can do to stop the decay?"

"Cryo-sleep helps," said Antonia. "As does exercise of the memory circuits. It builds new pathways in the brain and stops the memory from fading away...but otherwise, the damage is permanent. Why didn't you see me earlier?" she asked Alfred directly. "About your failing implant? I've been here all the time you were on the *Green Dragon*..."

"I..." Alfred paused. "I was afraid..." He lay on his back and looked at the ceiling.

Artisius felt somewhat guilty about not introducing Alfred to Dr Antonia earlier.

"Well, we're on our way to Europa, and that will take the best part of a year, so cryo-sleep is on the cards for that." Artisius nodded.

"Take him to the cryo-pods now; he must have all the rest he can. He's been through a lot," Dr Antonia said before she was dismissed by Artisius.

"Sleep...blissful sleep..." Alfred said as he got off the medical table slowly and ran a hand through his messy hair. He sighed hard, then winced as he touched his implant.

"Oh, Dr Antonia!" Artisius called after the retreating doctor who paused and turned to face her captain. "Can he still zet?"

"I don't see why not, if it's done in moderation. Nothing too strenuous or involved. However, every zet will advance the decay. But then, the decay is at such a point, that it will progress anyway, whatever is done..." Antonia waited and then was dismissed again. She walked away back to her other duties.

"Well, that's shit," Alfred said, matter-of-factly. He gave a little chuckle. "Because apart from a desperate desire to sleep right now, I also really want to zet."

"If I have to give up drugs, you'll have to give up zetting..." said Draz. The look of worry still had not left her face.

"That may not be possible..." said Artisius.

"What do you mean?" snapped Draz and Alfred together, but for different reasons, and with different tones.

"I mean," said Artisius. "That he's our only zetter, and he's one of the best zetters in near Solar Solutions space, if his own boasting serves correctly." Artisius nodded to Alfred, who grinned a little.

"So, we just let him destroy himself? While I have to abstain?" said Draz, a note of hurt in her voice.

"Drug addiction is not helpful, zetting is, and I believe we've been through this before..." is all Artisius said. He began to leave the room followed by Alfred.

Draz stood, arms folded, and seemed to sulk like a small child. "I see..." she said after a short time. She then followed the pair.

"One thing," Artisius said as he walked. "What actually did happen on *Florida Station* all those years ago? I was part of your interrogation, and for that I am sorry, but what did happen? Why did it explode? The reason I ask is we're heading back to Jupiter's moon Europa which was near the orbit of *Florida Station* and there may be questions as to why you're free...I mean, I trust you, and I've reported that you're innocent to the Europa high command, but I'd like to know what actually happened," Artisius paused, waiting for an explanation.

Draz followed a little behind in the corridor, she could still hear the conversation and caught up with the pair in an effort to listen.

"Ah..." said Alfred. "At the moment, I can still remember that, I guess because it is newer in my memory," he paused.

"It was the Head Trader...Virtus was his name. He plotted the whole thing and I suppose he blew up the station himself..."

Artisius stayed silent, his eyes scanning the movement of Alfred's face. The destruction of *Florida Station* had cost the life of a dear friend of his, General Hestra, and he still felt the pangs from her death. He knew that he could now trust Alfred, but it was still hard to hear.

"I was taken prisoner before I could stop him," continued Alfred. "We were in the reactor module and a tech-slave incapacitated me and then I ended up in the interrogation and then on my way to the Moon even when it was clear," he paused and glared at Artisius, who smarted a little at the returned glare, "that I was innocent."

"So, it was the chief priest? Why?" asked Artisius after a few moments thought.

Draz watched on intently and silently.

"He had some cult, some...Sect? I don't know what to call it. He tried to recruit me into the thing and that the main aim of it was to 'free the computer from human control'" Alfred shrugged. "It was all madness. The computers of ships and stations are not sentient, they don't need freedom."

Artisius chuckled, "That's true...if the computers all turned sentient, we'd be in trouble..."

"But," said Alfred. "There was something..."

"What?" asked Draz, unable to stay silent any more. She seemed intrigued.

"The computer core of the station, *Florida Station*...it...talked to me..." Alfred paused, "this sounds mad I know...but it did..."

"When did you hear it?" Artisius said.

"In a zet, and when *Florida Station* blew up." Alfred stared at the wall of the passageway, his expression blank.

"Hmm, should we go back to the doctor and ask about this? Was this to do with the other voice you heard on the

199

pirate base?" Artisius half turned and indicated back where they had come.

"No. Too tired. I have to sleep now. I can see the doctor when we approach Europa. There's nothing that can be done for me immediately," Alfred said, the fatigue evident in his voice.

Artisius nodded and listened to his passenger. "Then we'll head to the cryo-pods." Artisius turned to Draz. "You don't have to enter cryo-sleep just yet, but Alfred is tired."

Draz nodded silently. A look of worry, not for Alfred, crossed her face. It was plain that she still feared cryo-sleep.

As they headed to the cryo-pods, Alfred asked, "Something's been bugging me..."

"Yes?" said Artisius carefully.

"Why did you help us?" Alfred stopped in the corridor and looked hard at Artisius, his fatigue etched across his features but the desire for a truthful answer was in his voice. Draz switched her vision from Alfred to Artisius and back again. "I mean," Alfred continued, "you didn't have to, and yet you threw away everything for us, in an instant..."

Artisius was silent for a moment as they waited in the corridor; they had all stopped walking. "I'm sure I said when we were fleeing Earth, perhaps you do not remember? I can say now in more detail. Basically, the Collective Zone gave me no choice...back when I questioned you, Alfred, and blamed you for the destruction of *Florida Station,* I assumed you were guilty out of hand. I found myself on the brunt of a decision like that. And as for your past, Draz, false imprisonment and all that, it all sounded too familiar. In short, I had no love lost for the Collective," he said after a while. "I had to choose a side. At my time of life that's hard, but sometimes...it's necessary..." He laboured the last words and smiled at Alfred. "Does that answer your question?"

"Basically...sort of...what did the Collective Zone do?" Alfred pressed the issue.

Artisius sighed. "They were going to take my trading rights and blame me for part of the Earth Moon rebellion...for bringing you there, if you must know..." He fell silent.

Alfred and Draz shifted uneasily on their feet at this revelation.

"So...we destroyed your life?" said Draz carefully after a pause.

"In a way...but in a way you gave me some purpose in a pointless existence. So, in a way I am grateful." Artisius stared down the corridor, not meeting either of their gazes. "Your two lives were destroyed before mine, and many more have been and will be destroyed by the war that broke on Mars and is heading to Solar Solutions space...so...what's one more life in a mess. We have to survive, that's all, and I think we're doing okay for the moment..." Artisius' gaze snapped back to Alfred and Draz. "So, enough of that...let's get you to your pod." He looked at Alfred, who looked back with a grateful expression.

The trio headed down the corridors of the *Green Dragon* to the cryo-pod room. Already it was in use as some of the non-essential crew began to enter the long sleep to Europa. They would be in suspended animation for around a year.

Alfred undressed to his underwear. He stashed the clothes and items in the locker next to the pod.

"And here we go again, sweet sleep..." Alfred said as the pod opened with the attention of a tech-slave. He climbed in and gave a smile to both Artisius and Draz as they stood outside the pod. The pod closed on Alfred and within seconds the lights had all gone green on the pod's side and it was clear he was in cryo-sleep.

"To sleep, perchance to dream..." muttered Artisius.

"He looks at peace. And now we hope he survives," said Draz. She looked in through the small porthole in the outside of the pod at Alfred's face. It was lit with a bluish light.

"He will," said Artisius. "Will you?"

"If you're referring to my addiction and withdrawal, it's hard, but I'm managing. The gnawing is there. You say it always will be..." Draz trailed off in thought. She stared into the distance in the pod room.

"I can offer moral support if you ever need it," Artisius put his hand on her shoulder. She shook it off.

"Thanks, but I'll be fine. I always am." She grinned at him. "So, I guess I should get in a pod..." she started to get undressed to her underwear before Artisius could say that she did not need to immediately. She replied to his unspoken words. "I'll just get it over with...I hate all this waiting..."

Draz climbed into the pod next to Alfred's after storing her gear and, with the help of the tech-slave, the pod shut and was activated.

Artisius checked the lights on the side, and they were all green. He breathed a sigh of relief.

Artisius watched the pods for a short time, and observed his crew progressively getting ready for interplanetary travel. After a while, he headed back towards the bridge, he still had some jobs to complete before he could be put into cryo-sleep.

***

Artisius walked briskly to the bridge. Now that the Collective Zone fleet knew that something had happened in their area, his crew could not waste any time getting to Europa.

"Captain on the bridge!" came the cry from the First Officer as Artisius marched to his command dais.

"Send this message to the Europa Colony," Artisius snapped to the Communications Officer. The man sat attentively, waiting for the command. "The Supply Frigate designated *Green Dragon* will be arriving in Europa Colony space in about a year's time. We are towing with us some...unwelcome guests in the form of the whole Collective fleet. Some time ago I already warned the Solar Solutions Headquarters about such a thing. Now I have seen what the Collective Zone has done to Mars: they crushed it. I fear the Collective Zone want a full invasion of Solar Solutions space. I cannot be certain, but I suspect it to be true. They will be following us with maximum force. Be ready. End message."

The bridge had gone silent but for the quiet bleeps of computer holo-screens and system readouts. The crew had stopped and were focused on their captain.

Artisius could see from their holo-screen illuminated faces that they were apprehensive but would follow him to Hell and back if he ordered them to. It was clear that they trusted him absolutely. Nevertheless, Artisius knew that what he was doing was very risky.

He was going to be branded as the scapegoat for bringing war to the Solar Solutions Sector. People would blame him; because the Collective Zone fleet wanted his ship. He was convinced that the Collective Zone fleet would have found a reason for invasion, regardless of his actions, but now, the war would be on his shoulders.

"Got that?" Artisius barked.

"Yes, sir!" replied the Communications Officer.

"Right! Send it!" Artisius snapped. "This day we all become part of a war that has been brewing for decades," he addressed the bridge crew. "Just know that whatever happens, I trust you all to do your duty to this ship. When the ship is ready for interplanetary flight, get to your pods and turn the ship over to the computers, we can't stay cloaked during this year long journey as the cloaking only lasts a few days, so we'll just have to out run the enemy." And with that he turned on his heel and marched smartly out of the bridge with the First Officer's voice saying he left the bridge ringing in his ears. "I hope we all survive this..." he said to himself as he walked down the corridors to his cryo-pod.

Chapter 24

CEO Uxus stood on the bridge of the *Old Monarch*. Acting Commander Tyyz was at his side. "And so, the planet is being subjugated as we speak?" said the raspy voice of Uxus to the divisional commander of his forces on Mars and the space stations.

"Yes, CEO Sir!" came the uncompromising response.

"And the Family that helped the *Green Dragon* escape? What are we doing to them?" asked Uxus.

"They will be punished, CEO Sir. We have rounded them up and they will be punished..." replied the commander.

"Good. Continue your actions here commander. Extract resources from the planet as you see fit; we must grow our Collective. You are placed in full command of Mars. I believe our fleet's attention lies elsewhere, but we will be back for you..." Uxus' attention was diverted.

The divisional commander, now in control of Mars, looked crestfallen. Although he had now earned a planet, his part in the war was over already and it would be many years before he saw the lights of the Great Fleet again. The communication went dead.

Uxus turned to Tyyz. "What do you think now?" he asked malevolently.

"Now, CEO Sir, I think we should--" Tyyz said before being interrupted by an orderly.

"CEO Sir, ma'am, we have something!" the man said running up to them.

"What?" snapped Tyyz, angry at being interrupted.

"Auto-turret and missile fire from sector theta nine! A ship just appeared there and..." the orderly withered under the gaze of his two superiors.

"Appeared?" asked Uxus, "You mean just appeared in space?"

"Yes, CEO Sir, on our scanners...it must be some sort of--"

"That's them! That's the *Green Dragon*!" yelled Uxus. "Lock on to their position and follow them. Don't lose them again! They must've..." he trailed off.

"But, CEO Sir, how could--" the orderly said again.

"Just do it!" yelled Tyyz. She was beaming. "You see, CEO, we have them!"

"All about turn! Follow that signal. Wherever it goes, we will follow!" Uxus yelled to his bridge crew.

He turned on the spot and paced the length of the bridge. Suddenly the sound of Fleet Commander Boltha chimed into the bridge.

"CEO, what is going on? The fleet is deviating from pre-planned attack patterns. We were meant to be heading to Solar Solutions space..." the crisp voice sounded a little peeved.

"We have found the *Green Dragon*, Boltha," said Uxus testily. He looked at Tyyz who rolled her eyes as an indication that she, too, did not like Boltha. "Now that we have found our prey, we can pursue it into Solar Solutions space. They will be heading for Europa, which is my best guess, the next colony in our long hop out of our controlled territory," continued Uxus.

"But CEO, the battle plan was to smash the Solar Solutions fleet that would be meeting us--" Boltha was cut off by her CEO.

"They will meet us around Jupiter, which is where Europa is, is it not?" Uxus smiled to himself. He could see Tyyz smiling too. "I will have no more of it, Boltha. We will follow the *Green Dragon* to Europa. Prepare the fleet; get the troops and crews to their cryo-pods and make the ships ready for interplanetary travel."

And with that, Uxus, glancing at Tyyz and giving her command of the bridge, left the bridge and headed to his quarters to get ready for another long distance travel.

**

Trooper Grox readied himself for cryo-sleep. He looked around his comrades who were also all preparing for the long trip to Jupiter. Some bunks and cryo-pods were empty, and would remain empty. Their occupants had been killed on Mars.

They knew they were heading to Jupiter as the orders had been passed down already: follow the *Green Dragon* and besiege Europa where they will probably dock. Then they were to wait for the Solar Solutions fleet to arrive and strike a decisive blow by defeating it. It all sounded so easy, so mathematical, so unlikely.

Now that Grox had actually fought in combat, he viewed it differently. His mind was forever changed. He realised that it was not some wonderful, exciting experience that he longed for. It was horrid, messy and brutal.

Althar stood beside him again, also getting ready for cryo-sleep. "What?" he asked as he saw Grox pause in his preparations.

Grox was holding his copy of *The Collected Works of William Shakespeare* in his hands and thumbing through the pages. "It's all nonsense," he said absent-mindedly.

"What is? Poetry?" Althar continued stowing his gear and undressing.

"No, all that rah-rah let's go to war, let's fight, let's win rhetoric...war isn't like that...it's..." he trailed off, staring into the middle distance.

207

"Look, we had a bit of a bad time on Mars, that's 'cause it was mostly civilians and criminals. Next time will be different! When we board a Solar Solutions ship, then you'll feel good!" Althar said calmly. He had been in the thick of the fighting too, but it was plain to see that Grox had been badly affected by it.

"Yeah...and then there's this gnawing feeling, like I really want that stimulant again, from the battle..." Grox sighed, "ah well...next time will be different. It will be glorious!" Grox laughed. It was a hollow laugh, and it scared him.

Lieutenant Vauz stepped into the barracks and the remaining soldiers snapped to attention.

"At ease, soldiers," their commander said. He seemed less driven this time. He seemed more reserved. "Well, you already know we're going to Jupiter. Mars was not very pleasant, and some nasty things happened there, but when we engage the Solar Solutions fleet it will be a proper combat between soldiers and we will prevail!" There was a faint cheer from the soldiers. "Carry on!" and their commander left the barracks.

The troops, somewhat less enthusiastically this time, began to get into their cryo-pods. They knew what their job was, and they would do it to the last letter of the last command. However, the glory of war had been lost to them. Now, it was only a bloody mess.

Chapter 25

The *Silver Ark*, flagship of the Solar Solutions fleet, forged quickly through space and slid past the frozen rings of Saturn. The supercharged engines of the Solar Solutions fleet, which they had developed because of the extreme distances throughout their portion of the Solar System, gave them a better travel speed than the Collective Zone fleet that was heading outwards from their home planet.

The rest of the fleet that was massing around Saturn and that had fallen back from Jupiter, joined with their brothers in the *Silver Ark* and the Home Fleet and forged a new path towards Jupiter. They thought that strength in numbers would carry the day.

The Solar Solutions fleet still had many millions of kilometres to go before it would reach its target planet of Jupiter.

The tech-slaves and the skeleton crews that were onboard the ships of the fleet as the majority of the crews slept peacefully in cryogenic storage, had no idea yet of the Collective Zone's plans to attack Europa.

Gunter and the Solar Solutions High Command had reasoned that their Corporation could make a stand at Jupiter, and then fall back, if necessary, towards Neptune.

Perhaps Fleet Commander Boltha would have bypassed Jupiter and struck deeply into the heart of the Solar Solutions Empire, but Uxus and Tyyz were heading after the *Green Dragon* and thus, they headed to Europa.

Therefore, it was, almost by chance in the vastness of space, that two powerful fleets were on a collision course.

Chapter 26

Virtus cursed. He withdrew the zetting needle from his implant. This was the fifth time he had tried to interact with the computer core on Europa, but it was resisting. There seemed to be safeguards in place that were blocking his attempts.

"Damn Anya," he said under his breath. "She suspects too much..." He stopped speaking when he sensed someone behind him in his private rooms within the Church building. "Yes?" he said without turning around.

"Do you want me to take care of it, master?" came the soft voice from the shadows.

"No, we cannot do that. We cannot go that far. It would raise too much suspicion," Virtus said, turning on his chair to look into the gloom of the room. He could see a figure standing in a black robe. Its eyes glinted in the light coming from the computer monitor that Virtus was using.

"Then what do we do?" the figure said in a measured tone.

Virtus pondered for a moment. This acolyte of his was obviously keen to prove himself in his master's eyes. Virtus had amassed a number of cultists around him that all wore black robes and answered only to him. They would do anything for him. They believed in the Sect absolutely and they were all computer augmented zetters. Yet even their skills could not bypass the safeguards Commander Anya's head zetters had put in place on the computer network of Europa.

After a time Virtus said, "You know that Guide? That pest in the dark red jump suit? That informant that I have grown to despise and who informs Anya about everything I do? I think he's been following me in my zets. Kill him. Make him disappear and remove that annoyance from my life."

"I will do it, master. But won't Anya know what's happened and blame you?" the acolyte responded devotedly.

"It's becoming too late for hesitation. The Collective Zone fleet will be here soon enough, and they will want to spread our religion throughout this part of the Solar System. I have their CEO's word on that!" Virtus spoke in a reverent tone of his distant commanding officer. "We must act and act soon. The *Green Dragon* will be here with unwelcome guests, and we cannot allow them to derail out great plan!" He finished with a flourish that was lost on the devoted acolyte. Virtus sighed.

"It will be done, master." The acolyte, whose name Virtus did not know, backed into the shadows and left the room silently. Virtus felt a shiver run up his spine. If he felt a little worried about his devoted followers, what must other people feel when they see them going about their secret business in the colony?

"Time to try again," Virtus said as he reinserted the zetting needle into his temple. He felt the rush as the world dissolved around him and he soared through the colony's computer network.

*** *** ***

It was a much larger and more complex network than the one on *Florida Station*. It stretched across the length and breadth of the colony on Europa, which, being a moon of Jupiter, was much larger than an ancient space station.

Virtus revelled in his freedom. Every time he zetted he loved it. However, he was recognising some disturbing signs. The edges of his vision were becoming fuzzy and his desire to zet was becoming unquenchable. His memory was also starting to fail; he sometimes could not remember things

211

from his past. He had not been to a doctor, as he should not be zetting very much as Head Trader, but he knew that these were signs of impending zetting sickness. This made him anxious. He had to complete his mission before the madness claimed him. He had to complete his task of spreading the Sect to as many places as possible, for his CEO, for the computers!

Virtus angled towards the computer core of Europa. He sensed something in the network. Something was following him. He craned his vision around and saw a coloured mark following him along the network. It was the Guide. He could never be rid of him. The creature always knew what he was doing and it infuriated Virtus.

As Virtus neared the core he, again, came up against the safeguards and blocks that Anya had put in place. He tried route after route to approach the core and its critical systems but every path he tried was somehow blocked with either a blank spot in the pathway so he could not progress or some form of required password.

Virtus sensed the Guide behind him, close this time. Virtus turned, he spun on the electron stream. He faced the Guide. Then there was something different. There was another mark, another stain on the network of glowing pathways. It came closer and closer to the Guide. The Guide tried to get away. Virtus knew the dark purple marking was the acolyte, it had to be, there was no other person who would try such a thing.

Virtus watched as the Guide tried to outrun the acolyte, but it was impossible: the Guide was not as skilled at zetting as the acolyte and could not outrun him.

The acolyte caught up to the Guide and in a flash of light and a release of energy, the two colours on the network annihilated each other.

Virtus felt relieved. The Guide would be dead, his brains fried on the end of a zetting needle. What the acolyte had done was sacrifice himself and overloaded the neural input of the Guide, killing himself and the Guide in the process.

Virtus did not know if this would make things easier or harder. It would be easier as he would have no shadow, harder because Anya would find out eventually what happened to the Guide. Virtus would play dumb about the Guide's death and a neural overload was difficult to pin on another person. Virtus would argue that the Guide had simply been careless in zetting after him.

The acolyte's body would never be found, Virtus would make sure of that.

Getting back to the task at hand Virtus probed the pathways of the network for an unguarded way into the computer core, he found none, Anya's technicians had been meticulous and left no pathway unblocked.

"You will serve me!"

There it was! The computer core! Virtus jumped at the sound that unfolded in his mind, but he knew he could not get close enough to enact its desires.

Virtus cursed again and began the log out procedure. He would have to make an appearance in the Church. Things were happening on the markets.

After logging out, Virtus exited his private rooms within the Church, his heart racing at hearing the computer again.

He headed out onto the trading floor where people were making their benedictions and in a flurry of activity. People were withdrawing their savings en masse from the worshiping terminals around the room. The screens around the edge of the room were full of red numbers.

Virtus knew why the panic was setting in and the people were withdrawing their money and the charts showed a mass of red. The Bear God was in ascendance. War was coming,

213

so went the rumour. The people knew it. War was coming and people wanted to escape.

Virtus smiled. He knew war was coming. It was no rumour.

Chapter 27

Alfred dreamed. Images and thoughts raced through his head as he slept in cryo-storage. But the dreams were more like nightmares. He saw himself tortured by pirates and repeatedly he saw Draz and Artisius on the other side of a bulkhead trying to rescue him but failing at the last second. He screamed in his sleep.

He saw the splattered blood of Crathka over and over. He saw Draz executing him. And then the dream morphed into him executing Grekthax. He saw the blood fly. He felt the kick of the pistol in his hand.

Then there was something else. There was always this presence in his dreams now. He knew that he should know who it was. It was a young woman. She was standing on top of coolant pipes. She turned to him and looked sad. Then she threw herself off the top of the structure. Alfred screamed in his sleep again. He knew that she was important to him, but he could not quite remember who she was.

Alfred felt the implant fizzing in his sleep. He was then at the zetting terminal of the *Green Dragon* in his dreams. He licked his lips. He inserted the needle into his head and the pain was immense. He screamed again. The computer interface in front of him began to spark and melt. He felt the feedback of the zetting system as it overloaded. He died as the system overloaded and fried his circuits and brain. He died over and over again.

Suddenly Alfred was conscious. He coughed hard in the cryo-pod. The door began to slide open, and he saw the silhouette of a tech-slave checking his vital signs on the pod.

"All. Clear." the tech-slave spat and stumbled towards the pod next to him.

"Blinky..." Alfred whispered to himself. He ran a hand through his hair, which had regrown before the cryo-pod journey. "It was Blinky. How could I forget?" But his thoughts were snatched away as the dream faded from his consciousness and he could not quite remember what had happened in them. All he knew was things were not right.

Alfred, still in the pod, reached up and touched his implant in the side of his head. It hurt. He needed to zet. He knew that Draz did not want him to zet. There was a strange fuzzy feeling in his head.

Alfred got out of the pod stiffly, and began to dress from the clothes in his locker next to his pod. He turned to see Draz stagger out of her pod. She coughed.

"This floor's freezing," she said, stepping from one foot to another.

"Not as cold as in there." Alfred indicated the pod she had just come out of. He grinned. Draz gave him an unimpressed look but said nothing.

Draz began to dress, and Alfred realised just how attractive she was. He had known she was physically attractive a long time ago, but now that he knew her better, he knew her resolve, and that she had supposedly given up drugs; Alfred found her attractive.

"You're staring..." she said, stopping mid dress. She gave him a look that meant: I know what you're thinking.

Alfred blushed and said nothing. He looked at the floor and then continued dressing. He had been caught gawping and it was clear that Draz knew exactly why.

They finished dressing and as they did, Artisius appeared in his dress uniform. "Ah, good, you're both okay," he said with a genuine note of relief in his voice.

"We're fine," Draz said as she put her boots on. She sat on the edge of the pod to balance herself.

"Yes..." said Alfred, not knowing whether to divulge his vaguely remembered dreams or not. He shifted uneasily on his feet. He knew the dreams meant something. His brain was telling him something. However, if he said anything it may become obvious that he could no longer zet, and that would be the worst thing for him. He could not give that up, not now...

Artisius gave Alfred a concerned look, indicating that he did not quite believe the answer, particularly with the way Alfred behaved, but he said nothing else about it.

"Good, let's head to the bridge. There's quite a sight up there for you..." Artisius smiled and beckoned with an outstretched arm after they had finished dressing.

The trio headed towards the bridge and when they got there much of the crew were already on duty and readying for the approach to Europa.

"Captain on the bridge!" shouted the First Officer. Artisius nodded to him and took up his position on the command dais.

Draz and Alfred entered behind the captain. As Draz saw what was ahead of them through the observation dome she stopped suddenly, her mouth open.

"Wow..." is all Draz managed.

Ahead of them was the massive form of Jupiter. Its huge bulk filled the dome. It was marbled with colours and the massive red spot spun and churned. It was an awe-inspiring sight, and it was clear from Draz's reaction that it was quite moving.

Alfred had a different reaction. He felt all the pain of the loss of *Florida Station* come rushing back. He stopped too, but said nothing. His eyes would have betrayed his emotions, but no one was looking at him. He was home, but with no home to go to.

"Impressive isn't it?" said Artisius to them, taking a break from barking orders.

"It's...It's," Draz said. "It's wonderful..." She stood next to the command dais, respectfully out of the way of Artisius.

"'Tis new to thee..." said Artisius quietly.

Alfred stood at the entrance to the bridge. He said nothing. His heart was pounding. He did not think that he would have this reaction on returning to Jupiter. He knew that they would have returned eventually on the way they were going, but he had not anticipated his emotions.

"Alfred? You all right?" asked Draz, she turned to him and noticed he was still at the doorway.

"I'm...fine," Alfred lied. "It's just, this was what I saw most of my life, and now I'm back. I never thought that I'd come back..." His eyes had welled up a little. He wiped them to hide his emotions.

"I'm sorry if this is too much? But we have to dock at Europa..." Artisius said carefully.

"No, that's okay. I'm okay. I just, didn't expect to return to a home that's no longer there..." Alfred wiped his eyes and ran his hands through his hair. "What now?"

"Well." Artisius indicated the zetting terminal. "You're our only zetter, and we've been on a long journey...."

Draz shot him a murderous glance. She said nothing but it was clear to Alfred that she was unhappy with the decision.

Alfred's pulse had quickened. He knew that it was possible that due to his condition, Artisius would not let him zet, but there was nothing else in the world that he wanted to do now. His brain screamed at him though. He remembered his dreams. He remembered the pain. He remembered that he did not want to forget. But he was addicted. He knew now, that he was addicted to zetting, and that nothing would fill the void. It would kill him in the end, but he did not care. He wanted to zet, and that is what he would do.

"All right..." is all he said as he moved to the terminal at the side of the bridge.

Draz looked like she was about to say something when Artisius interrupted. "We need him, Draz," is all he said.

Draz looked annoyed, but said nothing.

Alfred sat down and began the boot up procedure of the terminal. He heard Artisius barking orders and sending a transmission to Europa concerning their docking requirements. The response from Jupiter's moon was a welcome one.

"*Green Dragon*, this is Europa Command, we welcome your arrival. We will make a docking port ready for you. We have been experiencing some troubles with our computers, but things should be fine for your docking." crackled the communication.

"Please inform Commander Anya that it will be a great pleasure to see her again," said Artisius.

Both Draz and Alfred turned and gave each other a look that said all they needed to say about that last comment.

Alfred's mind suddenly clicked. He turned and realised that the Europa Command had said that they had had trouble with their computers. "Artisius, ask what trouble with computers!" He shouted to the captain.

Artisius looked at Alfred and saw the worried expression on his face. "Europa Command, what kind of computer trouble?" There was a pause.

"Just some tech-slave failures and various network issues: integrity and such. Some strange disappearances," crackled the comlink.

Alfred suddenly felt very afraid. His face went a whiter shade of sallow. "It can't be," he whispered. "He must have died in the explosion."

219

"Alfred?" asked Artisius. He saw the worry on his friend's face.

"It's probably nothing, but can you ask if there was a Virtus on the moon?" Alfred had stood up from the terminal and looked rather nervous.

"I'm sure there's nothing--" began Artisius.

"Just ask! Please," begged Alfred.

Artisius obliged. "Europa Command, was there a 'Virtus' on your colony?"

The reply chilled Alfred, and Artisius, to the bone. "Oh yes, we picked him up quite a while ago and instated him as our Head Trader..."

"Oh shit..." said Alfred.

Draz looked on.

Artisius paused.

"We've had him under surveillance for a while now, and--" continued the comlink.

"Arrest him! Immediately! He blew up *Florida Station*," yelled Alfred, quite beside himself.

"I'm sorry but we cannot..." came the reply from the colony.

"Why not?" asked Artisius, somewhat calmer than Alfred.

"He's...gone missing..." said the colony's Communications Officer.

There was a pause as all parties accepted this. "We'll be docking in about six hours, Europa, you can tell us more then," said Artisius after a while.

"Good, *Green Dragon*. We will await your arrival," said the officer and then the communications ceased.

Alfred was shaking. "How could he?" he said over and over. He had forgotten about the zet.

"Are you sure it's him?" asked Draz, trying to help. Artisius looked over at Alfred, apprehensively.

"It's him, he's doing it again. We have to stop him!" Alfred said. He breathed deeply trying to calm down. He knew that hysterics achieved nothing. "I'll zet, but I need to be there in the command when we arrive. I need to tell them what happened to *Florida Station*!" Alfred said, a little calmer. Artisius nodded his acceptance of these terms.

Alfred finished the boot up procedure and after a little pause, inserted the needle into his implant. The bliss that he felt was unsurpassed. It washed away the worries of Virtus surviving. He raced through the system, and he loved it. However, his implant was on the path to utter decay, there was the fuzziness on the edges of his zetting vision. The more he zetted, the more he lost memory. He knew this, but he could not stop. He was an addict, and it would kill him in the end.

***

Draz stood to one side as Artisius communicated with the Docking Master on the docking procedure. As the *Green Dragon* closed with its target, the small orb that was Europa grew in the observation dome. Draz was still mesmerised by the massive form of Jupiter that filled space in front of them. She had never seen anything like it.

"That's where we're going." Artisius pointed to the small moon that was growing in stature as they approached. "It's a small ice world that sits on top of a massive ocean. They've tapped the thermal vents for some of their energy needs. It's a delicate balance between survival and keeping the surface cool enough so that the massive ice sheets don't move and crack."

Draz nodded her understanding, even though she did not quite understand. She had never experienced space travel like this and everything she encountered was a combination of marvelling at nature, and being terrified at what lay out there in the Solar System.

After a time, the orb of Europa grew sufficiently to allow Draz to see the colony that crawled across its surface. It was a mountain range of towers and valleys all the product of human labour and all wrought in steel and glass. There were still some parts of the moon that had the ice sheets visible, and Draz tried to imagine what the moon would have looked like before humans had moved onto its surface. It would have been one pristine ice sheet, and now a substantial portion of it was covered with human activity. Draz smiled. What humans will do to survive, she thought.

Draz felt Artisius watching her, and she turned to him. He had stopped speaking to the docking controller.

"What?" she asked him.

"Oh, I was just watching you to see your reaction to the first time here." Artisius smiled. "I remember my first time to Jupiter. It blew my mind." He laughed. "The wonders of nature!"

Draz smiled. "Yes, indeed. It is quite spectacular..." she trailed off and looked out the observation dome again. But it was not Earth, she thought to herself. It might be magical, but it was not Earth.

Draz suddenly felt very homesick. She missed her planet. Even though it was unremarkable, and a toxic war torn wasteland, she missed it. And standing here so many millions of kilometres away from it left her feeling very alone. Artisius and the space travelling crew of the *Green Dragon* could not understand her position. She was new to all this, and as remarkable as it was, it made her feel sad.

She looked over at Alfred, still zetting at the terminal. She saw his bared teeth, and his bolt upright posture. She looked back out at the now large orb of Europa that had replaced Jupiter in the observation dome. They were obviously on final approach and Artisius and the Helmsman were guiding the *Green Dragon* in to the docking terminal.

She felt the gnawing pangs of the withdrawal return. She tried to shut them out, but they came back stronger than ever. She sighed. Where had the confident and headstrong Draz gone? The head scavenger of the Corporate Wing seemed so far away now. Draz shook her head to clear it. Self pity would get her nowhere. She bit down on her inner cheek and the pain caused a rush of endorphins that somewhat alleviated the drug withdrawals. She stopped biting and tasted a bit of blood in her mouth. Self pity would get her nowhere, she thought again. She had to be strong. She had to survive.

They entered the thin and almost nonexistent atmosphere of Europa and managed to dock safely at the landing pad at the top of one of the tall towers that jutted out into space high above the icy surface.

Alfred, just at that moment, finished his zet and slumped in the zetting chair while withdrawing the needle from the side of his head. "System...integrity...restored..." he gasped. Then he got to his feet and leaned on the wall of the bridge while he tried to get his footing back.

Draz looked at him. She had grown fond of the scruffy fool. She considered him a friend. She said nothing however as she knew that he would respond assuming she was chastising him for feeding his addiction.

"Good," said Artisius. "How's the memory?"

Alfred paused for a few seconds before regaining his balance and moved away from the wall. "All right, I think...I know who I am and who you are...so that's something I guess."

Draz noted that Alfred still looked paler than normal. "And Blinky?" she said testing him.

"What about...her?" He smiled. "Look, my memory isn't that bad. The decay will be slow and steady. When I forget

223

Blinky, my parents, and my home I will be too far gone, but at the moment things are okay!" he tried to reassure Draz.

Draz was not totally convinced and looked carefully at Alfred as he seemed to turn and listen to something that only he could hear. He seemed to focus on a sound that was not audible to anyone but himself. But as quickly as the distraction had happened, with a shake of the head, he returned to normal and faced Artisius and Draz.

"We're docked at one of the towers, and cleared through customs in this emergency circumstance. They know me and we have a direct appointment with the Colony Commander Anya," Artisius said, breaking the concentration Draz had. Artisius turned and addressed his crew. "All crew are to disembark for some R and R but be ready for immediate departure when necessary. The Collective fleet is not far behind. We out distanced them, but they will be coming. We must refuel, though, so get on to that!"

The crew responded instantly, and Alfred and Draz nodded silently, and they all headed to the docking tube.

Draz noted they did not head to the armoury. "No guns?" she asked.

"Our guns wouldn't be allowed on Europa," Artisius said.

Chapter 28

They headed to the docking tube and disembarked onto Europa.

After a short hover train journey, the trio came to the command complex of Europa Colony and were let through the security checkpoints. Commander Anya was there to greet them.

"Commander Anya, what a pleasure to see you again." Artisius bowed a little and took her hand in his.

Draz and Alfred looked suspiciously at each other.

"Okay enough of that Artisius, I know you too well. I'm not swayed by your charms," Commander Anya said, withdrawing her hand.

Draz and Alfred noticed that Artisius seemed a little hurt, but he recovered. "Indeed, well, down to business then..." he said, straightening up.

Draz looked around the command centre. It was a large collection of walkways around a central dome that was made of glass for observation. A little like the *Green Dragon's* bridge but much larger due to the larger staff required to control the colony.

She looked at Alfred who seemed to want to blurt out something but was having a hard time trying to contain himself. Draz knew this was about Virtus.

"What's this about the Collective Zone fleet?" said Anya.

"Well...we might happen to be towing a rather large Collective fleet..." said Artisius a little sheepishly.

"How large?" snapped Anya. It was obvious that she was rather annoyed and Artisius.

"About thirty ships," Artisius said, definitely sheepishly this time.

"WHAT!?" shouted Anya. "And the command ship?" She quietened herself.

"Um...well..." said Artisius. "Both of them, the *Old Monarch* and the *Iron Bastion* are both in the fleet...We detected both signatures on our scanners..."

Anya glared at him. "We cannot fight that off!"

"We've sent a message to the Solar Solutions Command, and they should be on their way..." Artisius said.

"Good, how long ago?" Anya calmed herself.

"A couple of years ago, when we left Earth. Which means that they should be here in about a month or so, given the Solar Solutions fast engines," Artisius placated Anya.

Anya glared at him again, and then looked out to the massive form of Jupiter in the dome above them. "Now I don't know if this is to do with anything, but we've been having trouble with our systems and apparently one of your crew said to one of my communications staff that he might have known why?"

"Virtus!" blurted out Alfred.

"Ah, was it you?" snapped Anya, focusing her piercing gaze on Alfred.

Draz felt sorry for him to be under her gaze.

"Yes, did Virtus survive *Florida Station*?" Alfred seemed unfazed by Anya's gaze.

"He did, we thawed him out from his pod and instated him here as our Head Trader as our old Trader was on a pilgrimage to Neptune. He has not returned yet--"

"Where is Virtus?" interrupted Alfred.

It was apparent from Anya's expression that she was not often interrupted. "He's...disappeared..." she said calmly.

"And the trouble?" pressed Alfred. "Was it tech-slaves failing, people disappearing, and systems failing; along with zetting not ironing out bugs?"

"All of those!" said Anya; she seemed impressed by his knowledge of the situation. "Can you help us with those things?"

"It's Virtus, it's all Virtus. We need to stop him and arrest him. He did the same to *Florida Station* and then he blew it up!" Alfred said.

Anya was silent for a moment. She stared at Alfred. He shifted uneasily in her vision and scratched his implant. "Ah, you're Alfred...Yes Artisius said you were on *Florida Station* and were innocent in an earlier communication. I see you're a zetter," she did not ask a question, Alfred nodded. "Can you fix our current troubles?"

"But we must find him..." blurted Alfred again.

"We can do that," said Draz. She put a hand on Alfred's shoulder.

"Yeah, we can find him," said Artisius. "With help," he looked at Anya.

"If you let your friend zet the system and fix it, I will aid your search," Anya said in a measured tone.

Draz and Artisius looked at Alfred, who looked at them tensely. Alfred nodded.

"Good, then we will prepare. And if you try anything funny," Anya pointed at Alfred, "I'll have you shot."

Alfred swallowed hard. He loved zetting, but this was pressure that he did not need. And Virtus was missing.

"Where will he be, Alfred?" asked Draz.

All eyes fell on Alfred. He paused for a minute and thought. "The reactor complex, he'll be in the reactor complex. That's where he was when I found him on *Florida Station*." Draz and Artisius nodded.

"I will give you a Guide, but so as to keep things quiet I cannot give you any extra manpower," said Anya. "The Guide will be waiting out those doors," she indicated to where they came in. "And don't even think of leaving this colony until I make a thorough security check of you, and your crew. I also want Virtus found. No ships leave until that man is apprehended!"

As they were about to leave Alfred grabbed Draz and Artisius' arms and said to them carefully, "Go armed! He will be protected!" They nodded.

"Come, zetter, it's time to begin," snapped Anya to Alfred and Draz saw him follow Anya to a zetting terminal on one of the long catwalks around the command centre.

Draz and Artisius left the command centre and found their Guide waiting where Anya had said.

"We need weapons before going to the reactor complex," said Artisius rather awkwardly to the strange man in front of him. "I suppose we're not allowed to bring weapons from our ship?"

The man shook his head silently and beckoned. They followed him.

Draz knew that the Collective Zone fleet was coming, and they did not have much time.

***

Draz and Artisius armed themselves in the armoury, which was situated near the command centre. It was a small armoury compared to Lady Hangara's on Mars. It was meant simply for peacekeeping purposes, not all out gang war. They kept to small calibre pistol weaponry and Draz eschewed her customary grenades due to the fact that she did not want to breach the reactor core and cause a catastrophic meltdown. They armed themselves quickly as they knew that any delay meant that Virtus could escape.

Draz thought it odd that they were given no backup. But she understood that Anya would want to keep this operation quiet and trying to sneak up and ambush someone hiding in the bowels of the colony would be hard with a security detail stomping about everywhere. Still, Draz felt a little tense. Even though they were going to obtain an old man, Alfred's anxiety at detaining him had rubbed off on her a little and if Alfred had been so nervous, what could this one old man do?

"Ready?" asked Artisius. Draz nodded and they followed the Guide to the nearest hover train station.

On the hover train, they remained silent. Draz was mesmerised by the giant orb of Jupiter that she could see through the glass shields on the hover train, and she stared at its vast expanse above her.

The colony seemed to stretch out endlessly around them as they made their way through and around towers of steel. Then there were the small patches where the surface of the old Europa was visible. It was a gnarled and cracked ice surface that seemed so ancient. It was, Draz mused, as it had been there for billions of years, and would be there billions more.

Draz mused as to what it would be like to live for billions of years. To see the stars live and die; to watch planets boil away into the ether. She smiled. The thoughts took her mind off the gnawing feeling in her soul. The emptiness was juxtaposed against the massive form of Jupiter that filled her vision. She had to be strong. She had been before, she could again; but it would never go away.

The train carriage they were in was pretty empty; Draz looked down the length of the compartment they were in.

"Where are all the workers?" she asked the Guide. She did so quietly, so as not to be heard by other people around her. She felt a little embarrassed asking the question, she did not know why.

"Night cycle," the Guide said breathily and softly. "We are in our night cycle, so this is the skeleton crew to keep the colony going. During the day there would be a lot more."

Draz nodded her understanding and wondered if the command centre crew ever slept. Commander Anya seemed to have no sense of going to sleep.

They rode on in silence. After about forty minutes, the train stopped, and they disembarked after the Guide beckoned them to do so. They stood in front of a large lift door with a radiation symbol etched onto it. The train departed, taking the people onboard to some unknown job.

"Down that lift," said the Guide.

"Right," Draz said, "that's the reactor complex?" she pointed to the large door.

The Guide nodded.

"No security?" Artisius asked. He had not spoken the entire train journey.

"No need," said the Guide. "The security is down there; any unauthorised entrant gets terminated by the guards."

Artisius raised his eyebrows. "That's a strange security system."

The Guide did not reply but stared blankly at them.

"What's your name?" asked Draz after an awkward pause.

"I do not have one. I am simply a Guide..." the Guide said somewhat confused.

"Right...well, wait here for our return," said Draz. "We'd better get on..." she walked over to the large door and triggered the mechanism. Artisius followed her. The Guide stood back watching and waiting obediently.

When the door opened, Draz and Artisius stepped into the large lift and pressed the only button on the side panel. Next to it was the word "Reactors" with a radiation symbol. The lift thrummed into life and began the descent after the door closed.

"You've been very silent..." said Draz, breaking the silence as she saw Artisius staring into space.

"I've been thinking..." Artisius said.

"Really? That's new," Draz smiled.

"Oh haha," said Artisius, he seemed amused by her jibe and smiled.

"No really, what are you thinking?" Draz asked genuinely curious. She had not seen Artisius retreat into his own mind so much before.

"About Alfred, and the man we're hunting," Artisius said. "If I'd believed Alfred back on *Florida Station*, then all this may have been avoided..." he paused.

The lift kept rumbling.

Artisius continued, "But then if I had not taken Alfred to the Earth Moon then I would never have been on Earth to pick you up, and that would mean that I would never have been in a position to warn Solar Solutions about the pending invasion, which would have happened anyway..." he trailed off. His face betrayed that he was deep in thought. "So many had to die..."

"Indeed," said Draz after a moment's contemplation. "I'm not one to believe in fate, but sometimes things happen just the way they should. If you hadn't rescued me from the Earth and brought the red hard drive with you, then things may have been very different," Draz paused, pointing a finger at Artisius. "Where is that hard drive, by the way?"

"Remember, that's my insurance policy," he smiled. "But I'm intending to give it to the Solar Solutions people, when I get there."

"But the Collective Zone fleet is almost here, it will take years to install the cloaking devices on the Solar Solutions ships?" Draz was confused. "And can you trust the Solar Solutions high command not just to invade Collective space with that technology and the war would be prolonged?"

231

"Hence the insurance policy," Artisius said. "If they think it's in Solar Solutions' hands they'll be more careful. I know it won't be installed for years, but the Collective Zone command don't know that...Also, they'll follow me to the ends of the Solar System to get that drive, they won't risk blowing up my ship if they think they can get the drive. See? Insurance. And I'll assess whether to give it to the Solar Solutions Command at all when I meet up with them. It will be insurance against their acting rashly as well..."

Draz's face showed she understood, but she said nothing. It was clear that Artisius was still a mercenary.

***

Then the lift rumbled to a halt and the door slid open. They drew their pistols. The corridor beyond the lift door was dark and brooding. The light in the lift shone and diffused into the dark space beyond, causing eerie shadows to be cast along the hallway's length.

Draz stepped out first into the darkness, thumbing the little light on the end of her pistol, which sent a beam of bright light down into the darkness. Artisius followed her and did the same with his pistol.

"Handy these have torches on them," Draz whispered.

Artisius nodded.

They proceeded carefully down the corridor. Condensation was dripping from overhead pipes and their torches cast shadows down the corridor.

After a short walk, they came to a largish room with no door. It was some sort of control room, but there were no people in it. Artisius, who followed Draz into the room, triggered a light switch and the room was flooded with light.

Over on one side there was an unoccupied zetting terminal and near that there was a large, armoured door that had a massive radiation symbol on it and a red light on the door controls indicating that the door was locked. Around the room were control terminals, clearly meant for tech-slaves due to the lack of chairs and the computer inputs that were displayed at every place.

"There are no tech-slaves here!" Draz whispered again.

"There's no one here," said Artisius, louder. "No guards..."

Suddenly there was a fizzing and clattering noise. Both of them spun around to face a tech-slave that had got up from behind a control terminal. It was wounded and was bleeding from a number of places. Its yellow jump suit was stained red.

Draz raised her pistol. "Stop!" she shouted. "What happened here?"

Artisius also brandished his pistol, but said nothing.

"V-v-irtussss..." the tech-slave fizzed, still staggering towards them.

"Yes, Virtus, where is he?" Artisius yelled at the approaching tech-slave. "Stay back!"

Draz's heart was pumping hard. Her grip on the pistol was firm. It was plain to both of them that the tech-slave was not fully functioning and may have gone mad. Its circuits may have been fried by Virtus and thus it could not be trusted. Its skull mesh looked damaged. It might attack them at any moment.

"G-gone," the creature said, staggering towards them. It tripped over a loose cable and went sprawling across the floor with a loud crash. It kept crawling towards them with its hands. "To the Collective Zone..." The tech-slave stammered.

Draz and Artisius looked at each other.

"He's escaped!" Draz said.

The tech-slave was almost on them by now and they backed up towards the wall.

"Now what?" asked Draz, her back against the reactor wall.

Artisius opened fire with his pistol and Draz followed his lead. They emptied their magazines into the thing crawling towards them but due to the low calibre of the pistols, the shots did little to stop its implacable advance. Its skull mesh circuits overrode the pain and damage from the bullets. It clawed itself upright. As it did so it grabbed a sharp piece of metal from a nearby damaged console and held it as a weapon.

"Shit! That didn't work! It's in our way!" Draz swore as the creature blocked their one and only exit from the control room.

Draz and Artisius backed up against a wall in the control room. The creature staggered towards them. Draz fanned out on one side of it and Artisius on the other. Draz looked at Artisius and they made the unspoken communication for each of them to try to pass the thing on each side of it.

With a nod, Draz dashed past on the left while Artisius made the attempt on the right. He swore as the tech-slave caught him a glancing blow with its outstretched weapon. Draz heard Artisius' clothing rip as the sharp metal tore into Artisius' arm.

Artisius swore and both he and Draz made a dash towards the lift at the end of the corridor next to the room. The tech-slave turned and clomped its way after them. It was surprisingly fast for the damage it had sustained.

"Shit...shit!" Draz swore as she pressed the button for the lift and the doors opened slowly.

Both of them rushed inside and positively willed the doors to close faster as the tech-slave approached, it stumbled on, and blood seeped from its damaged parts. Its skull mesh fizzed and sparked as it tried to catch them.

Finally, the door to the lift closed at the last second and they began their ascent away from the deadly creature. Draz was breathing hard. Artisius held his arm.

"You okay?" Draz asked, noting the man's pained expression.

Artisius grimaced in pain. "It got me a good blow..." he said, lifting his hand off the wound and some blood ran down his forearm and dripped onto the floor of the lift.

"Nasty..." said Draz, genuinely concerned. "We'll need to get that seen to."

"Don't worry about me," Artisius said, grimacing. "We need to tell this information to Alfred and Anya."

"Why should we believe just a tech-slave? About where Virtus has gone, I mean," asked Draz.

"If a tech-slave is damaged like that, with its skull mesh malfunctioning and almost disconnected from the network, they often tell the absolute truth. They cannot think properly so they revert to base function. What it said was believable, I think," Artisius said with a grimace.

"I wonder how Virtus overpowered the guards..." Draz said to herself.

Artisius said nothing.

The rest of the ride up was made in silence.

Chapter 29

Draz and Artisius radioed in the information they had found out and returned to the command centre with the Guide.

Alfred was just coming out of a zet and to Draz he looked strangely at peace.

"So, he's gone?" snapped Anya. She had been waiting for them to return.

"Yeah, a friend told us that he had disappeared off world before he gave me this souvenir..." Artisius said through gritted teeth.

"You're hurt!" Alfred said as he regained his senses. Artisius was still holding his arm and blood was still seeping from the wound.

"It's minor, just messy," said Artisius, grimacing. "I'll be fine."

"But you're bleeding on my command centre floor," said Anya bluntly. She waved over an orderly who ushered Artisius away towards the medical section of the colony. Artisius delayed, and only moved slowly.

"What's up, Anya?" Artisius said just as bluntly. "Why are you so--"

"Cold?" she said. "Because you've brought the whole Collective Zone fleet to my doorstep that's why and I thought you were a responsible captain! Ha! You've brought us war! And you expect me to fall for your charms?..."

Artisius was silent and pursed his lips.

Draz had moved over to Alfred and was helping him stand. It was obvious he was exhausted from the zetting. She shot Anya a glance, which Anya did not see.

There was an awkward silence for a short period of time. Then Alfred spoke. "System integrity is being restored, slowly..."

"Good, then go again and get it better, and then again, and then again. We need the problems sorted if we are going to resist the Collective Zone fleet," snapped Anya.

"Can't you see he's exhausted?" snapped Draz with more force than she intended.

"I don't care," said Anya. "He's the only one who has known Virtus' system corruptions and you brought the Collective Zone fleet here so it's his job to get things sorted so that we can put up some sort of defence." She turned to Alfred. "How are the defence networks?"

"Only at fifty per cent," Alfred said with a sigh.

"Then go again. We don't have much time..." the note in Anya's voice was one of fear and desperation.

"And what of me and my ship?" said Artisius, still resisting the orderly's imploring him to leave the command centre.

"Go...or stay...it doesn't matter," Anya said with a sigh. "But Alfred stays with me," she said with resolve.

"We can't leave him!" blurted Draz.

Artisius looked at her, a pained expression on his face, not just from the wound in his arm. "Can't we?" he said with a grimace. He looked at Alfred who had moved back to the zetting terminal again and was preparing to re-enter the network.

"We can't," pleaded Draz. Her face was pained, and her eyes were begging Artisius to reconsider.

Artisius paused for a while in thought. He mumbled to himself a few things. "What's that?" snapped Anya.

"Am I a good man?" Artisius said louder this time.

"I have no idea," snapped Anya. "Bringing the whole Collective Zone fleet to Solar Solutions space doesn't seem very good to me..."

Artisius ignored Anya and looked at Draz.

Draz nodded. "I think you are, when you want to be..."

"Do I want to be?" Artisius asked softly.

"It'd be a shame to quit now..." Draz said with a smile. "Pick a side, remember?"

Artisius looked torn, torn between his own survival and duty to his friends. Draz saw the pained expression on his face.

Alfred was about to log in again. If he knew about the difficult decisions going on in Artisius' mind he did not let on that he did. He was busy with the zetting terminal. "Next zet ready, commander," he said with practiced precision. As tired as he was, Alfred seemed at home where he was zetting for the Europa Colony and undoing Virtus' damage.

"Stay or go, it's up to you, but he stays." Anya pointed at Alfred. "I can have a Guide show you to your temporary quarters."

Turning to Alfred, Anya gave him permission to log in and he did with enthusiasm. His features peeled back, and he began his next foray into the computer network.

Artisius looked over at Alfred, and then at Draz. Anya had walked off around the command centre's walkways to do her job and prepare the colony for the coming fight.

Artisius looked at the ground. "All right, we stay," he said.

Draz heard him and smiled. "I know this is hard, and you want to run, but maybe we need to fight a little. The Solar Solutions fleet is coming. They'll make the Collective Zone fleet think twice, and then we can escape..."

"I wish I had your confidence," Artisius smiled. "Now, I need to get this wound tended to!" He looked over to the orderly that had almost given up trying to help him and they went off together to the medical wing of the colony.

Draz stood alone on the command centre catwalk and looked up at the large form of Jupiter that filled the dome. "I hope I...we...made the right decision," she said. And so, they waited for the Collective Zone and Solar Solutions fleets to arrive.

Chapter 30

CEO Gunter dreamed. He was oblivious to the world around him and the space sliding past the *Silver Ark* as he was in his cryo-pod.

Gunter dreamed of many things; many women; many drinks; many good times. However, as was customary with his dreams, on the journey, something kept returning to his mind. A sinister threat always invaded his consciousness and chased him down. He would run through the corridors of the *Silver Ark* in his mind, and yet it would always catch him; always find him. It sought him out without mercy or remorse. He was always held to account by this unknown force, and he was found wanting.

Gunter dreamed, as did many of the other crew of the *Silver Ark* and surrounding fleet that had gathered in the void and was progressing back to Jupiter. They all dreamed fitful dreams.

They would all be tested soon.

***

This story is continued in the next novel *Neptune's War: Broken Cosmos Volume Three* by Ian Kennedy:

Fleeing Mars for Europa, a moon of Jupiter, the crew of the *Green Dragon* become the spark which ignites the war between the Solar Solutions Corporation and the Collective Zone as the Collective Zone Great Fleet invades Solar Solutions territory.

Alfred fears losing all hold of his sanity as his zetting becomes increasingly self-destructive.

Draz tries hard to maintain her sense of who she is.

The war that has been brewing for decades forces Artisius to confront his demons and make choices that test his true character.

Things take an unexpected turn as Virtus discovers the truth about his calling.

Soldiers on both sides clash for the glory of their corporation and blind survival.

Everyone must ask themselves: what price are they willing to pay for victory?

**

Author details and sites:

Website: www.ikennedyauthor.com (mailing list link on website / contact email at bottom of website)

Amazon: www.amazon.com/author/ikennedy

Twitter: twitter.com/ikennedyauthor

Facebook: www.facebook.com/ikennedyauthor

**

Please leave a review of this book on (*Martian Flight*) Amazon, I would really appreciate it. Please see the Amazon link above for the link to the book.